# BREATH
## of *Air*

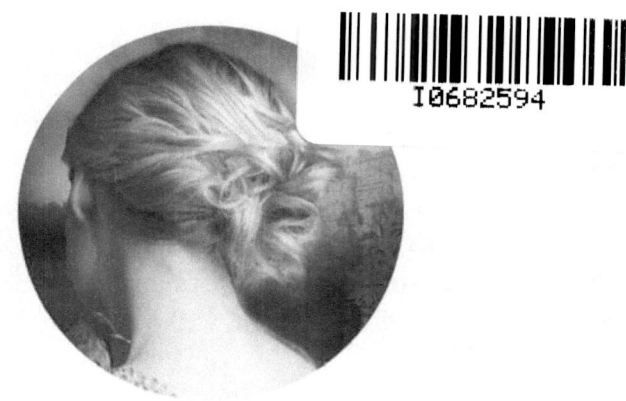

## FIRST OF THE DRYAD QUARTET

# KATIE JENNINGS

Sapphire Royale
publishing

Cover design by Katie Jennings
Interior book and eBook design by Blue Harvest Creative
*www.blueharvestcreative.com*

Published by
Sapphire Royale Publishing

ISBN-13: 978-0615709680
ISBN-10: 0615709680

Visit the author at:
*www.katieajennings.com*
*www.facebook.com/katieajennings*
*www.twitter.com/dryadquartet*
*www.katieajennings.wordpress.com*

"Wow. Such an amazing book. The detail is amazing and so beautifully written. It is as if you are right there with Capri."

*– Sara Daniell, author –*

"Katie Jennings weaves a beautiful tale filled with vivid characters, intrigue, romance and adventure. The world she creates for the mystic beings that reside there and rule the elements around us and our very lives, is wonderfully rich. The Furies, the Fates, the Dryads, Mother Earth and Father Sky - this author can handle a large cast and each character retains their individuality, their voice. Capri is a wonderful heroine, so damaged but with such a wealth of untapped strength. She, an orphan (or so she thought), is thrown back into a world she had forgotten existed filled with people who know her, but whom she doesn't remember. Who can she trust? Who can she love? Why do the demons want to destroy her happiness so badly?"

*– Natalie Gibson, author –*

"I really liked her style of writing and the story kept me engaged throughout. The author writes in a way that really captures your imagination [...] There are plenty of twists and turns. I can imagine the series being adapted into a Television Series where all the characters are beautiful, this is how I imagined them to be whilst I was reading the story."

*– Becky Sherriff with The Kindle Book Review –*

"Jennings has created a world unlike any I have read about. By the end of the book I wanted more of Euphora....and jumped straight into the next book in the quartet."

*– Cassie Deaton with Shadow Kisses Reviews –*

"This is a story that truly captures the imagination from the start. Capri's story of love and loss draws you in and you can't put it down. With plenty of twists and turns to keep you on the edge of your seat, this book will make you want to find out what will happen next and leave you anxious for the next installment. A definite must read!"

*– Allison Kappen, editor –*

## Also By Katie Jennings

### The Dryad Quartet Series
Firefight in Darkness
A Life Earthbound
Of Water and Madness

### The Vasser Legacy Series
When Empires Fall
Rise of the Notorious
*Coming Spring 2013*

*For my mothers,*
*who read every word and*
*didn't complain once!*

# THEA & SEBASTIAN
## MOTHER EARTH & FATHER SKY

**ROHAN & SERENDIPITY**
EARTH DRYAD | MUSE

RHIANNON
EARTH DRYAD

SIENNA
MUSE

**CLYNN & HEIDI**
AIR DRYAD | HUMAN

CAPRI
AIR DRYAD

**BROCK & NYXA**
FIRE DRYAD | FATE

BLYTHE
FIRE DRYAD

**LUCIAN & CLARITY**
WATER DRYAD | MUSE

LIAM
WATER DRYAD

CILLA
MUSE

**ROARKE & ERIN**
FURY | ENFORCER

RIAN
FURY

**TRINITY & JEAN PAUL**
MUSE | HUMAN

TOBIAS
MUSE

**BALGAIRE & NYXA**
FURY | FATE

NOVA
FATE

**BALGAIRE & OLIVIA**
FURY | HUMAN

BROGAN
FURY

**MORGAINE & WYNN**
FATE | ENFORCER

MABLE
MUSE

**ANGORA & ALAN**
FATE | HUMAN

ALASTOR
FATE

## DRYADS

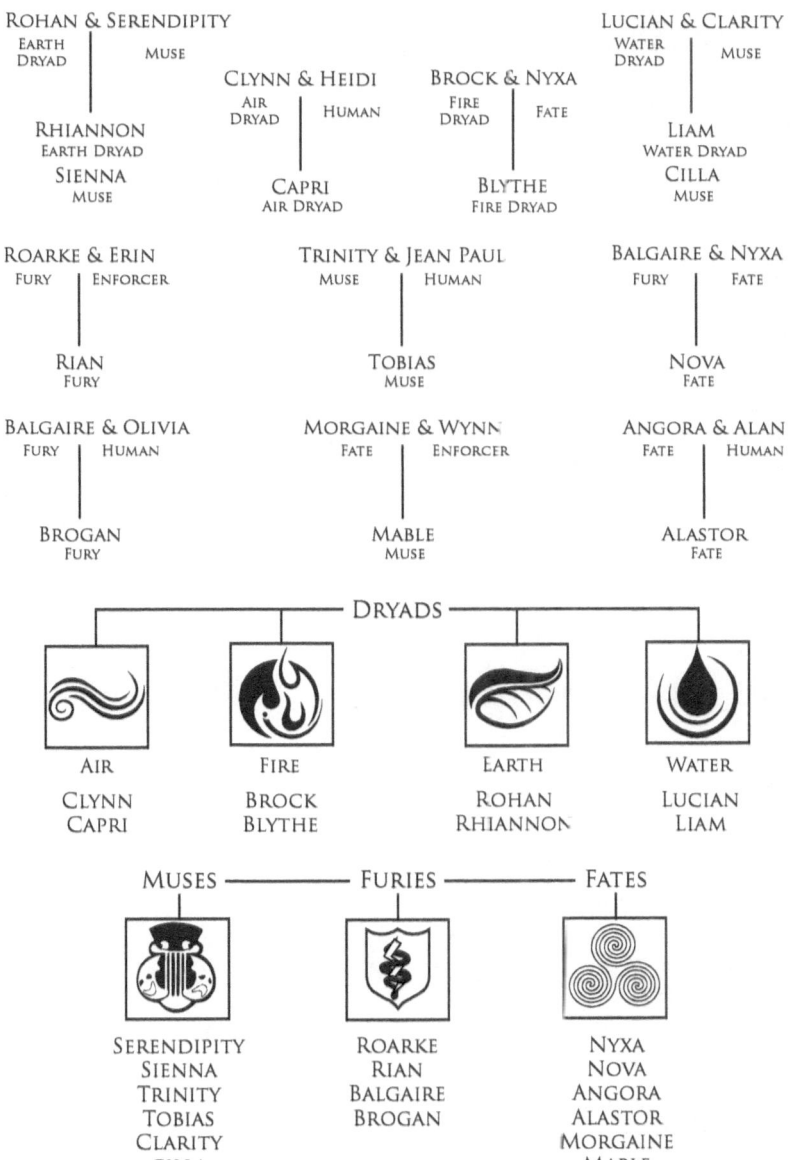

AIR
CLYNN
CAPRI

FIRE
BROCK
BLYTHE

EARTH
ROHAN
RHIANNON

WATER
LUCIAN
LIAM

## MUSES —— FURIES —— FATES

SERENDIPITY
SIENNA
TRINITY
TOBIAS
CLARITY
CILLA

ROARKE
RIAN
BALGAIRE
BROGAN

NYXA
NOVA
ANGORA
ALASTOR
MORGAINE
MABLE

# Prologue

*And it seems to me from the dreary night,*
*I am going up there to a world of light,*
*Away from the world and the tempest so wild,*
*There, I am sure, I'll be somebody's child.*

*Her name was* Capri, and she was Air.

She was eighteen, and for the first time since she could remember, she was home.

Home was not in Virginia, where she had floated through life like a leaf on a faint breeze. No; home was here, on this floating Eden with its larger than life trees and glorious meadows that were in a constant state of spring. Home was in the elegant stone castle, with its rising towers and glittering windows. It was, to a girl who had always had luminous and extraordinary dreams, nothing short of a fairytale. And if she thought herself to be something of a princess, then it was for her to revel in. No one had to know.

An orphaned girl was bound to dream of being a princess at some point in her life. Especially an orphaned girl who had no past.

But all was not well. The dark dreams that had plagued her since childhood–since that one night so long ago–had begun to resurface with astonishing clarity. The dreams where she hides under the cover of jasmine flowers, listening with trembling fear while a woman screams and dies, and cruel laughter rings out into the crackling air.

# Chapter One

*March 8th, 2010*
*Richmond, Virginia*

*Today was a* special day. At least she supposed that normal people with normal families would consider today to be special. Didn't most people celebrate their birthdays with loved ones and friends? Maybe open some presents, blow out a handful of colorful candles adorning a sugary chocolate cake. Most people probably took the fact that birthdays existed for granted. It was just something that happened every year. Something to be excited over, but still something very normal. Yes, that was how most people must feel.

Capri Summers had never known a normal birthday, at least not from what she could remember. She supposed that perhaps before she had been brought to the orphanage, she must have had a family. Maybe she had even had parents who celebrated her birthday with her. She might have even eaten cake once or twice and blown out those silly candles. If she had, it was a memory long gone.

The truth was, she had no idea who her parents had been, or where she had been born. Her earliest memories were of living at the orphanage in Richmond, which had been her home for as long as she could remember.

Now she was finally eighteen and legally an adult, free of the orphanage for good. For the first time in her life, she could venture out into the world and actually try to be somebody.

And, since today was her first official birthday as an adult, Capri decided to treat herself to a slice of pie at the local diner. Maybe she would even ask the waitress for a candle to blow out. Why the heck not?

As she walked along the wet sidewalk, dampened from misty rain that had fallen the night before, Capri felt the odd and unfamiliar sensation of freedom. She could go wherever she wanted, be whoever she wanted to be. She was not entirely fond of the person she had become, a ghost drifting through life with no real passion or goals. It had been hard for her to find the motivation to do much more than drift, so she had never really put down roots or committed to much of anything. All she had achieved thus far was a basic high school education and a job as a library page. Not much to build off really, though she supposed it was a start. And for a girl who had no beginning, a start was as good as it was going to get.

Most of the children she'd grown up with at the orphanage had a reason to be there, and a story to go along with it—parents that had died in a tragic car accident or a mother who was single and sixteen, unable to take care of them. Capri had no reason and no story. All she had were recurring nightmares so outrageous that she had long ago convinced herself she had made it all up.

How could she explain her vivid dreams about an enormous castle with ivy crawling up its massive stone walls? And of a courtyard, flanked on all sides by abundant flowery plants with butterflies that floated freely on a warm and gentle breeze? Of a woman's laughter, musical and sweet, just like the jasmine flowers that surround her, star shaped and smelling like Heaven?

And how could she rationally explain the darkness that seemed to swallow up this paradise in one greedy gulp? The screams echoing as rough hands lifted her away...away from all sound...all light...all being.

Stolen. That was what she always realized when she woke up from the dream. She had been stolen from that paradise.

As she had matured, she had confessed this dream to countless psychologists, explaining how it recurred several times a month, and that it never varied. Over the years, she had come to accept their explanations that it was merely a childish fantasy projecting her fears and her denial of being abandoned. Not that they ever referred to her as being *abandoned*, but she knew that was the truth.

Fifteen years ago, with no explanation, she had been found in the middle of a dark alleyway by a rough and tumble rookie cop, who had brought her to the orphanage until the Richmond Police could locate her family. But no one ever came. Capri had given up hope long ago that she would ever find out who she was or why she had been left in that alleyway on that balmy July night. The only information the police managed to get out of her was her first name. Since she didn't remember her last name, they gave her the surname *Summers*, in honor of the season she was found.

She stopped in front of the diner, her hand pausing as she reached for the handle of the door. Staring at her reflection in the sparkling clean glass, she took in the long, pale blonde hair and guileless gray eyes set in an oval-shaped face with soft planes, and had the sharp realization that despite being eighteen, she still felt like a child. A child that was completely and utterly alone.

She suddenly didn't feel like eating any pie. Birthday or not, she didn't think she could stomach it. Stalking away from the diner, she dug her hands deeper into the pockets of her black wool coat. Tears brimmed in her eyes, blurring her vision. She quickly cut across the street toward the park. I just need a moment to myself, she thought, hastily wiping the tears with her palm. Just some time to adjust before I take the next step.

She headed toward her favorite tree, its branches hanging low to the ground over a lovely little pond still shimmering with bits of ice.

There was no bench, only supple, green grass that had absorbed the moisture from the constant March rains. Capri tossed down her duffle bag that contained all of her worldly belongings and reached in to dig out her only blanket. It was a faded brown and white plaid with a couple of holes in it, but it did the job. She spread it out under the tree, then plopped herself down, hugging her knees to her chest. Her head fell down as the tears began to fall freely. She desperately tried to control the sobs that wracked her body and to be as silent as possible. No one needed to know she was upset. It was a park after all, and it was the middle of the day.

After a few moments, the rawness that always accompanied the tears began to assault her throat and her chest. She sniffled, wiping her face dry with her sleeve, and with a heavy sigh she stared toward the pond.

She could see two middle aged women in the distance jogging along the cement path, their laughter drifting over the water. A man and a young boy played catch in the grass several yards away, the father calling out encouragement to his son as a broad smile graced his face.

How amazing it must be to have a father, Capri thought sadly. To have someone big and strong to protect you, to look out for you. Someone who loved you unconditionally and unequivocally. Yes, it must be the most amazing feeling in the entire world.

Deciding that she had wallowed in enough self pity for one day, Capri reached into her bag for her latest library book, *Jane Eyre*. She had read it several times before, but it still remained one of her favorites. Perhaps because she likened herself to young Jane, the lonely orphan who finds a home and love with the temperamental Mr. Rochester.

As she opened the book and began to read, Capri let herself drift beyond her own life and into the pages of the story. That was her favorite thing about reading: the fact that you could lose yourself in a different life, become someone else for a short time. She could discover what it was like to be intelligent and witty like Elizabeth Bennett, or volatile and mischievous like Catherine Earnshaw. Even the guileless Jane Eyre possessed so much strength in the face of adversity that Capri was always struck blind with envy.

She had never really thought herself to be any of those things. She wasn't really brave and she certainly wasn't very witty. Perhaps she was intelligent, since she had been above average in school, but she had yet to discover what to do with it. For now, she would content herself with reading about other people's triumphs and adventures, and hope that one day she would find the strength to be more than just an abandoned orphan.

An hour or so passed and the sun began its descent into nightfall. Capri set her book aside, marking her spot with her favorite bluebird bookmark. She gazed out at the expanse of grass beyond the pond in front of her, and watched as people came and went throughout the park.

She watched as a couple of small blackbirds chased each other in midair, flirting as birds do while they darted in and out between the trees. Capri had always loved birds. If reincarnation existed, she wanted to come back as a bird. How simple life would be if all you had to do was spread your wings and fly to avoid a bad situation.

One of the birds flew near her, landing in the grass a few feet away from where she sat. It stared at her inquisitively, as if gauging whether she was a predator or not. After a few seconds with Capri sitting still, the bird began to happily pick at the grass for seeds and small bugs to eat.

Yes, how simple life could be.

Biting her lip tentatively, Capri slowly reached out her right arm, fingers extended to the bird. She focused all her thoughts on the tiny animal, and suddenly, it stopped eating. It stood up straight and looked right at her, its tiny black eyes unmoving.

She pictured the bird lifting its right wing and spreading its feathers, and watched with silent glee as it did what she commanded. The bird tilted its head slightly as she imagined it lifting its left wing. The bird did as it was told, as though it were a puppet being controlled by strings. It stood regally, its wings spread out and its black feathers capturing the fading sunlight so they appeared almost iridescent purple and blue.

She didn't know why she could control birds, but it was something she had discovered as a young child playing outside in the orphanage courtyard. She had seen a hummingbird flitting around one of the white rose bushes, and she had sat watching it with admiration, enjoying its erratic movements. Then she had imagined it flying over and perching on her finger so she could pet it, and miraculously it did just that. It had nearly scared her half to death at the time, but when she realized she could control it, she was mystified by her gift. It was too crazy to tell anyone so she had kept it to herself all these years. She rarely used it anymore, but since she was feeling down it served to cheer her up.

Capri also discovered at a young age she could make leaves twirl in the breeze, and if she thought hard enough, she even had once caused the wind to shift directions during a massive rainstorm.

It was undoubtedly the most interesting thing about her, and yet it was also a source of dark embarrassment. The nightmares were bad enough but this made her feel even less than normal. But today she couldn't care less if people knew her secret. Maybe she should just pray that someone would see her, just so she wouldn't have to hide it anymore. Maybe there was even an explanation why she could manipulate birds and control wind, despite the hours of research she had spent in the library that proved fruitless. Yes, how wonderful it would be to have someone see and understand, and provide her with an explanation.

Perhaps it was chance, or fate, she would never really find out which, that at that very moment brought her someone who actually knew why she had this strange gift. And as he walked along the cement pathway a couple of yards away from her, his eyes watching the little blackbird do tricks no bird should know how to do, two likely explanations passed through his mind.

Either this girl was the first person in the history of mankind to teach a bird to do backflips, or she was the Air Dryad.

He figured it was worth five minutes of his time to find out.

"Hey there," he called out, waving a hand in greeting. The girl jolted at the sound of his voice and then froze, her haunting, lovely gray eyes wide upon his. Jumpy little thing, he thought, his eyes following the bird as it flew up into the tree.

"Hello," she managed, feeling her face redden in embarrassment. For the first time in her life, she had been caught red-handed. And to think, she had actually wished this to happen just seconds ago.

"I'm sorry to bother you. I was just wondering how you trained the bird to do tricks."

Capri studied the man, arguing inwardly with herself over whether or not she should run, or stay and try and make conversation. He looked harmless, she thought warily. Only a year or two older than herself. Actually, she thought he looked kind of like a prince.

He had full, black hair that curled around a handsome face with a cleft chin. His eyes were a startling shade of blue, almost too bright to be natural, flanked by generous lashes and dark brows that arched beautifully. With looks like that, he should be wearing a suit of armor and riding around on a white horse, she thought wistfully, not wearing simple gray slacks and a plain black coat.

"Um…what bird?" was all she could think to say in response. She saw the humor in his eyes, and felt like digging a hole and crawling into the ground to die of embarrassment. Of course he had seen the stupid bird; it was pointless to feign ignorance. "I wasn't doing anything; it was doing that stuff on its own. Weird, huh?"

"Definitely," the man replied, his face kind. "I'm Liam."

He stretched out his hand to her and she took it in her own where she sat.

"Capri."

His face split into a radiant smile as he shook her hand. "Of course you are."

"Excuse me?" she said, fear beating its way into her heart when she realized he wasn't going to let go of her hand.

"Please, stand up. Let me look at you." Liam pulled her to her feet without waiting for her consent, and proceeded to stare at her face, her hair, her body. She felt ridiculously exposed.

"Look, I don't know who you are or what you're planning to do to me, but if I scream that cop over there is going to come running over, and you'll go to jail. So back off. Please," she added with embarrassment when he just continued to look at her.

"I apologize, perhaps I should explain myself," he laughed, running a hand casually through his hair and grinning sheepishly at her. "It's just that I can't believe you're here, after all this time."

"You're surprised that I'm in the park?"

"No, I'm surprised that you're alive!"

"I'm going to scream." Capri bolted to the right to escape him, her mouth opening to scream, when he grabbed her arm and held her back.

"Please, don't go! I'm sorry I've frightened you." He had surprising strength as he held her in place in front of him, and she would have fought tooth and nail to run away if it hadn't been for the unshakable kindness in his eyes. She felt compelled to trust him, despite what her survival instinct was telling her. Something about him was…familiar, but she couldn't place what it was.

"Let me start over. My name is Liam and I come from a place called Euphora. I am a Water Dryad."

"A what?" Her eyes darted toward the cop, and she was relieved to see him still standing there. Just in case this lunatic was dangerous, she had protection.

"Water Dryad," he repeated, smiling at her again. "And you are an Air Dryad."

"Excuse me?"

"You have the power to control birds, do you not?"

"Yeah, but—"

"And let me guess, you can also move the wind, cause it to shift directions?"

"I did it once, but—"

"Then you are an Air Dryad."

She didn't know what to say. It was a better explanation then she had ever come up with for her gift, but it also sounded ridiculously crazy.

"Look, I'm sorry, but that's just not possible. I'm just an orphan library page with less than thirty bucks to my name, not some Dryad thing."

"Orphaned…" he murmured, sadness clouding his handsome features. "I'm sorry. It must have been hard on you."

"As if such a thing could be easy?" she said, more to herself than to him.

"You don't belong here, Capri. You belong on Euphora with your family."

"My family?" her brows furrowed in confusion, "but I don't have a family."

"Yes, you do." Liam let go of her arms then, confident that she wasn't going to run away. "We thought we had lost you fifteen years ago, that you had been killed."

"Killed?"

"Yes, you disappeared the night Euphora was raided by demons. We thought one of them had taken you and killed you."

"Demons?" How much more ludicrous was this going to get? Capri pinched her right arm, positive that she must be dreaming. She must have fallen asleep while reading, and at this moment she was imagining this ridiculously handsome stranger stating that he knew her family.

"It's not a dream." His voice was low, comforting. Despite it, Capri felt completely mystified.

"There's no way this is real," she managed, clutching her arms around her body defensively. How did he know she had been at the orphanage for fifteen years? Had she mentioned it? "Please, just leave me alone."

"Capri–" Liam led her back to her blanket and helped her sit down before sitting beside her. "This is going to be a lot to take in, but you must trust me. I can take you home."

"Home?"

"Euphora. That is your home."

"I don't know…" She felt tears welling up in her eyes again, and tried to will them away. She wanted to believe him, wanted to believe that she had a home, had a family. Had something.

"Would it help if I showed you what I can do? Would that make it more real for you?" he asked gently, motioning with his arms to the pond.

Capri nodded, despite her better judgment. Then she watched in amazement as he pointed at the water and it rose in a funnel out of the pond. The water spun and whirled seemingly on its own, sparkling in the last dying golden rays of the sun, and she turned to watch his deep blue eyes concentrating on the movement. He's controlling the water, she thought with wonder. Just like I can control air.

"But…how?" she whispered, watching as the funnel spun itself back into the pond. Within seconds the water was still again.

"It's complicated…it might be too much for you to understand right now," he paused, looking sheepish. "I'm sorry, I just don't think that I'm the best one to explain it to you. You'd be better off talking to Thea."

"Thea?"

"Mother Earth."

Capri snorted. "You're telling me that Mother Earth exists?"

"Of course she does," he patted her on the shoulder gently. "Come with me, and I promise you that everything will soon make sense."

"But...where is this Euphora place?"

"Again, it's complicated to explain..."

"So how do you get there?"

He grinned. "By tree, of course."

It took her several moments to realize that he wasn't joking. "Tree?"

"Yes, follow me." He stood up gracefully and reached out for her hand. She took it hesitantly, still not sure she was making the right decision in trusting him.

He folded up her blanket and tucked it inside her duffle, then swung the bag effortlessly over his shoulder. Taking her hand in his, he led her toward a different section of the park.

"What was wrong with the tree we were standing under?"

"Too many people around. Can't have someone see."

"Right...well, I hope you're not some sadistic serial killer and I've just fallen for the most ridiculous line in the book."

He laughed and smiled at her. "Don't worry, I'm a horrible liar. You'd be able to tell."

"So, if you're from this Euphora place, what are you doing in Richmond?" Capri asked as she walked beside him.

"You know, it's actually a funny story. I've been particularly moody these past few weeks, and so I consulted the Muses. They told me I'd find peace of mind if I came here. Guess what they really meant was that I'd find you."

"Oh." She didn't really know what else to say to him. She was still trying to wrap her mind around the idea that *Muses* lead him to find her. She must not have heard him right...

They stopped in front of a large pine tree in a denser area of the park. Capri could see a couple of people jogging off in the distance, but otherwise they were completely alone.

"Place your hand on the tree," Liam instructed, doing the same with his own hand. He watched patiently while she cautiously lifted her hand and laid it against the rough bark. Her eyes flashed to his, watching with uncertainty. She was still braced to run, just in case.

He smiled and turned back to the tree. He was so close to it that his forehead was nearly touching the bark, and his eyes were closed. When he began to speak, the words had an almost musical and otherworldly quality to them.

"Mother, I seek to return to you. Grant me entrance, and I will always be true."

Capri was so focused on his face that she almost didn't notice the bark beneath their hands begin to glow with vivid gold light.

"Oh, my God," she whispered. Capri would have yanked her hand away, but it appeared to be stuck to the tree by an invisible force. She sent a panicked look at Liam, who just grinned and winked at her.

Suddenly, the gold light flashed and the park around them dimmed, shadowed by a thick fog. Capri glanced around wildly, trying to make out something, anything in the mist. For a moment, all she could see was the tree in front of her, glowing gold, and Liam beside her.

Then, as if it had never existed, the fog faded away. There was still a tree in front of them, no longer glowing. Only it wasn't the same tree, and they weren't in the park anymore. They probably weren't even in Virginia. Instead, they were in a glorious meadow, filled with wildflowers and misty sunlight, flanked on three sides by enormous trees. Ahead of them rose a wall made entirely of pewter-colored stone. A wrought iron gate with intricately woven patterns was settled amidst the rock.

Beyond the gate Capri could see a castle. Not just any castle, she thought with an astonished laugh, pulling her freed hand away from the bark. It was the castle in her dreams. The one she'd convinced herself she had imagined all this time.

"Almost there," Liam said quietly beside her. He steered her toward the gate and placed his hand upon the wrought iron. It melted away at his touch as though it hadn't even been there.

"What's the point in having a gate if it just disappears?"

"It knows my touch, and yours too, actually, and will allow only those who call Euphora home to enter."

"Oh, well that makes sense," Capri said dryly. She blushed when he looked at her and laughed.

He led her inside a massive courtyard, overflowing with trees and plants and flowers. She saw birds fluttering in and out of the dappled light of the trees and even saw a rabbit dart beneath a bush to her left.

The castle rose like a god, massive and beautiful, at the far end of the courtyard, a cobblestone path leading the way to its doors. She thought it looked like something out of a fairytale, with its glittering windows and roaming ivy. Towers grew like limbs out of the magnificent base, rising high up into the air. The pale, blue sky was dotted with puffy, white clouds and graced by a gentle and misty sun, as if it were morning. Was it morning here, she wondered, confused as she continued to look at the sky. Where in the world had he taken her?

"I need to let Thea know that you are here," Liam said suddenly as he stopped walking, his hands held out in front of his face, palms cupped. What looked like a shimmering silver bubble began to form in his hands, and Capri watched in astonishment as he began to speak quietly to it. The small bubble grew as his lips moved, until it was roughly the size of a softball. He held it out in front of him, then blew it toward the castle. It flew with surprising speed, disappearing into one of the many windows.

"What did you just do?" she asked, despite herself.

"It's much quicker for me to get a message to her that way than for us to go searching the whole castle for her."

"Oh." Capri bit her lip, feeling extremely out of place in this fantasy world.

They stood for a few moments, and then suddenly a man and woman appeared out of the castle doors.

As they approached, Capri felt completely awestruck. They were both so beautiful, and so undeniably different.

The woman was tall and generously built, with wild, dark curly hair that nearly reached her waist. Her skin was olive-toned, and her face that of a gypsy. Her eyes were a deep, dark brown like rich soil, and were by far the most intense eyes Capri had ever seen. She seemed to radiate power with every movement, her body draped in a flowing off-the-shoulder white gown.

The man, in contrast to this dark gypsy woman, was light and pale, oozing elegance and class in crisp, white linen slacks and a matching long-sleeved shirt. He was tall as well, only inches above the woman, and his corn silk hair fell generously to the middle of his back. His eyes were pale gray, like the fog that settles over a lake at sunrise. When he smiled, she could see that his intensity, while cooler and smoother than that of the earthy woman, was just as potent.

Liam bowed his head at the couple. "Thea, Sebastian."

"Glad to see you safely home, Liam," the woman said tenderly. Her voice was sultry and thick, with a touch of rasp that only served to enhance her power. When she turned to look at Capri, her eyes were stern. "You tell me that this is Capri?"

"Yes. I witnessed her powers myself. It is her."

The man called Sebastian seemed to light up, his handsome face radiant. "Dear love, could it be she has been alive all this time?" His voice was lyrical and smooth as honey. He touched the woman's shoulder, his eyes on Capri.

"It appears it is so," Thea replied. "Do you remember anything about this place?"

"No…not really," Capri answered, blushing. The woman's stern gaze was unnerving. "I think I've dreamt of this place before."

"You think?"

"I mean, I know I have. I recognize the ivy on the walls and the giant trees. There are jasmine bushes somewhere nearby, or at least I think there are…"

"Very well. Sebastian, get Clynn. He will determine if this girl is really his daughter."

"Daughter?" Capri's eyes widened in surprise.

"Yes, you're obviously someone's daughter, aren't you?"

"Yes, ma'am." She averted her eyes and stared at the ground, the nerves rioting in her stomach. Less than thirty minutes ago, she had been just a slightly less than normal girl sitting in a park in Virginia, reading a book. Now she was in the company of total strangers in a bizarre place with no idea how to get home. And they were claiming she was some Dryad thing. Panic spread through her as her mind raced with questions and doubts. What was she doing here? How was she going to get back? What if this was some crazy cult and she'd walked right into it? Her boss had always told her that she was too trusting, too guileless. Maybe it was about to become her one fatal flaw.

A few moments later, Sebastian returned, a man racing beside him. Capri felt all of her doubts and fears fade to a numb denial. It wasn't possible.

She eyed the man carefully. He was nearly the same height as Sebastian, but older by fifteen, twenty years. His hair was the same pale blonde as her own, though it was neatly trimmed and receding slightly at his forehead. He had a thin face with worry lines around his eyes, and was slim and wiry looking, his legs covered in gray slacks paired with a matching gray sweater. As he approached, Capri saw that his eyes mirrored her own in both color and shape. She noticed awkwardly that they were already brimming with tears.

"Oh, Capri," the man stuttered, stopping a few feet from her, his eyes drinking their fill. "You're alive."

Capri was speechless. She could see with her own eyes that this man greatly resembled her in a way that no one else ever had. Had she really just found her father?

When he reached out to her hesitantly, she felt a tear slide down her cheek. Unable to do more, she stumbled to him, gasping as his arms enclosed around her, safe and warm. She gave in to the tears, the sobs shaking her as she held on. She didn't care who witnessed her tears this time. She was home.

It was by far the best birthday she had ever had.

The man named Clynn, who she was beginning to accept as her long, lost father, was taking her for a walk around the courtyard so they could get to know each other. The others that she had met, including Liam, disappeared inside the castle to give them time alone.

"So you have been living in Virginia all this time?" Clynn asked politely as they walked, the dappled sunlight bringing out the silver in his pale hair. He had a soothing voice, mild and quiet, giving her the impression that he was a man long accustomed to solitude. Funny, she was that way, too.

"Yes. In an orphanage," she replied quietly, biting her lip. It always embarrassed her to admit she was an orphan.

Clynn tilted his head down to look at her, and the sadness he felt showed clearly on his face. "I'm so sorry."

Capri shrugged. "I guess my only question is why you didn't try to find me?"

"We did," he insisted as he stopped, his hands reaching out to clutch her shoulders firmly. "We searched for nearly a year. But you have to understand, we had no idea where he had taken you."

"I see." Capri did, though it still hurt to think of how different her life would have been had she been found instead of lost.

"My darling," Clynn bent his head to kiss her cheek gently, a gesture that made her eyes well with tears again. "I didn't just lose you that day. I lost your mother as well."

"My...mother?"

"Yes. She was killed during the raid." He watched her face closely, gauging her reaction. She looked dumbfounded. "I'm sorry."

"I can't even imagine what that must have been like for you. I'm sorry I don't remember her."

"She was an amazing woman. The most kind, gentle, compassionate person I had ever met. It took quite a bit of persuading to get Thea's permission to allow her to live here with me."

"Why did you need permission?"

"Because Heidi, your mother, was human. She had no powers."

Her brows furrowed as she processed what he had just said.

"So because I have powers, does that mean that I'm not human?"

"You are partly human, but you are primarily an Air Dryad, just as I am," Clynn said kindly, knowing how difficult it would be for her to understand. "We have the appearance of a human, and the lifespan of a human, but we are not really human. We serve a greater purpose."

"Which is…?"

He sighed, wondering how to explain it to her.

"We were created by Thea, Mother Earth, to aid her in taking care of the planet. Our purpose is to maintain balance with the elements. As an Air Dryad, it is my responsibility, and soon it will be yours, to control the wind and the air. For example, every time there is a tornado, I am controlling it. Every time the wind shifts and a cold front sets in, I am controlling it. It is both our gift and our responsibility."

She stared at him for a long moment. She could hear birds chattering around her, could feel the light breeze on her skin and smell the honeysuckle just beyond them. But she couldn't process any of it. She was completely and utterly baffled.

"I'm still not convinced that I'm not dreaming this all up."

He smiled at her. "It will get easier to accept with time, trust me. This is where you belong. On Euphora, with me."

"But what about my job? And the apartment I had lined up to rent in Richmond?" Her practical side kicked in as she thought of her situation. "I can't just abandon the life I had and come live in this strange wonderland."

"We can arrange to have everything taken care of for you. Unless…you want to go back to Richmond? If you do, I will understand." Despite his words, Capri could see the concern in his patient eyes. How could she abandon her only family when she had just found him?

"No, I don't want to go back. All of this just seems…strange to me."

"You really don't remember anything from before you were taken?"

Capri debated for a moment whether or not to explain her dream to him. She had been told so many times that it hadn't been real, that it had been a figment of her imagination. But here she was, standing in the very courtyard she had long convinced herself didn't exist.

"I've been having this dream, always the same one, since I can remember," she began, her eyes meeting his. What a shock it was to look into the same cool, gray eyes that stared back at her out of the mirror every morning. "In my dream, I'm in a courtyard…this courtyard, actually, and I'm hiding beneath this huge jasmine bush. I remember it was jasmine because in the dream I play with the tiny flowers and think how they look like little white stars. I think someone told me that once," she paused, brows creased, the vague memory just out of reach. "Anyway, I hear this scream, a woman's scream, and then she falls to the ground. I never really see her, I just hear her fall. Then I feel hands grab me and lift me away, and someone, a man I think, laughs. It's a cold, ruthless laugh. And then I wake up with that horrible sound in my head."

For a moment, Clynn said nothing. He just stared into the eyes of his daughter, his little girl all grown up, who had witnessed the death of her mother without even understanding it. It pained him to think of how terrified she must have been, and how his own helplessness over the whole situation had nearly driven him mad. But, miraculously, his daughter had somehow made her way home to him. He would do his best to protect her, no matter what. "When you were here with me, I would walk with you around the gardens and I would pick different flowers and give them to you. I was teaching you their names, and I would help you remember by comparing all of them to something else."

He turned around suddenly and walked over to a nearby plant, plucking a flower from its branches. When he returned, she saw that it was tiny red blossom.

"What is this lovely, red butterfly called, Capri?"

"Red butterflies are honeysuckle," she answered immediately, then blushed when he smiled at her. "You were the one who told me that."

"Yes... yes I was." He pulled her into a hug, and she let her head rest comfortably against his shoulder. There was so much time that had been lost between them, and yet she had never felt more at ease with anyone before. She figured it was purely blood recognizing blood, something she had never felt before. It was an incredibly beautiful feeling.

# Chapter Two

*She heard the* footsteps of someone walking toward them and pulled away from her father. Liam was approaching, his face alight with a smile.

"How are you?" he asked politely.

"Fine. Confused and overwhelmed, I guess. But I'm fine," she replied, still feeling foolish and out of place.

"Thea wants to have a party to welcome you home and introduce you to everyone."

"What a lovely idea," Clynn responded, nodding at Liam.

Capri froze, dread rising in her stomach. "Everyone?"

She didn't like big crowds and she certainly didn't like being the center of attention. She instinctively crossed her arms over her chest.

Liam smiled easily. "Don't worry, there are only twenty-five of us."

"Twenty-five?" Capri spluttered, feeling suddenly nauseous. "Do I have to?"

"It won't be so bad, trust me. Most of them have technically met you before. They know who you are."

"I'm not good with people, especially a lot of people. Everyone's going to ask me questions and put me on the spot."

"I'll protect you." Liam grinned, patting her shoulder. "Serendipity has laid out a dress for you to wear in your room. I suggest you head up and change and then I'll escort you to dinner."

"I have a room?"

"Of course you do," Clynn asserted with a sad smile. "Did you think that I would give up hope that one day you'd return to me?"

Capri wasn't sure what to say. Had he really never lost hope in these last fifteen years? She herself had given up hope so easily that she felt ashamed.

"Come on, I'll show you to your room." Clynn wound his arm around her shoulders and lead her to the castle, Liam walking beside them.

She stared at the castle with wide eyes as they approached, taking in every detail. The marvelous stone walls, covered almost entirely with spiraling, twisting ivy. Row after row of large, pebbled glass windows, glittering in the sunlight. Towers, four of them, rising up from the main castle, each circular with pointed roofs the color of slate. The doors to the castle, she noticed now that she was closer, were huge as well, nearly twice as tall as a normal door and twice as wide. They were a deep mahogany, with wrought iron winding over its surface, similar to the entrance gate. Again, Liam began to place his hand over one of the doors, only to pause.

"Would you like to open it, Capri?" he asked encouragingly, motioning for her to touch the wood.

She nervously bit her lip, but stepped forward. As she laid her palm flat against the wood, she held her breath in anticipation. For a moment, nothing happened, and she felt mortification and embarrassment stab pitifully into her chest.

Then, like magic, the doors seemed to melt away beneath her hand, fading like the gate. Mystified, she stared at her palm, wondering how it was possible. Clynn had to press lightly into her back for her to look up and take in the magnificence of the castle's atrium.

It's like the garden has been brought inside, she thought as she simply stared, mystified. The circular walls were covered in plants, some of them in pots, others seeming to grow out of the walls and floor. The echoing chirps of birds could be heard as they flew overhead, and as she looked up she realized that where there should have been a ceiling, there were instead fluffy, white clouds glowing golden as though touched by the sun.

In front of her, past the atrium, was a large corridor that branched off to the right and to the left, each side flanked by several doors. Against the wall directly ahead stood a pair of larger, more impressive doors made of the same mahogany as the entrance. The walls and the floor were gray stone and iron torches lighted the way. Looking up, she noticed that the entire ceiling was covered in glorious paintings, depicting what looked like the Garden of Eden, with circular skylights throughout, casting lovely morning light upon the walls and floor.

"This way," Clynn said quietly, leading her to a door down the right corridor. When he opened it, she saw stone stairs winding up in a large spiral. "All of the living quarters are up here."

They walked up two flights of stairs before stopping at a landing that led off down a smaller corridor. Clynn motioned toward the first door, which he opened.

"This is your room, just as you left it. Though we upgraded the bed a few years ago." He smiled as he watched her mouth open in shock as she entered the room.

"Mine?" she gasped, twirling around in a circle to take in the lovely room with its stone walls and white canopy bed. Pale blue rugs graced the floor by the bed and near the fireplace, and beautiful oil paintings depicting various birds hung on the walls.

On the bed lay the most beautiful dress she had ever seen.

"Oh," she whispered, her mouth falling open.

"Serendipity has excellent taste," Clynn remarked, watching with pleasure as his daughter lifted the sapphire blue sleeveless gown from the bed. The material was silky and flowing, like smooth water.

"It's so beautiful," she murmured, admiring the bare hints of silver thread that shimmered throughout the blue silk.

"Please, take your time getting ready. Liam will meet you here in an hour to escort you down to dinner." Clynn walked over to her and kissed her forehead. "Welcome home, darling."

"Thanks." She watched as both men disappeared, closing the door behind them. She stood there, clutching the dress in her hands, feeling numb.

This was really happening, she thought wildly. She was really standing here, in a castle. She really had just met her father. And soon she would meet everyone else. Liam hadn't mentioned that they were related, so she guessed her only blood relative was her father. So who was everyone else? Was there a Fire and Earth Dryad too? Were there more Air Dryads? She had so many questions and hoped tonight would answer the majority of them.

Setting the dress upon the bed, she turned and noticed a door off to her right. When she opened it, she smiled. Her own bathroom...perfect. With a claw foot tub and everything. It was just how she imagined a bathroom would look in a castle: old fashioned and elegant.

Glancing in the mirror, she wondered how she would make herself look worthy to wear that gorgeous dress. Suddenly, she remembered she didn't have her duffle. Whirling around, she noticed it had been placed beside the bed. Thank you, Liam, she thought with relief, lifting it up and reaching inside for her toiletries.

Since she had an hour, she decided to indulge in a quick bath to freshen up. Slipping into the tub filled with frothy bubbles gave her a sense of tingling excitement.

After her bath, she applied makeup and tidied up her hair the best she could. Deeming herself worthy, she padded back into the bedroom for the dress.

Slipping into the gown, she zipped it and turned to stare at herself in the full length mirror by the door. The sight took her breath away.

I look like a princess, she thought wistfully, her lips curving in a feminine smile. She noticed a pair of silver high heeled shoes resting beside the bed, and made a mental note to thank whoever Serendipity was for lending them to her. They were a bit small for her feet, but she was too grateful to wear them to care.

Taking a deep breath, she analyzed herself once more in the mirror. She didn't look perfect, but she wasn't that bad. The dress fit beautifully on her willowy figure. And her height, which had always annoyed her in the past, actually added to the appeal of the gown. Feeling a little more confident, Capri opened the door to the hallway, meeting Liam's eyes as she exited.

He merely smiled. "You clean up nice."

"Thanks, I guess." Capri flushed, tugging at the skirt of the gown nervously. "I still don't really feel I deserve to be wearing a dress like this, but I'll take it."

"It suits you." He gallantly held out his arm and she wrapped her own around it. Completing the image of a modern day prince, he was wearing a handsomely tailored, three-piece black suit with a sapphire blue tie. "Ready?"

She took a deep breath. "No, but what can I do?"

"Suck it up." He grinned at her, leading her to dinner and what was surely going to be the most important night of her life.

"Today's my birthday you know, you should be nice and hide me for awhile."

"Not a chance." They reached the bottom of the stairs and he pushed open the door for her. "Happy Birthday though."

"Thanks," she murmured anxiously. "Oh, I hate being nervous."

"Don't be. They'll love you."

His words didn't make her feel any better, and as they walked together down the long corridor toward the large doors ahead, she began to feel a little faint.

She saw Clynn waiting for them outside the doors, his eyes filled with pride. He was also wearing a suit.

"Lovely." He smiled, taking her hands in his. "You remind me of your mother."

"Thank you." She blushed again, unable to help it. Her face was going to be red all night if she kept this up. She hated being the center of attention.

"Everyone is already inside. They're so excited you are home." Her father was glowing with such happiness that Capri began to feel cheerful just looking at him.

But when he pushed open the doors, she felt her confidence shatter and nerves return. Here we go…

The room was enormous, at least compared to the dining rooms she had seen. It was long and rectangular with a two-story high ceiling covered in beautiful paintings, just like the corridor, with windows entirely covering one of the walls. Outside, it was dark as night. Wait, hadn't it just been morning? Had she been in her room that long? It just wasn't possible…

The sudden movement of people rising to their feet made her notice the dining table, and the two dozen people who stood around it. They were all staring at her, and she felt her face flush once again with embarrassment.

Thea and Sebastian stood at the head of the table. Capri noticed that Thea looked much more relaxed, and her face much kinder than before.

"Welcome home, Capri," Thea said, her voice echoing throughout the room. She left the table and began to walk toward them. When she was a few feet away, she held out both her arms in greeting.

"We have been waiting for you." She smiled warmly, wrapping her arms around Capri in a hug. Capri hugged the woman back, feeling unsure. Thea pulled away, but held her at arm's length. "I'm sorry I didn't introduce myself properly earlier. My name is Thea. I am Mother Earth."

Capri attempted a shaky smile. "Nice to meet you."

"And this," she turned as Sebastian appeared beside her, "is Sebastian. Also known as Father Sky."

"Oh." Capri didn't know what to expect, but it hadn't been this. The mother and father...creators of Earth and Sky. She had studied Greek mythology and knew about Mother Earth and Father Sky. She just couldn't believe they were real and standing right in front of her.

"Welcome home, my darling." Sebastian lifted her hand and pressed his lips to it in a delicate kiss, his eyes on hers. "So lovely."

"Yes, she is," Thea replied. "It pleases me to have my long lost Air Dryad return. We have missed you dearly, child. You are greatly needed here."

Capri's eyes widened. Was she supposed to know how to be an Air Dryad right away? Thea gently grasped her arm lead her to the head of the table. She remembered all the people staring at her, and the thought fell to the wayside, nervousness flooding back.

She saw men and women, both young and old. The youngest was a skinny boy with jet black hair who appeared to be about fourteen and the oldest a man of about forty-five with long, white hair and vivid blue eyes. Liam's eyes, she realized with a shock. Was that his father?

Everyone was dressed magnificently and now she understood why she had needed the dress. Apparently formal wear was popular here. Even Thea was adorned in a shimmering silver gown that spilled onto the floor in a lovely train. Capri watched her step to avoid trampling on it.

The extravagance of it all caught her by surprise. Though, after meeting the princely Liam, had she really expected anything less than royalty?

"Sit here, next to me, and I will make a toast. We will do the introductions later, after dinner." Thea motioned to a plush mahogany and gold silk chair. Capri took her seat, and Clynn sat in the chair beside her. As they sat, the rest of the group took their seats, including Sebastian. Thea alone remained standing.

Capri stared dutifully at the white tablecloth in front of her, terrified to do anything more. All of these people made her uncomfortable. How did anyone get used to this? At least at the orphanage she wasn't required to socialize. She could just eat in peace, talk to someone if she pleased, and be on her way. She had a daunting feeling that she was not going to have that same luxury here.

When Thea began to speak, Capri looked up, her eyes focused on the woman she now knew as Mother Earth.

"Fifteen years ago, our home was violated. We were attacked by our enemies, and we suffered a great and terrible loss. One of our own was killed, and another stolen from us, presumably dead. I am thrilled on this night to announce that what was once lost has been found. And while the memories of the attack still plague our minds, I hope you all will take comfort in knowing that miracles do happen, and even a tiny three year old girl can have the strength and resilience to survive. Let us toast, to her return."

At that very moment, all across the table golden goblets appeared out of thin air. Capri watched as everyone casually reached for a goblet to lift in toast, as though everyday objects commonly appeared out of nowhere.

Capri reached for her own, glancing briefly inside to see deep red wine before lifting the goblet. She returned her eyes to Thea, who smiled warmly at her.

"To Capri," she bellowed powerfully, and all around the table everyone repeated the phrase, resounding in a deep echo. Capri blushed again, unable to look at all of the people who were toasting in her honor. She felt her father pat her gently on the arm in comfort.

Everyone began to drink, so she lifted the goblet to her lips and sampled the wine. Impressed, she took another sip, wondering if they got to drink wine like this every night.

She set the goblet down, just in time to notice that the table had suddenly been populated by gold rimmed plates and more food than she had ever seen in her life. Stunned, she simply stared while everyone around her began reaching for the food and filling their plates.

Sensing her discomfort, Clynn lifted her plate and began placing a few slices of turkey breast and some steamed vegetables on its surface. He added a buttered roll and set it down in front of her.

When he saw the look on her face, he looked sheepish. "I'm sorry, did you not want turkey? You used to love it before…" The sadness in his eyes broke her heart.

"No, I still love turkey. I'm just overwhelmed, that's all." She smiled at him, hoping she could mask her apprehension. The fact was, she did like turkey, but the thought of eating anything was sickening. Nevertheless, she forked a bite of turkey and began to eat. It wasn't until she ate a few pieces that she realized just how good it was, so juicy and tender, that within minutes her entire plate was cleared. Clynn looked extremely pleased when he noticed.

"After dinner everyone will head into the parlor and I'll introduce you," her father said, leaning toward her.

"Are they all Dryads?" Capri asked, her eyes briefly glancing around at the group, noting how easily they socialized with one another. They were like a family, she thought. And she was one of them. It was going to take a long time for her to get used to that fact.

"No, they are not all Dryads," Clynn replied, his eyes kind. "Some of them are Muses, others are Fates and Furies."

"Um…" Capri's eyebrows raised in bewilderment. So she had heard Liam right about the Muses…they did exist.

He gently patted his daughter's hand. "Don't worry. They don't all expect you to remember their names and titles right away. Just get through tonight and we'll take it one day at a time. You have a lot of training to catch up on."

"Right…" The idea of taking everything one day at a time made her feel slightly better, despite the fact that even more questions were racing through her mind. Muses? Fates? Furies? She had heard of them from her basic research of Greek mythology. But she had never believed in them. Though knowing that Mother Earth and Father Sky really existed, she supposed she shouldn't be surprised about the others. Might as well believe it all, she thought as she took another swig of wine. It couldn't get much crazier than this.

Oh, how wrong she was.

By the time everyone finished eating both dinner and dessert Capri felt relaxed and began to enjoy herself, quietly listening to the conversations around her. A few times she had been brave enough to actually look around at all of the faces, and as she did so, she silently made observations.

There were several young people, most of them within a few years of herself. Among them was a girl with wine-red hair that fell in curly waves inches above her shoulders. She had tawny brown eyes that looked almost like liquid amber, and a husky laugh that carried throughout the room. Capri could tell without meeting her that this girl was the most extroverted of the group, and easily the most vibrant.

Another girl sat across from Capri, a classic beauty with dark coco hair that fell straight down her back and wise, sage green eyes. She had an air of intelligence and quiet superiority about her.

There were also two young men sitting at the table and they both were about Liam's age, one older and one younger. They both sat quietly, neither one engaging in much conversation. One of them, the younger of the two, had wavy, black hair and dark, melancholy eyes. The other one seemed harder, stricter, almost like a soldier who's about to head into battle. He sat rigid in his chair and ate politely, but she watched with intrigue as his eyes continually scanned the table, watching everyone and everything. He had dark blonde hair that was cut relatively short and sharp blue eyes. Capri's first thought was that he was a cop, but she brushed the thought away. As far as she knew, there were no cops on Euphora.

She felt oddly ordinary as she glanced around at everyone. They all knew their place and knew the rules that went along with it. While everyone sat together at the table, they still were sectioned into groups. Where she sat at the head of the table, there were three older men, including her father, and four of the younger people, including herself, the red haired girl, the classically beautiful girl, and Liam. Looking at physical comparisons alone, she could assume that the older man with the white hair and striking blue eyes was Liam's father, and the man with the rich brown hair and elegant poise was the father of the dark haired girl. Then there was her own father, Clynn. Where the redhead's father or mother was, Capri wasn't sure.

Further down the table from where the two young men sat, were two tough looking older men she assumed to be their fathers. The older man sitting beside the dark haired young man had equally dark features and seemed reserved, but polite. He had an oddly harsh and sour looking face, despite his pleasantly blank expression.

The other older man seemed charismatic and boisterous, if not a bit domineering. He was talking animatedly about something, his hands waving around in avid gestures. He had a full dark blonde beard just going gray to match his hair, and his face was scarred in places, from what she didn't know, but it was handsome nonetheless. He had a bark of a laugh and the same intelligent blue eyes as the young man she assumed was his son.

There were also others toward the end of the table, though they seemed to only speak amongst themselves. Among them were three extremely beautiful women who had fluid movements and lovely smiles. Sitting beside them were three bored looking teens.

Across the table from them sat a group of people who looked so morose that Capri felt an involuntary chill run up her spine as she looked at them. They all had dark hair, wildly curly, and they all seemed quite content to keep to themselves. Again, it was three older women and three teens, including the fourteen year old Capri had noticed earlier. He had the face of a gypsy, with wide, dark eyes.

Graciously, the people around her seemed content to let her eat in peace which she silently thanked them for. She figured it was either her expression or her father's doing that kept them from badgering her with questions. Either way, she was content to sit in silence and observe.

After dessert was cleared, however, her anxiety returned. She felt her stomach tighten as she realized it was time to socialize.

Thea rose from her seat and suddenly everyone stopped speaking at once. They all turned to her with avid eyes, as though awaiting instructions.

"Let us all move into the parlor," she announced, her arms motioning with a flourish and her face beaming with a smile.

With the sounds of chairs scraping against the stone floor and idle chatter, everyone turned and left through another set of large doors that were off to the right hand side of the dining hall.

Capri stood and was about to follow them, when Clynn stopped her. "Are you feeling alright?" He asked kindly, his eyes on hers.

Capri tried to smile. "Yes, just fine."

She knew he could tell she was lying, but he lead her to the parlor anyway, his hand placed comfortingly on the small of her back.

"I'll just take you around and introduce you, then we can go outside and get some air."

"Oh! Before I forget," Capri began, stopping her father before they reached the doors. "How did it change from morning to night so quickly?"

He looked amused. "Thea's favorite times of day are early morning and night, so you'll rarely find it any other time of day here."

"She just changes it whenever she feels like it?"

"You'll get used to it, trust me. You could say we are in our own little bubble here on Euphora, unaffected by the outside world."

"Oh...so how did the food just appear out of thin air? Who cooked it all?"

He chuckled, smiling down at her. "We have a...staff that cooks and cleans for us," he paused, his eyes twinkling. "Have you ever heard of fairies?"

Her mouth fell open as she gawked at him. "You're kidding. If there are fairies here, why haven't I seen them?"

"They are invisible to those who don't believe in them, Capri," his eyes clouded with sadness as he continued, "you used to be able to see them..."

Her heart broke a little at the look on his face, and at the news that there was yet another thing she had lost. She sighed, knowing there was little she could do.

"Let's go, darling. They are waiting for you."

With that, he led her into the parlor, and into the throngs of people who had been waiting fifteen long years to see her again.

# Chapter Three

*The parlor was* nearly as large as the dining room, with high ceilings and dozens of windows. It was filled with plush furniture in rich earth tones, and there were plants and flowers gracing nearly every inch of the room that wasn't covered with furniture. The ceiling was coffered with gold and white accents, and in the middle was the largest crystal chandelier Capri had ever seen. The only difference was this chandelier appeared to move, or at least the lights inside it did. They were flitting around like fireflies, and for a moment she considered the possibility that they actually *were* fireflies...

As they had done earlier at the table, everyone was sitting or standing in groups, just like the cliques she remembered from high school. She also remembered that rarely did the cliques ever intermingle...would it be the same way here?

Clynn led her over to the first group, which included the redhead and Liam.

Liam smiled warmly and gave her a light kiss on the cheek as he greeted her. "Hope you enjoyed dinner."

"It was really more of a feast," Capri mused, feeling increasingly more comfortable in his presence.

"Capri, this is Rohan and his daughter Rhiannon, they are the Earth Dryads," Clynn introduced as Capri turned to look at the graceful, dark haired girl and her father.

Rohan politely held out his hand and Capri took it in hers. It was soft and elegant, not unlike her own father's hands. His hair was dark brown, but feathered with pewter gray that only made him look even more handsome and distinguished.

"I am pleased to see you safely return home to us," he said smoothly, his voice deep and confident. His eyes were the same sage green as his daughter's, if not a touch darker.

"Yes, I can't believe you've been living amongst humans all this time," commented the girl named Rhiannon, shaking Capri's hand as well. Her beauty was striking, from her smooth ivory skin to her slender, graceful femininity. "It must have been awful."

"Um…well, it wasn't all bad," Capri replied, flushing with heated pride. She didn't like how this girl spoke, as if she was superior in every possible way to everyone in the room. Classically beautiful, maybe, but Rhiannon sure had that perfect nose of hers held high in the air.

"Rhiannon, you're such a brat." The red haired girl said loudly, shoving Rhiannon out of the way, despite being half a foot shorter. Rhiannon looked extraordinarily insulted, and Capri felt a tinge of pleasure. The red haired girl smiled brightly, her amber eyes glittering deviously. "I love hanging out with humans, they know how to have more fun than all these boring people." She rolled her eyes dramatically as she laughed. "I'm Blythe, by the way. Fire Dryad."

"Oh!" Capri's eyes widened as she shook Blythe's hand. "I should've guessed, the red hair and all."

Blythe laughed again and Capri blushed.

"Honestly, the hair thing is a fluke. Though I guess it's fitting, huh?" Blythe smiled warmly and winked, brushing away a curly strand of wine colored hair that had fallen in front of her foxy triangular face. It was a face that had more sharp angles than soft curves and was graced with a light dusting of freckles which only served to heighten her charm. "So Liam found you! I always knew he'd amount to something."

"Oh, shut up," Liam said, playfully pulling her into a headlock with his arm. "Someone's gotta be the role model around here."

"Dream on, buddy." Blythe elbowed him in the gut and wrestled her way out of his strangle-hold. It was obvious to Capri that they were not only close friends, but as close to being brother and sister as two people can get without being related. She felt a hot rush of envy come over her just thinking about it.

Clynn cleared his throat, looking amused. "Anyway, this is Liam's father, Lucian."

The man with the long white hair nodded at her, his smile quick and infectious just like his son's. His blue eyes were bright and humorous, set in a long face that was youthful despite his age. "Welcome home, dear. You'll have to excuse the children; I don't know why we keep them around."

"Hey!" Liam called out as he and Blythe stopped wrestling each other. "You love us, don't lie."

Lucian sighed heavily, but his eyes twinkled with amusement. "I fear my love for you dried up long ago, son of mine."

Liam pouted playfully. "Capri, convince your father to adopt me. Mine clearly doesn't appreciate me."

Capri grinned. "I want him all to myself, sorry."

"Let me introduce you to the Furies, darling," Clynn interjected, pulling her away.

They approached the rough and tumble looking men, who now sat together near one of the windows. The four of them stood up simultaneously when they saw Capri.

"We thought we'd never see you again, girl," said the older man with the scarred face in a booming voice, holding out his hand and grinning. His hand was as scarred as his bearded face, and he was muscular and powerfully built, towering over her and her father. "I'm Roarke, and this is my son Rian."

Roarke shook Capri's hand vigorously, and she noticed that his hand was much rougher than Rohan's. She was interested to learn the reason why. Roarke nodded to his son, the young man with the dark blonde hair, who took her hand in his firmly. He was slightly shorter than Liam, with a stocky build, and while he wasn't as boyishly handsome as the Water Dryad, his face was compelling in a different way. It was sharper, harder somehow, as though he rarely had the occasion to laugh or even smile. His serious blue eyes bore into hers, and she had the distinct impression of being assessed. He said nothing, but merely bowed his head in acknowledgement. He let go and shifted aside to allow the other two men to approach.

"This is Balgaire and his son Brogan," Clynn introduced, and Capri shook their hands in turn. Balgaire was tall like Roarke, but leaner and sparer. He had a full head of dark hair and thick brows that arched over eerily dark eyes, with a clean shaven face tanned and lined with age. Unlike his partner, this man projected neither charisma nor power, but rather a quiet and sharp intellect, which led her to wonder if Balgaire was the brains behind Roarke's brawn.

His son was also slender and his handshake more gentle than that of his fellow Furies. When his eyes met hers, he seemed a bit nervous, as though he would have preferred quiet solitude to this impromptu party. He looked away from her the moment she let go of his hand, returning his stare resolutely to the floor.

When her father continued, Capri turned her attention away from shy Brogan. "They are Furies, basically like the police force here on Euphora."

That was why he acted like a cop, Capri realized, her eyes shifting to Rian, who was still watching her closely. He basically was one.

"Clynn, we're much more than your run of the mill *human* police force." Roarke chuckled and patted Clynn heartily on the back. Capri could sense the power and pride emanating from him, and it was no wonder why he seemed to be the leader of this small group. "You see, Capri, we not only preserve the peace here on Euphora, but we also hunt down demons throughout the world and bring them to justice. Damn bastards like to wreak havoc sometimes, and it's our job to stop them."

"Sounds dangerous," Capri said before she could catch herself. She caught the brief flicker of amusement in Rian's eyes before she looked back at Roarke, who was nodding in agreement.

"It is, which is why we have to be tough. Isn't that right, son?" He patted Rian on the back, though to Rian's credit he barely seemed to feel it.

"Yes, sir."

"Damn straight." Roarke beamed proudly at his son, then turned to Capri. "Rian trains every day, both physically and mentally. He's going to be the best damn Fury we ever had on Euphora. Next to his old man, of course."

"No one doubts that Rian will make a fine Fury," Clynn said politely, and Capri understood that he wanted to move on to the next group. Capri could tell that Roarke enjoyed boasting about his accomplishments, and about those of his son. She imagined he could probably go on about the subject for a very long time.

They continued on, heading toward a group of women and teens who sat around a lovely white grand piano. One of the women was playing, while the two other women were singing. Their voices were hauntingly lovely, and Capri had a brief image of sirens singing their songs to shipwrecked sailors on some far away island.

Clynn waited until they finished the song and then approached.

"Capri, meet the Muses."

The three women walked right up to Capri and hugged her one at a time, placing gentle kisses on her cheeks. They were so lovely, and their movements so fluid, that Capri almost thought they floated on water.

They all had waist length hair, ranging from blonde to chestnut brown. When one of them spoke, it sounded like lovely, lilting music played from a harp.

"We always hoped you would find your way back to us," the honey blonde said, clasping her hands together as she wistfully eyed Capri. "Thank goodness it has happened."

"This is Serendipity, the one who lent you that dress. She is Rohan's wife and Rhiannon's mother." Clynn smiled encouragingly and Capri's mouth fell open in surprise.

"Oh, thank you so much, it's a lovely dress," she said politely. She noticed the resemblance between this woman and the coolly superior Rhiannon. They were both heartbreakingly gorgeous.

"It looks like it was made for you, my darling," Serendipity commented serenely, turning to her fellow Muses, "don't you agree?"

"Yes, it suits her slender figure perfectly," the brunette replied. "I am Trinity and this is Clarity."

"We are so happy you are home," Clarity said, gracefully shaking back her mane of strawberry blonde hair. "I am so proud that my son found you."

"Liam is your son?"

"Can't you tell? Handsome boy, don't you think? Gets all of his good looks from me." Clarity smiled wistfully, and Capri couldn't tell if the woman was being serious or not.

"These are their other children, the future Muses...Sierra, Tobias and Cilla." Clynn motioned to the three bored looking teens, who sat side by side on the sofa next to the piano, still looking indifferent.

"Nice to meet you all." Capri smiled. She saw one of the teens, presumably Tobias, since he was the only boy, roll his eyes. She tried to ignore it, although it left her feeling as though not everyone was thrilled to see her return.

"The Muses are in charge of providing inspiration to the world, both in arts and music."

"Darling, we provide clarity of thought as well, don't forget!" Serendipity laughed musically, gazing fondly at Capri. "If you ever feel stymied, come to us."

"I will, thank you," Capri muttered, smiling faintly. She was beginning to feel overwhelmed as her father led her to the last group of people, sitting beside a large, roaring fireplace.

"Lastly, Capri, these are the Fates." They approached the morose looking women and Capri noticed the beauty of the Muses contrasted darkly with the gloomy Fates.

The three women all wore black to match their wildly curly dark hair. Their faces were pale and rather gaunt, and their deep brown eyes seemed to hold a legion of dark secrets.

"Capri, this is Morgaine, Nyxa, and Angora."

The three women looked at Capri, but none of them held out their hands. Instead they sat there, eyeing her knowingly.

"We knew she wasn't dead, Clynn, I don't know why you didn't listen to us," one of them said, her eyes still on Capri. Her right hand was opening and closing reflexively.

"Now, Nyxa, we both know that it's much harder for you to examine the thread of one on the Council."

"Rubbish. The threads do not lie. I knew she was alive. And despite what you may believe Clynn, we feel it when one of the Council perishes, and it is excruciating. It's something the rest of you couldn't possibly understand."

"You Dryads never trust us," one of the other women said suddenly. She was shifting constantly as though she couldn't sit still. Her voice was low and raspy, like she hadn't had water for days.

"We do, Morgaine," Clynn replied, and Capri could tell that he was lying through his teeth. He clearly thought all three of them were prone to exaggeration, and thus not worth taking seriously. "Now, where are your children?"

"They are taking care of business. Not a minute goes by without at least one birth or death, Clynn; we can't all take time off of work for a party," Nyxa responded haughtily, her eyes flashing with bitterness.

"Right..." Clynn turned to his daughter. "The Fates, as Nyxa has so graciously just explained, are in charge of spinning the thread of life for every individual on Earth. Then they measure it, and subsequently cut it when the time is right."

"Just like in the Greek myth," Capri noted, eyeing them curiously.

"Yes, but this is reality, girl, and serious business. The Greeks only knew what we wanted them to know because at the time we thought we'd try and introduce ourselves to them. Horrible idea that was, backfired on us. Took us hundreds of years to recover from *that* mistake."

"I think Thea would like to speak to you, darling," Clynn interrupted, leading Capri away. "Nice talking with you, ladies."

"There is so much more to this than I ever imagined." Capri sighed as she walked with her father.

"I know it's a lot to take in, but you will understand everything in time."

"I hope so."

Thea turned as they approached, her rich brown eyes warm. "How did the introductions go?"

"Everyone is very nice." Capri replied.

When Thea burst into laughter, Capri felt heat flush her cheeks.

"Oh, Clynn, you must have only introduced her to half the group!" Thea exclaimed, her face bright with humor. "You must've skipped Balgaire, the sour faced old coot."

Capri was completely taken aback by Thea's humor, so she stayed resolutely silent. There was still so much she had to learn about this place and the extraordinary people who lived here.

"He was polite, thank goodness." Clynn chuckled. "We barely escaped the Fates without a winded discussion about the Greeks."

Thea laughed again. "Oh, bless the Fates. Can't live with them, can definitely not live without them."

"Love of my life, can't we move this party outside? It's much too stuffy in here," Sebastian chimed in as he appeared behind Thea, lazily draping an arm over her shoulders, a snifter of brandy in his other hand.

Thea lifted one dark eyebrow at him, her lips curving into a smile. "Darling, you read my mind."

Within minutes, everyone was gathered outside in the courtyard on a large patio. Capri wasn't sure where they came from, but someone had conjured up glowing balls of light to float high in the air over what had become a dance floor. Tables were scattered around the edges, and everyone seated was laughing and talking. What looked like champagne bottles were opened with festive pops and poured generously into lovely crystal glasses. Music was playing, though she had no idea from where. She recognized the throaty voice of Van Morrison asking to have one more Moondance, and she wondered briefly if the Muses had influenced this jazzy number. She wouldn't be surprised if they had.

The whole thing had all happened so quickly, so smoothly, that Capri wondered if they did this every night.

"My fair lady, will you join me in a dance?" a voice said from behind her. Capri turned and saw Liam, bent over in a bow with his hand extended, a playful grin on his face.

"I don't really know how to dance," Capri said, feeling awkward.

"That is why the man is always the leader." Liam took her arm in his and led her onto the floor. Other couples were dancing already, including Blythe and Lucian who were spinning around and pulling off complicated movements Capri had no hope of mimicking.

"They're professionals," Liam remarked, taking Capri's hand in his and placing his other at the small of her back. "We'll just dance normal."

"Thank God." Capri laughed as she gazed upward, reveling in the beautiful star studded night sky. Had the sky ever been filled with that many stars in Virginia?

"I feel like I'm not even on the same planet." She hadn't meant to say the words out loud, and she blushed when Liam chuckled.

"I forgot to mention to you that Euphora is an island."

"Really?" Capri looked at him inquisitively. "In the Atlantic?"

"Not really…" He grinned mischievously at her. "We're technically over the Pacific Ocean."

"Over?" Her brows furrowed in confusion.

"Yes. Euphora is a floating island."

Capri's mouth fell open. "You're joking."

"Nope." He twirled her around to give her a second to process the concept of a floating island. When he brought her back into his arms, she felt laugher bubble in her throat.

"Alright, fine, we're floating, it's all good." She laughed openly, feeling free as he dipped her low to the ground. "I'm just going to accept that I'll never stop being surprised about this place."

"It will keep life interesting."

She smiled up at him. "Yes, it will."

After they'd danced through three whole songs, Liam led Capri over to an empty table. She collapsed into a chair, gently lifting her aching feet out of the shoes she was wearing. Liam went off to dance with Blythe, and Capri wondered how the two of them seemed to have endless amounts of energy. As she sat rubbing her feet, she noticed the Furies were sitting at the table next to her. Roarke was deep in serious conversation with the other Fury, Balgaire. Balgaire's son Brogan was out on the dance floor, slow dancing with Rhiannon. Both looked stiff and way too serious, a brutal contrast compared to the lively Liam and Blythe. Thea and Sebastian were dancing as well, Thea's silver gown shimmering like diamonds in the golden light. The way they moved seemed so graceful, so fluid and natural, that Capri couldn't help but imagine them dancing like that for thousands of years.

When she turned her attention back to the Furies, she spotted Rian sitting quietly across from his father, sipping champagne. Before she could do more than glance at him, his eyes shifted and met hers.

They held gazes for a moment, and she once again felt as though he was examining her. Because the feeling was uncomfortable, she turned away and shakily lifted a glass of champagne to her lips.

She'd never had champagne before, but she found the dryness of it didn't appeal to her. She'd set it down before she'd barely tasted it.

"Isn't it the most wonderful champagne you've ever tasted?" Rhiannon said as she sat suddenly beside Capri. She reached for a bottle herself and poured generously into a glass.

"Honestly, I've never had champagne before so I wouldn't really know," Capri replied, annoyed that she felt foolish.

Despite what Capri had been expecting, Rhiannon smiled. "Well, then take my word, this is as good as it gets."

"It must be an acquired taste," Capri said, her brows creasing as she tried another sip. It really did not taste very good, but then again, neither had coffee the first time she'd tried it...

"You're probably wondering if this is all we do around here, huh?" Rhiannon said as she propped her elbow on the table and rested her chin in her hand.

Capri glanced around at the dancing couples and at the others who were all laughing and drinking. A few, including the three Muses, were already visibly drunk and giggling with chorus bell laughter.

"If you do, then I've really been missing out."

Rhiannon laughed openly, and Capri felt a stab of envy at her beauty. "You will be so happy here, Capri, trust me. You are where you finally belong, after all these years."

Capri sipped at the champagne again, lost in thought. Every-one was saying that she was finally where she belonged, that she was home. She felt certain that she didn't belong here, not yet anyway, and she certainly did not feel at home. It would take time, like her father had said, for her to adjust, to accept.

"You know, when we were girls, you, me and Blythe were inseparable," Rhiannon said suddenly, her lips forming a deli-cate smile. "I'm only two years older than you, and Blythe is one. We used to run around in the courtyard pretending we were princesses."

Capri couldn't help but smile at the thought. "I bet Liam felt pretty left out."

"Well, being the only Dryad boy had its advantages. When we allowed him to play he was always the knight in shining armor, out to rescue the three princesses." Rhiannon sipped some champagne, her eyes glittering with humor. "I think the idea has gone to his head after all these years."

"He's very kind." Capri glanced out at the dance floor, where Liam and Blythe were still dancing.

When she looked back at Rhiannon, she saw that her eyes were filled with regret. "That was always his fatal flaw."

"How can kindness be a flaw?"

"People can easily take advantage of you when you are too kind."

Their eyes held a moment, pale gray and sage green. Capri didn't say anything, so Rhiannon continued.

"Unfortunately, when you were gone, the three of us couldn't cope with each other. It was like a piece of us was missing and we didn't know how to act anymore." Rhiannon reached out for Capri's hand and held it in her own firmly. "A divide had formed, most notably between Blythe and myself. It left Liam standing in the middle, but in the end, even his kindness wasn't enough to bridge the gap. A part of him was destroyed by it. Both Blythe and I knew it, but I suppose we were both too self absorbed by our own pride to care. In many ways, we still are. We barely speak to each other. And the only one who suffers is Liam, because he is kind."

Capri felt the helplessness rise up within her, and she squeezed Rhiannon's hand in an attempt to comfort. "I'm so sorry."

"It hurts to think how different things might have been had you not been taken from us, had you been here to keep us together."

"I wish I had been here, too." A tear slid down her cheek, but Capri didn't attempt to wipe it away. It felt appropriate, so she let it cling to her skin, a symbol of everything she'd lost, everything *they* had lost. "You seemed sort of stuck up before. I'm sorry I made that assumption."

Rhiannon smiled. "We all have our armor." She paused and took another sip of champagne as eyes drifted over to the dance floor and tightened. When she turned back to Capri, her smile was gone. "You'll soon learn that not everything is fun and parties on Euphora. What we are responsible for is very serious, and should be treated as such. If you need any help, I'm here for you."

"Okay," Capri said quietly as Rhiannon stood and walked away, carefully skirting the dance floor where Liam and Blythe were slow dancing.

She was astonished by how much she had learned in just one night. To know that her fellow Dryads had needed her, had shattered into pieces when she had been stolen, literally broke her heart. She knew that there was nothing she could have done to change it, but she hoped there was still time to repair the damage that had been done.

When she went to bed that night, curled up warm inside the bed that now belonged to her, Capri let the tears of both relief and sorrow fall freely until she drifted off into a wonderfully dreamless sleep.

# Chapter Four

*The sudden presence* of golden sunlight upon her face had her waking, her eyes gradually opening and her lips curving in a contented smile. Her bed was so warm, the blankets and pillows so fluffy and soft that it felt like sleeping on a cloud. She had never slept in a bed this comfortable and part of her almost wanted to stay in bed all day.

Then she remembered where she was and sat upright with a jolt, pinching her arm so hard she winced. It's all real, I didn't dream it up, she thought shakily, exhaling the breath she had been holding. Thank God, she sighed, eyes welling with tears again. Thank God it wasn't a dream.

Getting out of bed, she padded into the bathroom and splashed water on her face. Glancing at herself in the mirror, a huge grin greeted her back. She bit her lip to keep from bouncing up and down with joy. She was here, she was real, and she was home. Her father was alive and well and here with her, and she had a family. It was more than she could have ever hoped to receive in one day, much less at all. But the best part about the whole thing was that her childhood dreams had been based in reality. She hadn't imagined this place, she hadn't conjured it up subconsciously to explain away her abandonment issues. No, it had been real, and what she had experienced was real. The castle, the courtyard, the jasmine flowers…everything. If only she could remember more about the person who took her, maybe she could give closure to her father and the others.

Shaking away the thought, she brushed her hair and finished getting ready, throwing on a plain pair of faded jeans and a white t-shirt. She didn't own that much clothing and she hoped no one would be offended by her casual attire. She wondered briefly if everyone on Euphora went out into the human world to buy clothing and other necessities, or if they somehow made their own there. Deciding that it was just another mystery she would one day solve about her new home, Capri left her room and headed down the stone steps that lead to the atrium.

Her father had instructed her to meet him there so she could begin her training. She felt nervous about it all, hoping that she could live up to whatever expectations everyone had for her.

When she stepped into the atrium, Clynn was waiting for her. She approached him and he opened his arms, enveloping her in a big hug.

"Good morning, Capri," Clynn greeted as he released her, his eyes warm and kind. "Would you like something to eat?"

Capri nodded, realizing how hungry she was.

He led the way to the dining hall, and as they entered she noticed a few other people sitting around at the table, a host of breakfast essentials gracing its surface. This was obviously an informal breakfast, and everyone looked somewhat less polished and more bleary eyed than they had the night before. Capri kept her gaze lowered, shyly not wanting to meet anyone's eyes as she took a seat. Clynn sat beside her and automatically reached for a white pitcher.

"Coffee?" he asked, gesturing to the coffee cup that sat in front of her.

"Yes, please." Capri added sugar and creamer to the coffee after he had poured it for her, stirring it gently with a solid gold spoon.

"Good mo-ho-horning!" a sleepy, cheerful voice said with a yawn behind her. Capri turned around and watched Blythe slide into the seat next to her, her red hair curled wild and free around her face. Her amber eyes were sleepy. "Ugh, need coffee. Now."

Capri passed the pitcher over, watching as Blythe not only poured coffee, but simultaneously reached over and grabbed a bagel slathered in cream cheese, a chocolate chip muffin, a scoop of scrambled eggs, a few chunks of golden hash browns, and several pieces of bacon and sausage. She set down the coffee pitcher with her left hand, and with her right hand reached for what looked like maple syrup, pouring it all over everything.

Capri couldn't hide her shock as she watched Blythe rapidly and efficiently prepare a breakfast that would surely clog the arteries and stop the heart.

When Blythe tilted her head and noticed Capri looking at the food with wide eyes, she let her head fall back, laughing so hard her body shook. Gasping for air, she looked at Capri again, who was still staring at the plate in alarm. "Your face...it's so... funny...!" Blythe snorted with more laughter, and when Liam sat down across from them, his eyes danced with amusement.

"Blythe's eating habits are...unique," he remarked as he gathered his own breakfast, an egg white omelet and fresh fruit with orange juice. "But don't worry about her, she's got the metabolism of a five year old."

"But...you're so tiny," Capri managed, eyeing Blythe's slim, athletic figure with awe. "I just don't get it."

Blythe looked smug. "I have a lot of energy and I'm constantly running around, if you didn't notice. Trust me, I'll be hungry again in about an hour, and I'll need to refuel."

Capri shook her head and couldn't help the amused smile that spread over her face as she reached for a plain bagel, pausing to take a small bite. It was the most delicious bagel she had ever tasted, but she knew she shouldn't be surprised. She was going to have to get used to the idea that everything seemed to taste and look better on Euphora.

As they left the dining hall after breakfast, Clynn stopped in the corridor and turned to her, his eyes bright. "Would you like a tour of the castle before we get started?"

"Of course!" Capri smiled as she glanced around, wondering where they were off to first.

"Follow me." He turned right down the main corridor lit with morning sun from the skylights and led the way as they passed several doors on both sides. At the far end, there were beautiful stained glass windows casting multicolored light upon the stone floor. He stopped at a door on the left hand side with a large symbol emblazoned on the front of a golden lightning bolt with a black snake coiling around it. Beneath the symbol was the word FURY in bold, black letters.

"Oh," Capri said as she stared at the symbol, feeling her heart jump into her throat. So it would be the Euphora *police force* first...

Clynn opened the door for her and beckoned her inside before him. She stepped into a long, dark hallway with torches lining the stone walls. There were blank doors flanking both sides, as well as one large door at the very end. Her father led her down toward this last door, and when they reached it he pushed it open. The sudden brightness of the room startled her, and her hand shielded her eyes.

The room was enormously spacious and rectangular in shape, with white walls and white ceiling and pale stone floor. Along the right wall were four desks grouped together, each piled with paperwork. A large screen, nearly eight feet long and six feet high, hung on the wall near the desks with a digital map of the world on it. There were dots scattered throughout the map, varying from green to yellow to orange to red, the majority either green or yellow, and were more heavily populated over certain areas than others. Above the map were the words *Demon Tracker.*

There were three smaller screens flanking the side wall, but they were blank. Above them were the names: *FBI*, *Interpol* and *United Nations*.

On the opposite side of the room was a large indoor shooting range with cages and targets against the wall, coupled with a gym, complete with free weights, treadmills, and punching bags. On the side wall were lighted display shelves with row upon row of different weapons. Pistols, rifles, revolvers, whips, ninja stars... nearly every weapon imaginable was there including others she couldn't name.

In the shooting cages were the four Fury men.

"Good morning, Roarke, Balgaire," Clynn called out as he and Capri walked over to the cages. Roarke, who had been watching Rian target shoot, turned and smiled broadly at them.

"Clynn!" he bellowed, laughing as he stepped out of the cages and shut the gate behind him. He shook Clynn's hand genially, his grin wide and his scarred face cheerful. "Showing your baby girl around this morning?" he asked, winking at Capri.

"And this is our first stop," Clynn told him as he glanced over to where Rian and Brogan were both still shooting. "Maybe you could show Capri how you operate here."

"My pleasure." Roarke turned to Capri and placed his hand at the small of her back to lead her to the desks. She suddenly realized just how big he was. Tall, built like a tank, and heavily scarred. And yet he seemed to be completely in his element, as if he wouldn't do anything else in the world. She admired that about him and that he appeared dedicated to his work.

When they reached the desks, Roarke shuffled around on one of them a moment, lifting papers and pushing aside pamphlets and books until he unearthed what looked like a remote control. He pointed it at the *Demon Tracker* screen and pressed a button and suddenly the map moved and shifted, zooming in on the United States.

"See all those dots on there?" he asked, motioning to the screen.

She nodded, mesmerized as she scanned the map with its multicolored dots scattered all across the country by what had to be millions. What was even more interesting was how so many of them were centered around the major cities: Los Angeles, Chicago, Las Vegas, New York, Miami...

"Each dot is a demon and the color tells us what kind of demon it is. You have green for unlikely dangerous, yellow for possibly dangerous, orange for surely dangerous, and red for positively lethal. Obviously, we spend most of our time focusing on the last two." He turned to her and winked again, and she blushed. Something about him intimidated her despite his obvious politeness and good humor.

"What are those other screens for?" she asked, gesturing toward the other monitors flanking the side wall.

He pointed the remote, pressed a few more buttons, and the screens flickered to life. Visible on each was what looked like a boardroom, with a long table and chairs. They were empty.

"We communicate with a select few human organizations through live video feed, and they supply us with the extra manpower we need to hunt down the demons. It used to be that just two Furies could monitor and control the demons throughout the world, but within the last few hundred years, demon activity has spiked. Now we communicate with humans and get them involved, which makes our job easier and we get the added benefit of catching more demons. The humans who help us are specially trained agents, usually with police or military backgrounds, and are known as Enforcers."

Capri nodded as she glanced back at the *Demon Tracker*. "These Enforcers hunt down the demons for you?"

"They assist us with the more trivial cases, and alert us if there's a really bad case and then we swoop in and take the bastard out." He dragged his finger across his throat and grinned. "All demons are better when they're dead. And only we have the ability to banish a demon who has possessed a human, and the power to sense if a demon is nearby or has recently vacated an area. Many times the Enforcers require our help to finish the job."

"How do the demons live amongst humans and never get detected?" she asked curiously, "I never even knew they existed until I came here."

"A demon's true form is that of a serpent, or snake, and most of the time they search for an emotionally vulnerable human and latch onto them, possessing their body and living like that. Some of the most horrific murderers and dictators in history have been under the influence of a demon."

"Seriously?" Capri managed, looking horrified. "So I might have come across someone who was possessed and I wouldn't even know it?"

"Probably not. But then again, if you crossed paths with someone possessed by a demon and lived to tell the tale, you'd be damn lucky. They would have sensed your Dryad blood and known within two seconds what you were."

"Oh, well…" Her hand came up to her heart to steady herself. "That's terrifying."

"It's a harsh, cruel world out there, girl. Better get used to it." He chuckled and turned his eyes back to the *Demon Tracker* screen. After a moment, he spoke again, and his voice was kinder. "But you'll be safe here, on Euphora. It's the safest place there is."

Capri looked at the screen again and her eyes focused on Richmond, Virginia, where there were three or four tiny red dots.

"Let me show you how we fight these demons!" Roarke said suddenly, his booming voice startling Capri back to reality. She nodded, still feeling disturbed at the thought of *positively lethal* demons living within miles of her just yesterday…

Roarke led her to the shooting cages, where Clynn was busy watching Rian firing off rounds from the largest revolver Capri had ever seen.

As they entered the cage, Roarke laid a hand on Rian's shoulder, and he pulled the ear plugs out of his ears and turned to face Capri.

"Hold out that revolver, son, let's give the girl here a lesson in demon weaponry."

Rian skillfully removed the rounds from the revolver, and Capri noticed that they were not ordinary lead bullets.

He noticed her staring at them with wide eyes, and his lips twitched into a smirk as Roarke began to speak.

"In case you're wondering, these are called Demon Fire Rounds, or Eternal Fire Rounds, depending on who you ask." Roarke chuckled, grabbing one of the rounds as his son passed it to him. He held it up to Capri's face, so she could see it up close. "See? It has a lead casing at the bottom that holds an extremely flammable liquid, much more potent than anything humans use, trust me. And above it is eternal fire encased by glass. Eternal fire is something that can only be found in the Underworld, and only demons can control it. It needs no oxygen, no fuel, nothing. It burns, just like its name suggests, eternally. When this round is fired and hits a target, the eternal fire combines with the liquid underneath, and BAM!" He swung his arms out, simulating an explosion, and despite herself, Capri jumped in surprise. Roarke laughed at her reaction. "Pretty damn scary, huh?"

She nodded, her eyes still on the round, her imagination running wild with images of burning buildings and epic destruction.

"Anyway, we come across demons who have these sometimes and we confiscate them. It's good for us to test them out, and see how we can defend ourselves against them. The revolver itself is something we confiscated from a demon recently, and we're testing it out to see if they've modified it in any way. It's your basic double action, old west style revolver with an eight inch barrel. The only modification we can see so far is that they've enlarged the openings for the rounds, since these bullets are much larger than the kind normally carried in a revolver like this one. Why don't you go ahead and fire this one off again, Rian, so Capri can see it in action."

Rian nodded, reloading one of the rounds back into the revolver and clicking it into place. He replaced his ear plugs and then proceeded to point the revolver toward a target some twenty feet in the distance and then cocked it. Clynn motioned for Capri to step further back against the wall of the cage. She watched in fascination, realizing with a jolt that she had never seen a gun fired before.

After a moment of lining up the shot, Rian fired, and the bullet zoomed through the air with a loud pop, hitting the bull's eye on the target, which instantly exploded with fire. Capri's eyes widened with shock as sprinklers above the target sprayed some kind of white liquid over the fire, putting it out within seconds. All that was left of the target was smoldering remains.

Clynn and Roarke began to clap, so Capri followed suit, even though her hands were slightly shaking. Rian set the empty revolver down on a nearby table, turning to face his father.

"Good work, son. You'll never guess, but the one liquid we've discovered that can quickly put out eternal fire is milk. We think it's because milk means life and fertility and, well, the Underworld just means death." Roarke threw back his head and laughed at his own joke, and when he finished he was still grinning. "C'mon, girl, let me show you what else we have over here." Roarke motioned to the wall of weapons and led the way, Clynn and Capri walking behind him. Rian followed as well, silent as ever.

When they passed the other shooting cage, Clynn nodded to Balgaire, who tilted his head slightly in return. Capri caught a glimpse of his face before he turned away again, and she shuddered involuntarily. It amazed her how much of a contrast there was between the two older Furies. It was like night and day... Roarke was jovial and confident and Balgaire just seemed sour.

"These are most of the weapons that we not only use in the field, but that we've come up against in the past from the enemy." Roarke gestured to the wall, grinning. "As you can see, we have an expansive collection." He began to walk along the wall, pointing to each of the different groupings of weapons, his voice getting more and more excited. "You have your semi-automatic pistols, revolvers, much like the one you just saw; your shotguns, pistol grip, sawed off, and complete; your semi-automatic rifles, long distance sniper. Then we have the more unique weapons: your eternal fire whip, poisonous demon ninja star, and your full range of grenades." He paused at the end of the display case, which held nearly a hundred different sized and shaped grenades. He grinned again, even more excited. "But now I have to show you the best part."

He reached over and pulled a round from a box on the display case and handed it to Capri.

She stared at it for a moment, rolling it between her fingers. It looked almost identical to the demon fire bullet, only instead of there being fire in the glass casing, there was a smoky liquid.

"What is it?" she asked, glancing up at Roarke. His smile was that of a man who had all of the power in the world and knew it.

"Liquid nitrogen," he replied, winking at her. "Shoot a demon with that puppy and it freezes 'em from the inside instantaneously. Then, while their body is frozen, you smash them to pieces with either a hard object, or hit 'em with a normal lead bullet, and they shatter. Then, it's bye, bye demon."

Capri handed the round back, looking awestruck. "So they aren't really that hard to kill then?"

"Not if you know demons the way I know demons," he told her, looking smug. "And once Rian takes over for me, he's going to know everything I know, and maybe more." He wrapped his arm around his son and grinned down at him. Capri watched as Rian kept his gaze lowered, his face serious. He was certainly much more reserved than his father.

"Well, if that completes the tour here, we should be moving on," Clynn said suddenly, looking over to Capri. "Ready?"

Her eyes were still on Rian, but she nodded and turned to look up at Roarke. "Thank you for showing me everything. It's all very…fascinating."

"Come back and see us anytime. Maybe I'll even teach you how to shoot!"

Capri glanced over at the weapon filled display cases, feeling uneasy. She had never really thought about learning how to fire a weapon before...though it did look like it could be fun.

"Thanks, that would be nice," she said with a wave as her father led her back to the door and out into the hallway.

When they were back in the main corridor, he turned to her. "Feeling overwhelmed yet?" he asked, his kind, gray eyes twinkling.

Capri snorted. "Please, I've just learned that I've been living amongst demons my entire life disguised as normal people. I think I'm past the point of being overwhelmed."

Clynn just laughed and wrapped his arm around her shoulders. "Just wait till you see where the Fates work. Roarke at least makes the Furies' job sound adventurous, but the Fates are downright depressing. Just don't take them too seriously and you'll be fine."

"Great," Capri muttered as her father lead her toward another doorway further down the corridor.

The door they stopped at had the word FATES written across it, and when Clynn opened the door Capri noticed a similar hallway to the one that had lead to the Furies' workplace, only this hallway had no doors, only a staircase at the far end that spiraled up into darkness.

The torches supplied some light, and when Clynn shut the door behind them, Capri's eyes had to adjust to the dimness. They walked along, then up the spiraling staircase. Up and up they went, nearly two stories, until they finally came to a stop at the landing. There was a single door at the top, which Clynn knocked upon.

Nyxa opened the door a few moments later looking extraordinarily annoyed. "What is it?" she barked, looking from Clynn to Capri with dark eyes.

"Good morning, Nyxa," Clynn began, trying to be polite. "I am giving Capri a tour of the castle, and I was hoping you could spare a moment of your time to show her around."

Nyxa rolled her eyes and sighed. "Clynn, we never have a moment to spare, you know this. It's only ten a.m.; I still have a hundred thousand more deaths to do. Show her around, but don't expect me to play tour guide," she scoffed, her raspy voice bitter. She immediately turned back around, leaving the door open, and headed back inside the room. "Nova, stop getting distracted, you're getting backed up!"

Clynn motioned for Capri to enter, and when she did, her eyes immediately shot straight to the ceiling.

They were inside one of the four circular towers of the castle and where there would normally be a pointed dome ceiling, there was instead a swirling black hole. She saw silvery figures floating up into the black hole from the right side of the room, while others seemed to float back out of it on the left side, forming a weird cycle.

The walls of the tower had a few slitted windows that let in limited sunlight, and were made of plain stone, as was the floor. More light came from several torches lining the walls, though when combined with the tiny windows, the room was very dim in comparison to where the Furies worked. Centered in the room were three work stations, complete with the Fates busily working away.

The room was quiet except for the sounds of work and Capri decided to just watch and not ask questions.

If she hadn't known better, she would say that the Fates were seamstresses, busy making clothing. But, of course, she did know better, and instead she watched with awe as the Fate named Angora and the young teenage boy with the gypsy face were busy spinning thread on a traditional looking spinning wheel, feeding what looked like wool into it as Angora pressed a pedal with her foot, thus spinning the wool into thread as it wound around a spindle. Capri noticed that when the thread reached the spindle, one of the silvery figures would descend out of the black hole and attach itself to the thread, merging with it and changing it into a glowing silver strand.

From the spindle, the silvery thread wound its way down to the next station, where Morgaine sat with her daughter. They were seated at a long wooden table, and they appeared to be measuring the thread against a strange looking ruler with ancient looking symbols on it. They were marking their measurements with what looked like black chalk, and as they marked it, they would feed the thread onto another much larger spindle, nearly full, where the silvery thread was busy being unwound by Nyxa and her daughter, Nova, who were laying the thread on their own smaller table and cutting it with ancient looking metal shears. As they made each cut, the silvery glow would leave the thread and take form once more, flying back up into the black hole. The thread pieces were then discarded into a large pile on the floor.

"I'm sure it must be pretty obvious to you what they're doing here," Clynn quietly whispered in her ear. She turned to him and nodded. "Why don't we move on?" he whispered again, ushering her to the door. The Fates didn't even acknowledge them as they left, as they were intently focused on their work, and Capri figured that it was probably for the best.

Once they were safely out onto the landing and down the stairs, Capri finally felt like she could speak.

"I can't believe that they are real," she murmured, the image of the silvery thread still in her mind. "For some reason, out of all of this, they were the hardest to believe."

Clynn chuckled as they emerged back out into the main corridor. "The Fates are certainly unique and their purpose is extraordinarily important. They may be rough around the edges, but you saw how hard they work. Yet they refuse to bring in reinforcements like the Furies do. The Fates prefer to do everything themselves, that's just their way."

Capri stopped then, pausing midstep as she stared at her father. "Where does that black hole go?"

"It takes the soul where it belongs, whether it is to Heaven or to Hell," he said.

She nodded, feeling incredibly small.

"By the way, you saw the boy in there? With Angora? His name is Alastor, and he is the first male Fate in over a thousand years." Clynn smiled at her. "Needless to say, Angora and Thea were both thrilled to welcome him into the world. Male Fates tend to have powers that the female Fates don't possess, and so they are keeping a close eye on him, waiting to see if he is unique in any way."

"Wow, that's a lot of pressure to put on someone so young." Capri's eyes widened as she thought of the gypsy faced boy spinning the thread, so intent on his work.

Clynn smiled at her. "In many ways, we are all under more pressure than we should be, but that is just the way it is."

"I understand." Capri smiled, glancing around at the other doors. "Where to next?"

"Rohan is the last on this side of the castle, let's go visit him and Rhiannon. They should be in the greenhouse today."

# Chapter Five

*Nearly two hours* later, Capri had seen the rest of the castle and had walked what felt like several miles just moving from room to room. She had seen Rohan's greenhouse, with its glorious plants and luscious fruit trees. Lucian's tower, the walls covered in streaming water that pooled underneath a wooden platform floor. The Muses' tower, with burning incense and charming Celtic music. Blythe's dungeon of fire, equipped with a large, floating orb that showed the center of the Earth in its glowing core.

Her father had also shown her a vast library on the ground floor, with row upon row of hundreds of thousands of books reaching all the way up to a golden coffered ceiling, flanked by a solid wall of glittering windows facing the courtyard.

It was more than she could have ever imagined. And, it was her home. From now until forever.

"My office is up here," Clynn said cheerfully as he opened one of the few remaining doors in the corridor and led her up a long flight of stairs. When they reached the landing, there was a single door, leading to what Capri assumed was the last of the four towers.

When he opened the door and she stepped inside, her mouth fell open in honest surprise.

The walls were the same gray stone as outside, much like the other three towers had been. However, unlike the other towers, this room was open and airy, with natural light flooding in from several large, open arched windows that spiraled up to the ceiling.

Gracing the stone floor were several plush light blue rugs, and in the center sat what looked like a stone birdbath. Only, as she looked at it closer, it wasn't filled with water, but with what appeared to be white smoke.

Entranced, her eyes wandered up to the ceiling again, which to her delight was covered with misty clouds, the golden sunlight shining through them, just like the atrium. Birds flew in and out of the open windows freely, spiraling and singing as they flitted through the cylinder tower.

"This is where I spend most of my time, and where you will as well," Clynn said suddenly, his hand resting on her shoulder.

"This is beautiful," she murmured, her eyes following the birds as they darted through the windows.

Clynn chuckled. "It's been this way for centuries, every Air Dryad before me and you has worked in this very same room."

Capri smiled, her eyes shifting to her father. "I love it. It's perfect." She turned to look at the birdbath, pointing at it. "What does that do?"

"Ah, yes." Clynn walked over to it, chuckling and beckoning her to follow. "Why don't I just show you, since you wouldn't believe me if I told you?"

It was her turn to laugh, only it evaporated the moment he stood before the birdbath and raised his arms, his hands spread open. The smoke began to rise into the air, swiftly forming a shifting white column that soared swiftly up to the high ceiling.

The column started to swirl as Clynn motioned with his arms, his hands not touching the smoke but moving it as though it were solid mass. Appearing gradually through the mists, Capri could see images, clear as though they were photo-graphs. The smoke slowed in its movement as the images came sharply into focus.

She saw a bird's eye view of a vast forest, clustered with massive redwood trees, snow dusting the mountains in the back-ground. Then the plains, flat and filled with barley and wheat blowing gently in the wind. A bustling city...could it be Rome? With humans riding around on Vespas and in tiny cars on cobblestone streets. The streets melted away and were replaced by a long stretch of white, sandy beach with palm trees bend-ing almost to the breaking point by powerful winds. The sea rushed forward amidst angry gray skies, while rain pelted the sand mercilessly.

"A hurricane?" Capri muttered, her eyes entranced by the images she could see so clearly in the smoke column.

"Yes," Clynn replied excitedly. "I ordered it yesterday. Looks like it's coming along quite nicely."

"But...hurricanes are bad, people drown when there are hurricanes!" Capri was flustered, and turned to her father with pleading eyes. "Make it stop!"

He chuckled, his hands still outstretched, the image of the hurricane held in place. "Hurricanes are a necessary part of the balance of nature, darling. It's unfortunate that humans may perish, but the Earth needs destructive forces in order to balance out the harmonious ones."

Capri stared back at the image of the hurricane, trying to process it all. When Clynn moved his hands slightly and the image changed to one of a peaceful lighthouse far up the Eastern seaboard at sunset, calm waves lapping gently against the rocks, she felt she understood his meaning.

"Nothing is ever perfect all the time. You can't appreciate the bad without the good," she said quietly, her eyes still on the image of the lighthouse.

"Everything in life is balance: good versus evil, strong versus weak, hot versus cold...an equal amount of two opposites creates balance." Clynn motioned again with his hands, bringing them together as if in prayer, and the smoke dissipated and returned to the birdbath. He turned to face her. "And as I said before, it is our job to maintain the balance of air throughout Earth. We monitor wind patterns, cloud formations, hurricanes, tornadoes, most things involving weather."

"And rain?"

"Rain is Lucian and Liam's responsibility, though usually we work together to make it happen. Ever see it rain with hardly any clouds? Doesn't happen often, but when it does it's because we're not communicating properly. Thea gets upset when that happens." He smiled sheepishly at Capri. "We don't make mistakes often, but even we're not perfect."

"This is all so…overwhelming." Capri stared down at her own hands, feeling helpless. "Am I supposed to know how to do all this?"

Clynn pulled her into his arms, holding her tightly. He planted a small kiss on her forehead. "You were born to do this, Capri."

"It's like, my destiny or something?" She giggled, tilting her head up to look at him. When he smiled patiently and nodded, she felt an excited jolt run through her. "Wow, I never really thought about having some grand purpose in life before."

"You do. You will be the reason the Earth is able to continue functioning."

She processed his comment, feeling, yet again, extraordinarily small.

"That's a lot of pressure for one person to take on," she commented, her eyes shifting warily to the birdbath. "I don't know if I can do it."

"You can and you will," Clynn replied, holding her out at arm's length. "Why don't you show me what you can do?"

Capri blushed, twisting her hands together nervously. "I've never, ah, performed for anyone before."

"It's only me." He tilted his head to the ceiling and raised his right arm. Making a *come here* motion with his hand, a bird suddenly came zooming at them, landing in his palm gracefully. It was a tiny brown sparrow with darting black eyes, which it curiously focused on Capri.

She couldn't help but smile at the bird as she glanced up and met her father's eyes. He nodded, and she understood that he wanted her to try and control it.

Still feeling a bit foolish, she held out her hand shakily and closed her eyes, inhaling deeply to calm herself. She pictured the bird lifting its legs and tap dancing, and when she heard her father start laughing, she opened her eyes and saw that the bird was doing just that.

It was definitely comical, seeing the tiny sparrow's feet lifting and tapping to some nonexistent jazz music. Capri focused her eyes on the bird, staring intently at it, her hand still outstretched. She imagined it flying into the air and doing back flips, and when it zoomed out of Clynn's hand and into the air, diving and flipping, Capri smiled brightly.

"Very good," Clynn commented, his eyes warm on hers. "You have a way with birds. It took me a long time to figure out how to control them that well."

"Really?" She pulled her hand back and the bird, released, flew back up and flitted out one of the many windows.

"You're going to be fine, Capri." Clynn stared at her with misty eyes, just like any proud father would look at their child. Capri embraced the feeling it gave her, while at the same time she realized what was still missing…

"Tell me about my mother…I mean, if you want to," she hesitated. "It's just that I don't know anything about her."

He stared at her for a long moment, as though trying to decide where to start. With a sad smile, he began. "I met her by chance, or fate, I suppose, when I was up in Maine fixing a problem I had caused on accident." He flushed, looking embarrassed. "I was only nineteen and hadn't quite gotten the hang of everything yet. You're late grandfather was patient with me though, thank God, and let me fix the problem before Thea could jump down my throat.

"I was standing on this small, wooden dock by a lighthouse in the early morning hours, reversing the effects of this terrible storm that I had intended to send to Pennsylvania. This poor coastal town in Maine received my storm and it utterly devastated them, after they had already endured so much bad weather. It was too much so I had to fix it.

"Anyway, I was there, remedying my mistake, when this young woman walked up and saw me. I had thought I was alone, but she watched me as I calmed the wind and repaired the damages. Instead of running away, she approached me, and asked me questions. I had never spoken to a human before, much less a human girl…needless to say, I was very shy about her questions, but she was persistent and eventually she got the truth out of me. I was mortified and embarrassed, but she was impressed. She had the most beautiful smile I had ever seen, and I think the mere fact that she accepted what I was without question had me falling for her right then and there.

"We walked around her little town, and she showed me the café her parents owned that she worked at, the bookstore she spent all of her free time in, everything. And we talked, about nothing in particular, but we got to know each other. By the time I had to go home, I knew her favorite book, favorite color, favorite food…I knew how she took her coffee, how she liked her eggs, even the breed of her childhood dog, Rusty.

"She asked me to come back and visit her, and though I knew that I couldn't really promise something like that, I did anyway. Not very many of us here on Euphora end up having relationships with humans, and back then it was mostly frowned upon. But I didn't care; I wanted her more than I had ever wanted anything. I went to my father and Thea and announced that if they wouldn't allow me to continue seeing her, then I would renounce my position and my powers and live on Earth with her. Fortunately for me, Thea was feeling generous that day and granted me permission to visit Heidi. I went down twice a month for over a year and then I asked her to marry me.

"It was as though my soul had been searching for her, and when we finally found each other, my life was complete." Clynn smiled again, tears forming in his eyes. "I know you must think I'm a sentimental old fool, but having you here with me makes me feel like I'm with her again. Forgive me."

She threw her arms around him, tears in her eyes as well. "I'm glad it helps...me being here. Even if it's only a little."

"You have no idea how many holes you filled by coming home, Capri."

"I've never really felt needed before," she replied, nuzzling against his chest. "It's a wonderful feeling."

She felt more overwhelmed then she had in advanced high school calculus, but she also felt thrilled and determined. Her father showed her how to use her hands and her mind to schedule weather patterns throughout the globe, using nothing more than the column of smoke and images as her palette. It was almost like painting, she thought, as she walked through the courtyard, taking a short break between lessons. Painting the patterns of the wind with her hands, and using her mind to control the intensity and the direction. He let her practice on Richmond, and she felt as though she was doing her old hometown a favor by granting them three lovely days of sunshine to counter all the rain they had been getting the past week.

Feeling proud of herself and a bit giddy with accomplishment, Capri stepped out into the misty morning sunlight, closing her eyes and tilting her face skyward to drink in the warmth of its rays. She sighed, feeling content, as she walked under some large leafy trees, enjoying the way they dappled the light as it shone on her skin.

She had her long, light blonde hair pulled up into a ponytail, and she could feel the warm breeze tickling across her neck as she walked. Birds chattered nearby, the sound better than all the best music in the world to her. She continued walking down the cobblestone pathway that led to the front gate, taking in as much as she could of her surroundings.

There were so many trees; it was like the vast courtyard would be swallowed up by them. And so many different varieties, as if every species thrived in this paradise. Flowers sprung up around every corner, so many colors and shapes and smells. It was overwhelming, but so beautiful. A pond was nestled next to a low hanging willow tree, and she wondered if she would find goldfish inside of it if she looked. Content with walking along the pathway, she tucked her hands in her jeans pockets and kept moving.

She noticed the jasmine flowers off to the left, so she approached them and leaned over to get a better look, her lips curving in a smile.

She crouched down on her knees, examining them, lifting one of the flowers to her nose so she could fully enjoy its scent. As she pulled the branch toward her, she noticed the tiny alcove the jasmine bush formed beneath its branches. It was the perfect place for a tiny child to hide, so secret, so safe...

It hit her like lightning: hard, fast and vicious. The memory so clear, it could have happened moments before...of her hiding right there in that little alcove, smelling the jasmine, listening to the screams, feeling the terror rise in her throat as she suddenly realized something was horribly wrong.

Her breath hitched in her throat and her knees trembled as she backed away from the jasmine, her eyes wild. Her mother had died, right there in front of those flowers. Someone had stolen her, lifted her from her hiding place and taken her away. Had she cried out when her mother had screamed? Was that how they had found her, crouched helpless underneath some stupid flowers?

Her mind was racing and her whole body felt numb with shock and understanding. This was the location where her life had been cruelly destroyed, everything taken away from her by rough, greedy hands.

"Capri? Capri, are you alright?" A voice said from someplace far away. Her vision was blurring, going black, her head floating somewhere over her body, her stomach rioting in panic. She felt hands grab her just before she fell, gently lowering her to a sitting position on the cobblestone. "Liam! Get me some water! She's passing out."

Capri couldn't process what was going on, she felt lost, disconnected, confused. She felt tears in her eyes, but she didn't understand why she was crying. She leaned against the body of the person who held her, and she sobbed so hard her body shook.

"It's okay, honey, it's gonna be okay, I promise. Liam! For God's sake, hurry up!"

She could hear footsteps rapidly approaching, could feel the vibrations from them against her body, and suddenly something cool was touching her lips, pouring into her mouth. She swallowed instinctively, and once she had a taste, she grabbed the glass and greedily swallowed the rest.

Her vision was returning, the blurred outlines of the people in front of her sharpening. When she realized Blythe was the one who held her, she tried to sit up, embarrassment flooding through her.

"I'm s-so sorry," she stammered, her hands shaking. "I don't know what happened."

"It's okay," Liam said gently, smiling at her as he cupped her cheek in his palm. "You scared us, is all."

"Yeah, don't do that again," Blythe added with a quick grin. "You could've hurt yourself, passing out all of a sudden. Were you overheated or something? It's always seventy two degrees here, so I can't imagine how…"

"My m-mother…" Capri choked out, her eyes darting to the jasmine. Tears began to well up in her eyes again, and Liam looked at her knowingly, his expression kind.

"I see." He reached out and pulled her into his arms, and she held on tightly and started crying again, feeling like a fool.

Blythe seemed to understand as well, because she patted Capri's back comfortingly. "Maybe we should bring her inside, let her talk to Thea."

"Good idea," Liam replied. In one smooth move, he stood up and lifted Capri into his arms, cradling her there. "Don't be embarrassed, just relax, okay?"

"Oh, God," Capri laughed shakily, reaching up to wipe at the tears streaming down her cheeks. "My hero."

Liam beamed down at her. "That's what you used to call me when we were kids."

"I did?" Capri smiled, closing her eyes and laying her head against his shoulder. "I guess I knew, even then, that you would be the one to rescue me."

"Maybe I made a mistake waiting to talk to you about all of this," Thea concluded, sipping her tea and eyeing Capri over the rim of her cup. "I just wasn't sure how much you could handle all at once."

"I'm sorry, I don't know why I reacted that way…" Capri couldn't look at Thea, she felt so embarrassed. She clutched her hands tightly in her lap as she perched on the edge of the armchair she'd been instructed to sit in. They were in this enormous room on the far side of the castle, Thea and Sebastian's room, so she'd been told, with rows of open windows and plants growing everywhere. Sunlight drifted in through skylights in the ceiling, the gilded rays making everything inside the room appear to glow golden. Greek style columns engorged by ivy acted as supports for the high ceiling, which was virtually a straight look into the heavens above. There was an oversized gilded mirror that hung on one wall, and in it Capri could see flashing images: a dense rainforest filled with morning mist; a vast, open desert sweltering from heat; Times Square in New York City, overflowing with people and cars; and many more.

Exotic birds flew overhead, singing to each other in a song unique to their kind alone. Momentarily distracted by them, Capri jumped when Thea spoke again.

"I would have expected no less from you. Of course you should have been alarmed to revisit the place where your own mother had died. It's only natural. You shouldn't apologize for every little thing, it's unbecoming."

The harsh tone had Capri looking up, alarmed. "Are you angry with me?" she asked, her eyes wide.

Thea sighed and shook her head, waving her hand in front of her apologetically. "No, no I'm not angry with you. I just wish you would realize that you actually have a backbone." She leaned back against her chaise lounge, her legs curling up against her. She tossed back her mane of dark curls, her eyes softening. "I feel this is my fault, I should have discussed everything with you when you first arrived."

"How much more is there?" Capri wondered, mostly to herself.

Thea's lips curved into a knowing smile. "I should have brought you to that place myself, and explained the details of what happened the night you were taken, at least the details that we know. I went against my better judgment and instead let you stumble upon the spot on your own. However, we're here, so it's time we talked, asked questions, answered questions, etcetera."

"Okay," Capri replied, sitting up straighter in her chair, her eyes dry but still red from crying. Her hands were no longer shaking and her mind was clear. She was ready to hear the truth, no matter how painful it might be.

Thea took another lazy sip of her tea, looking relaxed and confident. Capri envied the power Mother Earth radiated, and the compelling feminine force that she embodied in every way. It was as frightening as it was awe inspiring.

"It was late summer, fifteen years ago. We were having a party, celebrating the birth of our newest Muse, Tobias. Everyone was inside the parlor, dancing and drinking. Your mother took you outside for fresh air, since you were fussy and tired. Your father offered to go with her, but she brushed him off, smiling in that way she had. She had a beautiful smile, your mother." Thea's eyes warmed at the memory. "Actually, your smile is very similar to hers, gentle and sweet."

"What did she look like?" Capri asked, leaning forward with her elbows on her knees and her chin in her hands.

"Different than you. You have your father's coloring, the pale hair and eyes. She was…simpler looking, I suppose. Mousy brown hair, unremarkable brown eyes…but despite her plainness, she brought so much warmth to this place. We can be foreboding to outsiders, but we all took to her like she had been meant to be with us. It was hard on all of us when she died, and losing you as well…I don't think we ever quite got over it."

"What happened when she brought me outside?"

"I don't know all of the details since I was inside at the time. Balgaire heard your mother screaming first and he ran out to help her. He says he saw her push you into the jasmine, a last minute attempt to hide you, I suppose. A group of very dangerous demons had been let through the gate, and he tried to stop them but they reached your mother before he could. They killed her and then one of them heard you crying and grabbed you. At this point, all of us ran out into the courtyard, only to find your mother dead and you gone. We never saw the demon who took you, and Balgaire didn't get a good enough look at him to know for sure who it was. In the end, we were able to chase out the demons, killing off a couple of them, but when we sent out a search party to find you, it was almost impossible since he could have literally taken you anywhere in the world. Who knew he would have chosen Richmond, of all places."

"Maybe Richmond meant something to the demon." Capri suggested.

"That may be so, but we never identified the demon, so it was fruitless from the start."

"Who let them in?" Capri asked, her eyes on Thea's, sterling silver into rich chocolate. They held for a moment, and when Thea spoke, her voice was dripping with anger and the sharp sting of betrayal.

"Blythe's father, Brock."

Capri's eyes widened and her mouth fell open in shock. "But...but why?"

"It's a long, complicated story better suited for a soap opera than for the Council. In any event, I banished him, so you needn't worry about him anymore." Thea still looked angry, but Capri could tell she was trying to reign in her emotions. Deciding it was best to avoid the topic of Blythe's father, she focused on the latter part of Thea's comment.

"Is that what you call everyone? The Council?"

"Yes, The Council is made up of myself, Sebastian, the four Dryads, the two Furies, the three Fates, and the three Muses. When your father retires, you will join the Council along with the other heirs. Those who retire live out the remainder of their days amongst humans, making room for the next generation."

"I see..." Capri bit her lip, a sudden idea occurring to her. But no, it probably wouldn't work...better not to suggest it and get laughed at...

"What is it, girl? You're thinking about something in that head of yours," Thea commented, eyeing Capri knowingly. "Your face is an open book, so easily read."

Capri blushed. "I'm sor- I mean, yes...the thing is, I told you how I'd dreamt of this place since I was little...and when I met the Muses, they said they can give someone mental clarity. I wonder if I talk to them, if they could help me remember more about the dream, and maybe more about the demon who took me. Then we could find him and get closure..."

Thea tilted her chin up and looked at Capri, considering. Her lips curved in a slow smile. "Interesting idea."

"Really?" Capri was honestly surprised and it showed clearly on her face.

Thea laughed, her smile bright. "So unsure of yourself. You are much stronger and wiser than you know, child."

"Oh, well, I don't know..." Capri flushed, smiling despite herself. "I have my moments."

"Well, this is definitely one of those moments."

*Chapter Six*

"*How did it* go?" Clynn asked as Capri closed the door behind her.

She looked at him with a smile. "It went fine… I'm going to talk to the Muses tomorrow about my dream. I want to see if they can help me remember more details about the demon who took me, that way we can finally have justice."

Clynn looked worried. "Are you sure you want to relive those memories? They may be more…brutal than you can imagine."

"I want to know who the demon was that stole me…the demon who was working with Blythe's father."

His face paled as he stared at her. "Thea told you everything, then."

"Yes, and I'm glad she did. I'm going to figure this out. I need closure and I'm sure you could use it, too."

He wrapped his arm around her shoulders as they began to walk toward the front doors, leading out into the courtyard. "As long as you are comfortable with this. None of us are pressuring you in any way to relive that night. It was difficult on all of us, but most notably you. Your entire life was changed because of that night."

"I'll be fine. I'm stronger than I look." Capri felt confident saying it out loud, especially since the all powerful Thea seemed to believe it.

As they stepped out into the misty morning sunshine, she had the sudden and overwhelming desire to go back to the place where her entire life had been changed in an unforgivable instant.

"Will you walk with me over to the jasmine?" she asked, looking up at her father. When he didn't say anything for a moment, but looked strained, she felt ashamed for asking him. "I'm sorry...if you don't want to, I und–"

"No, I should be the one to apologize, Capri," Clynn interrupted, stopping mid-step and clutching her arms in his hands. His face was desperate, his eyes sad. "For years I've been avoiding thinking about that night, because I decided that by ignoring it, I wouldn't have the need to be depressed anymore. It took everything I had to keep on living after what happened, and it was in my own self-interest that I avoided ever thinking about it again. Sure, in the back of my mind I would wonder about you, think about you coming home someday, but largely I avoided it at all costs. I'm sorry that this is not easier for me, and I'm sorry that I wasn't the one to tell you about what happened that night. It should have been me, not Thea. And maybe that was why she kept silent, because she had hoped I would bring you to that place, explain it all to you, and then we could find closure together. But I couldn't do it. I'm a coward, Capri, so much so that I couldn't tell my own daughter how her mother had died, and who was responsible. I'm so sorry."

"It doesn't matter." Capri looked into his eyes, searching. "It doesn't matter who told me the story, as long as it was told. We both need to go there, and we both need to relive this together, so that we can have closure. I'm scared, too...scared of the pain, of the misery, of the regret, but none of those fears change the fact that we both lost her, and we both need to remember her and avenge her. Please help me do that…Dad."

She felt tears brimming in her eyes as he hugged her tightly, but she also felt an odd strength rise within her. It was all so clear to her now…she would do everything in her power to find the demon responsible for ruining her life and she would avenge her mother's death. If she still had doubts and fears flashing like neon lights in her brain, telling her to let it go and forget, then she was just going to have to ignore them. This wasn't the time to be afraid anymore, it was the time to act.

"Let's go." Clynn smiled sadly as he pulled away and turned toward the path that led to the jasmine bushes. They walked together, arms around each other, and when they reached the jasmine, they stood in front of it as a unit, and mourned what had been lost.

It hadn't occurred to Capri how she was going to react to seeing Blythe again until she was seated at the dining table, ready to eat dinner, and the girl in question sat across from her, a bright smile on her face.

"You look a hell of a lot better," Blythe said as she grabbed a roll and bit into it happily. Liam sat beside her, shaking his head and chuckling.

"Thanks," Capri replied, finding it hard to look Blythe in the eyes. She wasn't sure why she felt so awkward…obviously Blythe knew what her father had done, and it didn't seem to stop her from being friendly.

"Man, I'm starving," Blythe announced as she swallowed and started piling slices of honey ham onto her plate.

"Big surprise," Liam grumbled as he forked up a bite of mashed potatoes. He winked at Capri as he chewed.

"Hey." Blythe pointed her fork at him, one of her eyebrows cocked defensively. "Lay off me and my food habits already, it's not like you haven't been living with me forever. You should be used to this"

"Yeah, but you seem to feel the need to announce it to the world every time your stomach grumbles," Liam retorted.

Blythe shrugged and patted her stomach happily, grinning at Capri. "What can I say? I'm a loud mouth. It gets me in trouble more often than not."

Capri avoided looking at Blythe again, and picked at the food on her own plate. She pushed around the carrots and peas, her mind elsewhere.

She noticed Rhiannon sit down a couple seats away from her, but when she glanced up and smiled, the other girl merely bowed her head slightly in acknowledgement and looked away. Unsure why Rhiannon was acting so coldly, Capri turned her gaze back to her food and sighed.

"Is something bothering you, Capri?" Liam asked, his kind eyes concerned.

Capri looked up, her cheeks flushing in embarrassment.

"No, it's nothing," she said, feeling foolish.

When her eyes shifted unconsciously to Blythe, Liam seemed to understand.

"If you need someone to talk to, I'm here for you," he said, eyeing her intently before returning to his dinner.

Blythe was busy in conversation with Lucian and didn't seem to notice the exchange, which Capri was thankful for. She wasn't sure how to act around Blythe since she knew what had happened, and even though Blythe had no responsibility what-soever for the actions of her father, Capri couldn't help but feel uncomfortable over the whole thing.

And so, when after dinner Blythe cornered her just outside the dining hall, Capri realized that she wasn't going to have the luxury of avoiding the confrontation any longer.

"So I assume that Thea told you that it was my father who was responsible for what happened to you and your mother," Blythe said, her lips curving ever so slightly into a dark smirk.

Capri bit her tongue, at a loss at what to say. Her hands twisted together in front of her nervously.

Blythe continued to stare at her, and after a moment, her pretty face contorted with despair and frustration. When she spoke, her voice was as heated as the temper that burned inside of her.

"It never sat right with me, what he did. I know that I'm not responsible for his actions, but damnit, he was my father, and he destroyed my family because of his petty hatred." Her jaw clenched and she took a deep breath as she bit back the rush of anger, averting her gaze in an effort to collect herself. When her eyes met Capri's again a moment later, they were steadier, focused. "Please don't think less of me because you know…we were friends once, and I'd like us to be friends again."

Capri reached out then, clutching Blythe's hands in her own. She squeezed tightly, the sorrow and forgiveness she felt so easily read on her face.

"I could never blame you," she whispered, shaking her head. She felt tears brim in her eyes as she recognized that the grief Blythe felt was the same that had plagued her own soul nearly her entire life. The grief of wondering what could have been had your life not been forever altered by someone else's bad decisions.

"Wow." Blythe laughed shakily, wiping away her own tears and grinning. "Liam said you would take it like this, and I thought he was dead wrong. I guess I just wouldn't blame you for hating me by association."

"I hope we can be really good friends. I want us to stay together this time," Capri said as she reached for Blythe's hands again. "We should both promise to not let anything separate us again."

Blythe grinned. "Deal."

When Rhiannon and Rohan walked by and saw the two girls clutching each other and sobbing, they both watched with very different expressions. Rohan looked annoyed at the fact that two girls were openly crying in what he felt was a formal court, while Rhiannon looked on with empty eyes and a ragingly jealous heart.

"Sit back and just relax, Capri," Serendipity said as Capri laid back in what was definitely the most comfortable recliner she had ever sat in. It was covered in smooth, buttery leather the color of natural silk, and when a button was pressed, a footrest folded out smoothly and Capri felt herself tilt back until she was so comfortable she could have nodded off to sleep almost instantly. If she hadn't been so nervous, she might have done just that, without even needing the Muses' help.

The Muses operated out of the far east tower of the castle. They had few windows, relying instead on hundreds of candles for light, and had decorated it with numerous jewel toned rugs, shawls, throws, and pillows, all scattered around with incense burning so that the entire tower was filled with the scent of sandalwood and vanilla.

Against the curve of the tower wall were three large, free-standing gold framed mirrors, which she had been informed were used by the Muses to search for those both deserving and in need of inspiration. She also learned that the Muses based their selection on destiny, and upon those who if given the right push, would create both art and music that would ultimately impact entire generations.

She sat in one of three recliners used expressly for the purpose of hypnosis and relaxation exercises. The three Muses stared down at her, their beautiful faces glowing in the candlelight.

"I want you to clear your mind of all thoughts," Serendipity began, her fingertips gently rubbing Capri's temples, soothing away any signs of stress. Clarity was busy putting light pressure on Capri's left palm, her fingertips light and cool as they moved in small, slow circles over her skin. Trinity was gently rubbing Capri's right calf, and the combination of all three had her entire body feeling limp and loose within seconds. When Serendipity continued, her voice seemed far away and distant, echoing somewhere in the depths of her mind. "Imagine throwing all of your thoughts into this great big box, one by one, emptying yourself until your mind is clear." She paused as Capri did as she was told, imagining every thought in her head being dumped into a big white box.

"When you've done that, I want you to imagine closing the lid and tossing that box down into a great big hole, down it goes, lost to oblivion. Picture lowering yourself into that hole as well, and slide down into it as if it were a slide. Down into the darkness, let it swallow you whole and cloak you. You feel so safe and cozy down in the abyss, nothing matters in the world. Feel yourself fade away, becoming one with the darkness…"

Capri felt herself drift off, her mind blank, the world silent around her. She thought she could still feel the gentle probing fingers along her skin, but everything seemed so far away, so distant, as though her body was feather light and floating on air.

Through the blackness, blurry shapes began to appear, gradually sharpening and forming together to create the courtyard, glowing with firelight from the torches on the wall of the castle as the night sky above lit up with stars. Plants grew wild and free, impossibly and vividly green in the limited light and lush with deliciously scented flowers. The air was quiet and tranquil, calming with a gentle westerly breeze.

She was in the arms of someone who was walking leisurely down the cobblestone path, and her head was resting against a shoulder smelling of gardenias. Coffee brown hair fell near her face, and she felt her small hand reach out to lightly touch it, marveling at how the firelight brought out the brassy toned strands.

The person holding her was humming quietly, and the sound of it was so hauntingly beautiful that it almost didn't seem real.

Her eyes felt wet and sleepy, as though she had been crying, but she couldn't remember what had upset her. Oh, that's right, that mean Fury boy had ignored her again, pretending not to see her as she offered him a flower she'd picked from the garden just for him. Even at three years old she could tell he needed a friend, but he had refused her offer like she had been invisible. The memory of it brought fresh tears to her eyes as she let out a hiccupping sob.

"Oh, baby, it's okay," the person holding her cooed, pulling her close and rubbing her cheek against Capri's hair. Then she started singing again, a song about life's little ups and downs, and Capri forgot all about the Fury boy.

Mother. That song…

There was a noise coming suddenly from somewhere ahead of them, a whistle and the sound of running feet. Heidi stiffened, her arms clutching protectively around Capri as her eyes scanned the darkness for the source of the noise. When she saw figures rapidly approaching her, she hastily slid Capri from her arms and into the nearest bush.

"Don't make any noise," she whispered as she straightened, facing the men, trying to hide the fear in her eyes. "What is your business here?" she asked, hoping her voice didn't betray her defenselessness. She had no powers, after all.

Capri couldn't see much more than her mother's legs from between the branches of the jasmine, but she just assumed that all would be fine once her mother made whoever it was go away. She started playing with one of the jasmine flowers, admiring its star shape and delicate scent as she twirled it between her fingertips.

She heard more footsteps approaching, and her mother's relieved sigh.

"Thank God you're here," she said. "I don't know who these men are, but they appear to have come through the front gate unannounced."

"It is none of your concern." The harshness in the tone sent shivers down Capri's spine as she listened intently, the jasmine blossom forgotten. "Dispose of her. And the child."

Before Heidi could even register the request, she screamed and was dead on the ground, fire erupting from her chest where the demon bullet had pierced her heart.

"Hurry, they will have heard the shot and the scream, take the girl and leave," the harsh voice spoke again, this time in agitation. Rough hands lifted Capri from the cover of the jasmine, and within moments she was carried to the front gate. She looked over the shoulder of the man who carried her as several more men spread out throughout the courtyard, lighting fires and cackling madly. She saw one man in particular standing over her mother's body, his body silhouetted against the glow of the flames, his head tilted back as he laughed wickedly at the sky.

Then the darkness swallowed her.

Capri jolted up in her seat, gasping for breath and clutching the arms of the chair so tightly her knuckles were white. The three women around her held her back, trying to calm her down.

"It's over. It's done," Clarity said gently as she placed a damp towel over Capri's forehead. "Relax. Breathe."

"Oh my God!" Capri exclaimed, glancing around wildly as if she expected to see the wicked man with the harsh voice appear in front of her.

"Shush." Serendipity soothed as she continued to rub Capri's temples. "The dream is over."

Capri pushed Serendipity's fingertips away and lay back against the chair, covering her face in her hands. She couldn't get the image of her mother's dead body burning in the courtyard out of her mind. It was a memory that would haunt her till the day she died.

"Thank you for doing this, but I need to go," she said as she sat up and tried to stand, only to have her knees give out beneath her. The women caught her, but she shook them off. "I'm okay, please, let me go."

With that she shakily raced out of the tower, slamming the door behind her as she went.

She didn't know how long she stayed locked up in her room. Hours. Days, maybe. It didn't seem to matter anymore. Her idea had failed, she had learned nothing of the demon by reliving her dream. Absolutely nothing.

Instead she had experienced something that was honestly better left buried within. What had she done but cause herself even more emotional pain? By reliving that night, she had brought back such vivid memories of her mother: the scent of gardenias, the soft brown hair, the song she always sang to comfort and soothe. She didn't think she would ever be the same again.

Thea visited her after some time, and Capri told her everything she had seen in her dream. Thea listened intently, never speaking, and when she left she thanked Capri for trying. As if it had been worth the time and effort, Capri thought miserably.

All of the strength she had convinced herself she possessed seemed to shrivel up and desert her when she needed it most. She felt so weak, both in mind and heart, and it seemed as though nothing could chase away the pain.

That is, until the most unexpected of visitors knocked on her bedroom door.

"Come in," Capri called out from her perch on the windowsill, her legs tucked up against her chest and her pale blonde hair spilling over her shoulders. She glanced up as the person entered, and her gray eyes widened with surprise and embarrassment.

Rian looked slightly embarrassed as well, and because of this he stood resolutely in the doorway, making no move to enter the room completely. He watched her carefully, noting the redness around those hauntingly lovely eyes of hers. She looked so frail, so defeated, that he was worried what everyone was saying was true: she would leave Euphora, and never look back.

But when she stood up tall and approached him, he saw more than just fragility in her eyes. He saw recognition.

"It was you," she said quietly as she stopped a few feet from him, her eyes searching his. "You were the Fury boy who ignored me when I tried to give you a flower I'd picked from the courtyard."

His eyes narrowed as he returned her stare, and he seemed to be measuring her.

"You remember me but you don't remember the demon who took you?" he asked, and she realized with a jolt that it was the first time she had heard him speak more than two words.

"I just remember thinking that you looked like you needed a friend, and I thought I could help," she replied, feeling sheepish and averting her eyes. Her hands subconsciously started to twist together in front of her, a sure sign that she was nervous. "I guess I was young and foolish."

He didn't say anything for a moment, but continued to watch her. She chanced a glance back up at him, and saw his hard face soften ever so slightly. "Thea asked me to bring you down for dinner. You need to eat something."

"Oh." Capri bit her lip and tried to hide her disappointment. She'd hoped he would open up to her, even just a little, but his wall seemed to be built as high as ever. "Okay, give me a second." She disappeared into the bathroom, shutting the door quietly behind her. She hastily fixed her makeup, hoping to cover up most of the damage her crying had done. When she opened the door and stepped back into the bedroom, he was still waiting in exactly the same spot as before. "I'm ready," she said as she walked to him and then out into the hallway. He shut the bedroom door and proceeded to walk down the spiral steps with her.

He didn't say a word, instead he walked, his back ramrod straight, and politely opened the door for her at the bottom of the stairs. She whisked past him, carefully avoiding his eyes again. She'd already embarrassed herself enough for one day where he was concerned.

They fell into step together as they proceeded down the long corridor that led toward the dining hall, and just as they reached the doors he stopped and turned to her. Thinking he didn't want to open the door for her this time, she reached for the handle herself, but he stopped her, his hand resting on hers for a split second before he hastily pulled it away.

She looked up at him, afraid she had done something wrong. His face was unreadable, his cornflower blue eyes serious, but when he spoke, his voice was much quieter than it had been before.

"You wouldn't have wanted to be my friend," he said quietly, his eyes intent on hers. She didn't know what to say, and when he suddenly pushed open the door and motioned for her to go inside, she had to focus on her legs to get them to move. Tearing her eyes away from his, she walked past him and kept going until she reached her father and took her seat beside him.

Clynn eyed her with quiet concern, but she forced her lips into what she hoped was a convincing smile.

"I'm sorry I worried you," she told him as the others began to file in and take their seats.

"Thea told me you were shaken up when she went to visit you. She told me what you remembered."

Capri sighed, chewing her bottom lip worriedly. "I'm afraid it wasn't very helpful."

Clynn patted her back gently. "Even if we never find out who took you, at least we can content ourselves that you are home at last."

"I suppose," Capri replied, though she knew that contenting herself on this issue was not going to be good enough. Hearing about her dead mother had been painful, yes. And knowing that the orchestrator of the plan, Blythe's father, Brock, had been punished was acceptable enough justice. But she knew it was always going to plague her mind knowing that the demon responsible for her kidnapping was still out there, roaming free, perhaps plotting more heinous crimes. And maybe, just maybe, he was plotting against Euphora, hoping to strike again.

Feeling disillusioned by just about everything at that moment, Capri tried to eat as much as she could, keeping her eyes down to avoid conversation. The moment she was done she excused herself and bolted out of the dining hall without looking back.

# Chapter Seven

*Against what many* expected, Capri did not run. In fact, she never once gave a single thought to leaving Euphora. Instead, she increased her determination to what she now felt was her duty and her mission: learn to be an Air Dryad, and find the demon responsible for her mother's death and her kidnapping.

She knew that neither task was going to be easy, but she also knew that she had never really had a purpose before, and the simple fact that she could wake up in the morning and know her place in this world was sufficient enough to keep her going.

Her first week on Euphora was filled with challenging training sessions with her father, who was endlessly patient with her, something she desperately appreciated. She was still so unsure of herself, so afraid of doing something wrong, that any normal person would probably interpret her caution as an unwillingness to learn. However, her father seemed to sense her true intentions, and as such, he was unfailingly kind.

On her fourth day back home, her father had shown her how to view a small scale model of the Earth through the smoke instead of individual places, and how to conjure up clouds and use wind to push them along to their destinations.

Capri soon discovered that it was not nearly as easy as he had made it sound.

"I think it's going too far north," she complained, her arms outstretched in the direction of the smoke, her eyes intent on the realistic looking globe. "It's going out to sea. But I think I want it to stay inland."

"Then concentrate on it, and with your right hand push it just slightly to the south. It will do the rest on its own."

She did as she was told, focusing all of her thoughts on shifting the storm clouds from the Indian Ocean back down into the western coast of Australia. The storm began to head south and Capri turned to look at her father.

"Is that good?"

"It's perfect," he replied, smiling at her. "They've been without rain for quite long enough. This storm will do them good."

"I can't believe I'm creating weather patterns for places I've never even been before." Capri giggled, looking back at the globe. It was nearly three feet in diameter, three dimensional, and looked just like what the astronauts must have seen from the Moon. And all the clouds gracing its surface were under her control. She felt giddy with power, while at the same time humbled by responsibility. The whole world was depending on her.

There was a knock on the door behind them, and when Capri turned she saw Liam and Lucian enter, both looking casual and in good spirits.

"Oh, just in time!" Clynn exclaimed, rushing over to Lucian and patting his old friend on the back. "Capri has just sent a storm over to western Australia that will need an extra boost of moisture. Drought, you see."

"I do see," Lucian commented, smiling serenely as he approached the globe. "Liam, my boy, why don't you assist the lovely young lady?"

Liam grinned as he walked over to stand beside Capri, winking at her. "No prob, Dad," he said before he turned his gaze over to the globe, his eyes focusing intently on the cloud formations Capri had created. His arms lifted, hands spread, and Capri watched his eyes as they seemed to darken to an even deeper, more intense blue. Entranced, she looked back at the globe and watched the clouds darken just slightly and grow, becoming more and more menacing as they absorbed moisture from the sea. When Liam lowered his arms, the storm continued its progression toward land, only this time it was a lot more ominous.

"Wouldn't want to be there tomorrow when that storm hits," he commented, grinning as he turned to Capri.

She couldn't help but smile too. "I wouldn't either."

"Children, why don't you build a supercell together? Its spring, after all, and Clynn and I have been hopelessly late in getting started on storm season in the Midwest."

"He's right," Clynn admitted, smiling sheepishly. "This will be good for you, Capri. It's one of the most challenging things we have to do."

"Um…is a supercell some kind of cloud or something?" Capri asked, her brows knit in confusion. She had heard that term from somewhere, she just couldn't remember where…

When Lucian and Liam started laughing, Capri blushed.

Clynn patted her on the back, smiling at her kindly. "A supercell is one of the most dangerous cloud formations we use. It takes a good amount of skill to do it correctly, but I'll help you. Besides, tornados can be fun!"

Her eyes widened in shock and she gulped, feeling a lump form in her throat. "Oh, I hate tornados!" she managed, her hands wringing together as she stared at him.

Liam and Lucian laughed again, but this time she wasn't embarrassed. Tornados were horrible; everyone knew that…she had always been glad that she lived in Richmond, where tornados were rare.

"It all goes back to balance, darling," Clynn told her. "Tornados have their purpose, just like everything else. We will make a smaller one, if it makes you feel better."

She nodded, looking at the globe again, her face pale.

"It's not too bad," Liam said as they stood side by side again, facing the globe. "Where are you thinking of putting this bad boy, Clynn?" he asked, lifting his arms and shifting the globe with his hands until the United States was visible.

"Nebraska is due for one," Clynn remarked thoughtfully as he eyed the globe as well. "Capri, let's start the formation near eastern Colorado, and have it shift northeast into Nebraska, then due north into South Dakota. We'll throw in a few tornadoes along the way, keep it interesting. Liam will drop some heavy rains, some hail." He stood directly behind Capri as she lifted her arms, focusing on the location he had mentioned she should start.

"Because this storm will take roughly two days to cycle through, we will construct it now and give it a direction, and it will take its course on its own. So go ahead and just as before, picture the moisture condensing in the atmosphere, forming the clouds. Okay, now begin a continuously rotating updraft into those clouds, mixing the warm and cold air. Looks good."

Capri watched the aerial view of the storm she was building, and it was growing in size as she concentrated on rotating the air through it, her hands guiding the motion. She could sense Liam beside her, filling the storm with moisture to not only help build up the clouds but also for the rain. She chanced a quick glance at him, and noticed his vivid cobalt eyes were focused intently on the storm, his face unusually serious.

She turned back to the storm, concentrating once again.

"Excellent, both of you," Clynn said then, his hand resting on Capri's shoulder. "Would you like to see how the storm looks from the ground?"

Capri nodded, and Clynn reached out his hands and with a flick of his wrist the globe faded into the smoke, and in its place the image of the plains of eastern Colorado appeared.

The storm was there, forming and shifting in the sky, darkening and growing in size as they watched. The grasses of the plains were blowing in the breeze as of yet untouched by the impending storm. The clouds were funneling upward, forming a mushroom shaped mass that was glowing eerily in the afternoon sunlight.

"Give it a direction," Clynn said from behind her, his voice excited. "Send it northeast."

Capri focused back on the image of the clouds and with her hands, shifted the current westerly breeze to the northeast.

When a spear of lightning crackled within the center of the clouds as they changed direction, Capri jumped, then giggled nervously at herself.

"I've always been jumpy around lightning."

"Keep the updraft going, rotating it clockwise, bringing the warm air up into the atmosphere so it mixes with the cold air. Nicely done," Clynn instructed, watching as his daughter continued to shift the wind. "Pay close attention, Capri, as the air you've just been sending up into the storm starts to create a funnel."

She kept her eyes glued to the image, seeing nothing but the storm hovering over the plains, darkening and shifting underneath, while up above the cumulous clouds were white and textured as they hovered high up in the sky. Every few minutes, the clouds would flash as lightning speared from within, the bolts shooting at the ground. She could even hear the faint roar of thunder as the storm became more and more ominous.

Then the rain began to fall, lightly at first, before pummeling the grasslands.

Capri glanced over at Liam, who was all concentration, his hands clenching as if he was squeezing the rain from the clouds.

Then his hands spread out and lay flat as he lowered them just slightly. The rain began to fall even harder.

Capri kept her arms out, her hands motioning cyclically to keep the air moving, and suddenly she watched as a funnel speared out from the clouds and touched down to the ground, sweeping up dust and debris into its depths.

She could feel the power of it in her arms, in her body, in her mind, as it twisted and fueled itself until it was three times, four times, ten times the size it was when it first touched down. She marveled at it for a moment, amazed that she could create such a monster, yet at the same time appreciating the beauty and the wrath of it.

"You can ease back, and it will continue on the path you've set," Clynn murmured, just as entranced by the storm as she was.

She gradually lowered her arms, and she could feel the power leave her as she disconnected herself from her creation. The massive tornado continued along its path, dark as night and spiraling with ferocity, while lightning flashed and hail began to fall all around.

Shaking with adrenaline, Capri turned to her father and threw her arms around him, laughter bubbling in her throat.

"I did it!" She pulled away from him, her eyes dancing. "That was just...incredible!"

"Well done, darling." He grinned at her proudly. "You are a fast learner."

"Yes, she is a natural," Lucian commented, beaming from beside his son. "You and Liam make a fine team."

Capri glanced at Liam, who was looking smug as he turned to stare at his father. "Better than you old farts," he joked, earning a playful punch in the arm from Lucian.

"Who're you calling old?" Lucian pretended to look insulted. "Clynn, our children think we are old!"

Clynn laughed and shook his head, looking resigned. "I fear that is exactly what we are, my friend."

"Nonsense!" Lucian retorted, his eyes dancing. "I may be old, but I am still young at heart."

"Keep telling yourself that, Dad." Liam laughed. "Maybe you'll live longer if you believe it."

"I may just outlive you, boy-o." Lucian eyed his son meaningfully. "Though, I think raising you and Blythe has shaved several years off of my life as is," he added thoughtfully, looking a bit forlorn.

Liam turned to Capri and shrugged. "The regrets of an old man, so sad."

"The ignorance of a young man is even worse!" Lucian wagged his finger at his son, looking just like a parent scolding a fussy child.

Capri giggled, enjoying the easy way Liam and his father teased each other. She turned to her own father, who was watching the interaction of the other men with wistful eyes. She realized then how hard it must be for him to know that she had been raised by someone else, in the human world, without his guidance or his love. Feeling suddenly sorry for him, she wrapped her arms around him and hugged him tight, hoping he would understand how glad she was to finally be home.

By the end of her first week, Capri had created a dozen or more storms throughout the world, and was in the process of monitoring her creations. Spring was a busy time for weather patterns, and so she and her father began working together once she got the hang of creating storms on her own. He would be on one side of the globe, creating a storm in China, while she was on the other side, working out wind gusts through the Rockies. Sometimes she would make a mistake, and Clynn would help her fix it, but for the most part she did exceptionally well.

He also taught her how to practice on a much smaller scale, creating mini storms right in front of her versus using the birdbath. They had practiced outside in the courtyard, and she had made a storm that only floated about two feet off the ground. She once again practiced rotating the air to cycle through the warm and cold, thus creating a mini tornado. She was delighted to watch the cyclone spin across the cobblestone walkway, picking up bits of leaves and dirt as it went. She also learned, if she really wanted to, she could create a real storm on Euphora. Of course, her father warned her that Thea would not be very pleased if she did so, and that therefore it was best to keep to the smaller versions.

After a long week of learning and practicing, Capri was excited to have Saturday to take a break and relax.

"What do you want to do today?" Liam asked her at breakfast that morning amidst the chatter around the table.

Capri looked up from her bowl of oatmeal and smiled, considering. "I'm not really sure…what is there to do?"

"Ooh! Let's show Capri what's outside the gate!" Blythe suggested excitedly, a piece of jellied toast in one hand and a banana nut muffin in the other.

"That's right, you haven't been outside yet, have you?" Liam asked, looking thoughtfully at Capri.

"What's out there?" she asked worriedly, unsure if she really wanted to know. She hadn't been outside the gates of the courtyard since the day Liam had brought her to Euphora, and all she remembered was a meadow surrounded by trees…

"Well, I told you how Euphora is a floating island, right?"

Capri nodded, feeling unsure.

"Good, then you won't be too shocked when you see it." He winked at her as he cut into his second omelet.

"It?" Capri managed, looking really worried.

Blythe had a mischievous twinkle in her eyes as she spoke. "The edge of the island, of course."

"Oh boy."

"Don't worry, we won't push you over or anything."

"What?" Capri's face paled as she looked back and forth between Blythe and Liam, who both looked incredibly amused.

Liam cracked first, laying a hand over hers. "We're just joking with you. We won't push you over the edge."

"I don't like heights." She pouted, pulling her hand away, nervously pushing her oatmeal around in her bowl. "I'll go see it, but if I don't want to stay you can't make fun of me, okay?"

"Scout's honor." Blythe pledged, holding a hand over her heart and grinning.

If Capri had a mental picture of what it would look like to see the edge of a floating island, it didn't come close to what she felt when she actually witnessed it.

Blythe and Liam led her out the front gates and through the meadow, the morning sunlight shining mistily around them. They trekked through the trees, walking several minutes through the dense forest with moss growing up the massive trunks and the sky becoming almost completely blocked out by the leaves. She even saw a deer eyeing her in the distance, standing as still as a statue.

Suddenly, she noticed a break in the trees ahead, and she could see the most vividly blue sky she had ever seen. As they approached, the opening grew larger and larger until they emerged from the forest and stood in tall grass with wildflowers that were blowing carelessly in the wind. About twenty feet in front of them, the ground dropped off into nothing.

Capri walked forward, eyeing the drop off point apprehensively. When she was roughly two feet away, which was as close as she dared, she leaned forward and peered down over the edge.

Nearly half a mile down she could see the blue waters of the Pacific, glistening like diamonds in the sun as the waves churned and shifted. The horizon was a straight line of sky meeting sea, and there was no other land in sight.

"So, what do you think?" Liam asked, watching her stare nervously at the sea below.

Capri backed up a few more steps, crossing her arms over her chest protectively. "That's a big drop."

Blythe snorted. "That's nothing. You should try skydiving."

Color fled from Capri's cheeks, her eyes huge. "You've gone skydiving before?"

"Hell yeah I have!" Blythe replied, looking excited. "It's the best adrenaline rush there is. I told you that humans know how to have more fun. They have all kinds of exciting ways to get the heart pumping and the adrenaline racing."

"I don't even like rollercoasters…" Capri shuddered, the very thought of it making her nervous.

"You're telling me you lived with humans your whole life and you never did any of the fun stuff?" Blythe looked astonished, and Liam patted her on the back consolingly.

"Not everyone is a daredevil like you, Blythe," he reminded her, smiling at Capri. "Some people enjoy hobbies that don't require their feet leaving the safety of the ground."

Instinctively, Capri dug her heels into the grass beneath her feet, as though ensuring she was indeed still safe. "I'm scared of a lot of things," she admitted, feeling foolish. "I would never have the courage to do half the stuff you guys have probably done."

"Hey, I never said I was a daredevil." Liam held his hands up defensively. "I hate rollercoasters just like any other sane person."

"Ugh, you guys are so boring." Blythe rolled her eyes and walked over to the edge, her feet literally hanging half off of it as she stood looking out at the sea. She held her arms out and leaned forward slightly, letting the gusty wind from the sea blow past her like she was flying.

Despite how free Blythe looked, Capri felt sick to her stomach just watching. "Oh God, please don't do that," she managed, covering her eyes.

Blythe laughed and backed away from the edge. She wrapped her arms around Capri and pulled her into a hug. "You're so cute."

"I'm timid."

"And the sweetest person ever."

"I worry too much."

"Oh, shut up and take the compliment." Blythe grinned as she pulled away from Capri. "Wanna go sit down? You still look a little sick."

"That would be nice."

They walked over to the left toward a wooden bench that faced the ocean. As they sat down, Capri watched the horizon in the distance, feeling far away from the world she once knew.

The three of them sat in silence, relaxing and enjoying the view. Blythe had her head back and her eyes closed, sunlight warming her face. Liam had his arms on the back of the bench and his right ankle resting on his left knee, looking utterly casual while still managing to look like royalty. Capri sat between them both, and for a few moments, she truly felt as though she belonged there with them.

"I don't mean to bother either of you with this..." Capri said suddenly, breaking the silence. "But it's been on my mind all week, and I just have to ask. If you don't want to answer me, I understand."

Both Blythe and Liam looked at her, each with concern in their eyes.

"What is it?" Blythe asked.

"You can ask us anything."

"Okay...well, the night I was taken...do either of you remember anything? If you don't...it's okay...I just really want to find out more, you know?" She looked down at her hands in her lap, feeling uncomfortable.

For a moment neither of them said anything, and Capri wondered if she had insulted them in some way. She glanced up at Liam, worried his kind eyes would be filled with anger, but instead he was smiling down at her with understanding.

"None of us really remember much from the actual night, but we all remember the aftermath," he said quietly, his eyes shifting back to the horizon. Capri followed his gaze, and listened quietly as he continued. "I was six years old that year, and all I remember from that night is playing this bubble game with my dad, where we would try and stick as many bubbles together in the air as possible without bursting them. Then someone rushed into the room, shouting and screaming, and the bubbles popped and I started to cry. My dad was so distracted he didn't even realize what happened, and he just grabbed me up into his arms and handed me to my mother, who took me and the other children away to one of the towers. We were locked in there for what felt like forever, and then finally my dad came to get me and explained that you and your mother were gone. I don't think I really understood what he meant at the time. I thought the two of you had gone on vacation or something. It wasn't until your mother's funeral that it really sank in that everything would be different from then on."

"Everything was different," Blythe commented, her eyes on Capri, irritation in her voice. "All I remember is my whore of a mother yelling at me about how my father had ruined everything, that it was his fault her life was in pieces. She even threw some of the blame my way. In her twisted reality, it was my fault my father turned to demons and waged war against Thea and Sebastian. That if I hadn't been born and spun my evil web around him, she could have kept him on track and stopped him before it got to that point. Mind you, I was only four years old." Blythe sneered as she stared off at the sea, looking bitter. "After the demons were killed and the raid was over, the Furies gathered the evidence against my father and he was banished and forbidden to use his powers ever again. I barely even remember his face, though I guess it's for the best. He was a real bastard, far as I can tell. Then after all that, good ol' mommy decided to disown me and Lucian took me in."

"Your own mother disowned you?" Capri asked, looking shocked.

Blythe nodded. "You've met her. Nyxa, the third Fate."

Capri's eyes widened and her mouth fell open in surprise. "Nyxa is your mother?"

"Yep. And within two weeks of my dad being gone, she was shacked up with Balgaire, marriage plans on the horizon and a new bun in the oven. Brogan is my step brother and Nova is my half sister, not that either of them want anything to do with me."

"They don't even speak to you?"

Blythe shrugged. "We're polite enough, I suppose, but they pretend we're not related, by blood or otherwise. It's for the best though, as I can't stand Balgaire and any offspring of his can go to Hell as far as I'm concerned."

"Why don't you like Balgaire? He doesn't seem all bad…"

"Because he's a Fury, and you can never trust the Furies," Blythe replied, her eyes meeting Capri's. "They may be good at what they do, but they're heartless people. You pretty much have to be if you're gonna be around demons all the time. Demons can sense weak emotions and will latch onto you if you're not careful. The Furies hunt them down and kill them for a living. Ergo, emotionless killing machines are not to be trusted. I would just stay away from them if I were you."

Capri had the sudden memory of the display wall with row upon row of deadly weapons, and the efficient way Rian had fired off rounds without even a moment's hesitation. With a jolt, she also remembered Rian when he'd said the words: *you wouldn't have wanted to be my friend.* Was this what he had meant? Did he think himself incapable of friendship?

"I don't know…Roarke didn't seem that way. He was very polite and generous to me," Capri countered defensively.

"That's what he wanted you to feel and think. Why do you think he's so successful? Why do you think he's the leader? He knows how to make you feel as though you're his best friend, while at the same time he's plotting ways to destroy you. Well, not you in particular, as he would never hurt you, but that's how he plays these demons. He goes in, convinces them to trust him, and then Balgaire sweeps in and takes 'em out."

"Wow," Capri managed, turning to Liam. "Do you not trust the Furies either?"

Liam shook his head. "Not really, no. I mean, like Blythe said, they are excellent at what they do, taking down demons and all, but I would err on the side of caution when it comes to dealing with them."

"Do you think they would tell me what they know about the demon who took me?"

Liam's brows lifted. "You really want to figure this out, don't you?"

"Of course I do!" Capri retorted, standing up suddenly and staring down at the two of them. "Wouldn't you if it had happened to you instead of me?"

"Of course I would," Blythe declared, tilting her head up with a fierce grin.

Liam chuckled at Blythe and turned to look at Capri. "Definitely."

"Okay then," Capri mumbled, feeling silly about her sudden outburst. She took her seat again, chewing on her lip. "I just need more information. Someone here must have seen something..."

"If you must, you could try asking the Furies," Liam suggested. "Just know that they might not like you meddling in a case that they never solved."

"But it's my mother; they can't expect me to just let this go," Capri argued, feeling frustrated.

"It doesn't hurt to ask," Blythe said, sitting back against the bench and resting her head in her hands.

Capri sat back against the bench as well, deeply sighing and watching the horizon again. She really hoped that the Furies could help her...they hadn't seemed so bad when she'd talked with them before. And if they could, then she would be that much closer to discovering the identity of the demon responsible for her mother's death...

"Do you think that if my mother hadn't been human, if she'd had some kind of powers, that maybe she wouldn't have died?" Capri asked, her eyes locked straight ahead on the horizon, her voice soft.

Liam slid his arm around her, pulling her close. "Just because we have powers doesn't mean we can't be fooled. Your mother had no reason not to trust Brock, and any one of us could have fallen for the same trick."

"Yeah, and she's not the first human to live on Euphora," Blythe put in, stretching her arms behind her head. "Though she has been the last so far."

"My father said it was uncommon for members of the Council to be with humans," Capri told her, looking puzzled. "But you say others have lived here, too?"

"Occasionally. I mean, all of us have to produce an heir to carry on our duties, otherwise Thea has to start over and she hates doing that, seeing as it's kind of complicated." Blythe shrugged, looking complacent. "Sometimes I think it would be better to just start over with some of the idiots around here, but they keep reproducing anyway."

"What Blythe is trying to say is that we are permitted to have children with others on Euphora or with humans. Sometimes the humans choose to live on Euphora, sometimes they don't. And in the worst of cases, the Muses have to step in and alter a human's memory when they don't accept our explanation of what we are. But if all goes well, like with your parents, the human accepts what we are and chooses this life."

"I see..." Capri murmured, silently hoping that whoever she chose to love and have a child with would accept her for what she was...

"The absolute only exception to the rule is that we are forbidden to procreate with a human possessed by a demon," Liam added seriously.

"Like anyone would want to." Blythe snorted, laughing.

"Other than the obvious..." Capri began, eyeing Blythe tentatively before turning back to Liam. "Can I ask why it's forbidden?"

Liam thought for a moment. "Honestly, I don't really know the specific reason. I assume it's just because they are dangerous."

"And disgusting." Blythe added with a grin.

Capri nodded with a sigh, wondering what she was going to do if she ever came face to face with the demon who took her, and whether she would be strong enough to stand a chance at surviving.

Later that night at dinner, Capri planned what she was going to say when she approached the Furies. She'd spent the rest of the afternoon thinking over the entire situation, trying to gather what she knew about that night and piecing everything together. And still she came to the realization that she just wasn't going to get any further unless she talked to the Furies and found out what they knew.

After dinner, when everyone drifted into the parlor for drinks and conversation, Capri hovered near the Dryads, waiting and watching for a good moment to approach Roarke and the others. She decided that Roarke would be the most forthcoming with information and since he was generally very talkative he might divulge even more than what he was asked for. Figuring that more information was always better than less information, she made her move toward Roarke.

She excused herself from her father and friends, who looked at her with concerned faces, and walked straight to him, trying to control her trembling legs.

The Furies were seated on their usual sofa and armchairs near the windows, and Roarke appeared to be discussing something with Balgaire on the sofa while Brogan sat by silently in one of the two neighboring armchairs. Rian was standing in front of the windows, staring out into the darkness with his hands clasped behind his back. She could see his faint reflection in the glass as she approached and could tell he was watching her.

"Excuse me," Capri said with a shy smile as she looked down at Roarke. He looked up at her from the sofa, his blue eyes twinkling.

"Well, hello there," he greeted gruffly, a glass of whiskey in his hand. He winked at her with a toothy grin. "Come to ask me for some shooting lessons?"

Capri blushed. "No sir, actually I was hoping I could ask you a question…regarding my mother."

Roarke's smile faltered slightly as he watched her, his eyes filling with pity. Capri knew she had made the right decision to go straight to him with her questions, as both Balgaire and Brogan seemed incredibly uncomfortable and sat in silence.

Rian turned around and leaned against the window, arms crossed over his chest, his eyes sharp and focused.

"What is it you'd like to know?" Roarke asked, gesturing for her to sit in the armchair across from him. She took a seat and folded her hands in her lap, hoping she didn't look as self-conscious as she felt.

"Well, I'm sure you've heard that I went to the Muses to try and remember more about the night I was taken, and that I still didn't really get a good glimpse of the demon responsible for my mother's death. I guess I was just hoping that maybe you could tell me what you knew and, if it's alright with you, I want to try and figure out who he is."

Roarke looked extraordinarily surprised. "I can tell you everything we know, but I doubt you'll be able to do anything more than what we've already done. The only person out there who knows the identity of that demon is long gone, withering away amongst humans. And if we couldn't get the name out of him, I doubt you'd be able to."

"I understand," Capri replied, biting her lip as she pondered what he said. "But it wouldn't hurt if you could at least tell me what you remember. I'm sorry if I'm being too bold, but my entire life was changed because of that one night and I'd like to know as much about it as possible."

Roarke watched her carefully, measuring her exactly as his son was doing behind him, and for a moment Capri began to doubt whether he would tell her anything at all. But when he spoke, his voice was kind.

"You were such a tiny little thing back then," he said, rubbing his bearded chin in thought. "We were all so protective of you kids." He glanced over at his own son, who was still leaning against the window silently, and his face seemed to tighten when he turned back to Capri. "As you already know, your mother was walking with you in the courtyard when the demons came in. Brock was supposedly working late in the dungeon when in reality he had left to bring the demons to Euphora and let them through the front gate, which was when your mother spotted them. At the same time, Balgaire stepped out for fresh air, and he saw your mother speaking with Brock and the demons, but before he could do much more than be suspicious, the demon had shot and killed her, and was running away with you. Balgaire didn't get a good enough glimpse at the face of the demon since he was too far away, but he did manage to fight off a couple of other demons before the rest of us even realized what was going on." Roarke turned to Balgaire and patted him on the back proudly. "He may look stuffy, but he knows how to use a pistol almost as well as I do."

Capri watched Balgaire shift uncomfortably in his seat, as though he didn't like being the center of attention. His stony face was unreadable, but when his dark eyes met hers she tried to smile. This man was essentially a hero and he had fought off the demons as they tried to storm the castle. Who knew how many others might have been hurt if he hadn't been there to fight? And even though he had been too late to save her mother and rescue herself, at least Capri knew that he would have tried.

He nodded slightly as though acknowledging her silent thanks. She felt she liked him a lot better than she had before. He really was just shy, and being shy herself she couldn't hold it against him.

"How many other demons were there?" she asked, turning back to Roarke.

"Ten, all possessing humans at the time. The one who got away with you makes eleven," Roarke replied with a nod. "And good ol' Brock tried to pretend to fight them off, had us all fooled until the evidence surfaced and pointed straight to him. Then Thea banished him to live amongst humans for the remainder of his days. Too light a punishment if you ask me; I'd have taken care of him myself if Thea had given me the chance. It's just not right what he did, and I have never been okay with murdering innocents."

"And he never told you the name of the demon? I just wonder why he would protect one demon while letting the others get caught."

Roarke looked intrigued. "Well, we figured it was because the demon that got away was his partner of sorts, while the others were merely a means to an end. You see, Brock had a lot of dealings with demons that were, let's say, unethical. He enjoyed his vices more than most men, and had a weakness for demon weapons and demon booze, a bad, bad combination. Not to mention, both are forbidden by Thea except when used for training purposes by us." He smirked, smug and proud.

"Did you know any of the demons that he dealt with?"

"We did, we had a good, long list," Roarke replied, looking suddenly bitter. "And all the bastards' stories checked out. None of them were part of the raid."

"Oh," Capri sighed, pursing her lips in thought. "So that was it? That's where the trail goes cold?"

"Pretty much." Roarke shrugged. "There comes a time when a particular case goes cold, and fresh cases start building up until you don't have the time to focus on the old anymore. I'm sorry we couldn't do more, but if you think of anything else or remember any more details, be sure to let me know. Sometimes cold cases get solved, even fifteen years later."

"I understand." Capri stood up and took a deep breath, trying to smile and look stronger than she felt. "Thank you for your time."

"You should help us help you," Rian said suddenly from his spot by the window, his arms still crossed and his face stonily serious.

"What do you mean?" she asked, eyeing him cautiously.

"You should go back to the Muses, and try and remember more details. If we had more to go on, then we could help you. So instead of asking everyone else what they remember, try uncovering everything you remember first. You were the only person who witnessed the whole thing."

Capri wasn't sure what to say for a moment, shocked Rian was actually speaking in full sentences to her. She acknowledged his comments, though she wasn't sure she agreed. She didn't think she could bear reliving her memories again, considering how much pain it had caused her the first time. Plus, she didn't even know if she had seen the demon's face, and if she hadn't then she certainly wouldn't remember it, so what was the point in seeing the Muses again?

"I'll think about it. Thank you again," she replied quietly, her eyes leaving his as she turned away and walked back to her father and the other Dryads, feeling even more lost and confused than before.

# Chapter Eight

*She tried to* convince herself during the next two weeks that she wasn't being a coward. Surely she could visit the Muses again and relive her dream and survive, it's just that she didn't think it was necessary. After all, she'd witnessed it once, how many more details could she possibly pick up by seeing the memory a second time? She hadn't seen the demon's face, so that was that. Rian was just trying to turn this on her, as if she was being foolish by asking others what happened that night. What he said annoyed her, though she knew that he was most likely just trying to help. And maybe he was right, maybe she should be focusing more on what she remembered instead of pestering everybody else...it was probably starting to get on everyone's nerves.

Annoyed that she was still so unsure how to proceed, she decided to take some time off for herself. She'd been spending as much free time as she could in the enormous library, and the fact that it was empty more often than not made it even more appealing. She always hated trying to read at her old library with all those people walking around and distracting her.

She entered the library and smiled to herself, excited for some time alone. Wandering over to one of the many bookshelves, she perused the titles, debating which book to read. On a good day, she could polish off a couple hundred page book without breaking a sweat.

The morning sunlight slanted in through the large windows that graced one of the walls, dust motes glittering in the golden rays. The library had three full walls filled floor to ceiling with bookshelves, with a notch cut out for the door. The fourth wall was entirely dedicated to the windows, which provided excellent reading light.

There were desks, sofas, plush armchairs, pillows, and side tables throughout the room, all arranged in groups. When Capri had selected *The Picture of Dorian Gray*, she headed over to her favorite reading spot: a tall wingback armchair the color of summer squash with a cozy matching footstool that faced the windows, keeping its occupant completely hidden from view. It was the perfect place for reading, and she loved occasionally glancing up from her book to admire the view of the courtyard outside.

Content, she cuddled up in the chair and opened the book, losing herself within its pages.

After some time, she heard the library door open and shut behind her, and someone shuffle inside hastily. She froze, hoping the person would leave and not notice her sitting there. She already felt embarrassed having someone think themselves alone when really she was hiding out in silence.

Before she could turn around in her seat to announce her presence to the newcomer, she heard two sets of low voices and instead sunk lower into the chair.

Her heart started pounding as she listened, clutching the book, trying to stay completely silent.

One of the voices she recognized as Rhiannon's father, Rohan. He sounded irritated and desperate, and the combination struck Capri as odd. She'd never seen him act anything other than elegant and quietly superior, so to hear his voice punctuated with resentment troubled her.

"You say you have this under control and that you are keeping an eye out, but I need your word that this will be handled!" Rohan whispered viciously.

"You have my word, like I said before," the other voice stated. It sounded oddly familiar, and yet she couldn't quite place it. "You needn't worry yourself anymore."

"Good...good," Rohan said again, softer this time. "But I am trusting your word will be good. If I find out otherwise, I will not be so kind."

"I understand."

Capri heard the door open, and the sound of footsteps. When the door shut again, she stayed where she was, listening for any other sounds in case one of the men was still in the room.

After a few moments of nothing but silence, she let out a long breath and sat up gradually, scanning the library. It was empty. Feeling foolish, she sat back down in the chair and tried to regulate her breathing.

All she had witnessed was a simple conversation, nothing more. And yet she couldn't help but feel that what she heard was important in some way, especially since the two men obviously didn't want anyone else to hear. But what could Rohan possibly be doing that would require such secrecy? And who was he doing it with?

The other voice had been deeper than Rohan's, harder with a sharp edge to it. While he had said nothing threatening, something in his voice still implied danger.

When her eyes drifted toward the courtyard and locked on the jasmine plant beside the cobblestone walkway, she had the sudden realization where she had heard that voice before.

He was the man who had ordered her mother to die.

Terror shot through her body in vicious waves as she fought with herself for a moment. It just wasn't possible. Brock had been banished, he wasn't on Euphora...

But how else could she explain hearing his voice? She was positive it was the same voice she had heard in her dream…and yet, she supposed she could just be projecting…

Maybe she'd been stressing herself out too much over the past couple weeks by constantly dwelling on the night she was taken. And maybe she was imagining she had heard that same voice, when in reality it was someone completely different. It was possible, she supposed…though she couldn't be sure.

Shaken, she stood up and walked over to replace the book she'd been reading in its place on the shelf. She began to make a hasty escape out of the library, except when she opened the door there was suddenly a person there.

She bumped right into them, and instinctively retreated, her hands up in apology.

"I'm so sorry!" she exclaimed, focusing on the person she had bumped into. It was Tobias, one of the Muses.

He looked at her with such an odd expression on his face, as if he had come across a monster that was quite ready to eat him.

"Are you okay?" she asked without thinking, biting back the instinct to reach out and comfort him. He was only fifteen years old, after all, and she could remember how uncomfortable it was to be that age.

It was the first time she really got a good look at him. He was tall and gangly for his age, with chestnut brown hair and gentle, sea green eyes, and lips that formed a stubborn pout like a child who hasn't gotten his way.

"I'm fine," he said curtly, suddenly gathering his wits and glaring at her defensively. "You should watch where you're going."

With that, he pushed past her, shoving her slightly, and headed into the library.

Capri stared after him with wide eyes, rubbing her shoulder before she turned and left. She wondered what in the world was wrong with him as she retreated down the corridor.

First he looked like he had seen a ghost, and then he acted as though he was angry with her, like she had done something to offend him. She sincerely hoped that wasn't the case, as she had yet to get to know any of the younger Muses and didn't think she had done anything wrong. But then again, Tobias was the one who hadn't looked too happy to see her the night she had returned, so maybe he just didn't like her on principle.

Annoyed that she was overanalyzing the whole situation, she pushed it to the back of her mind. He was a teenager, after all, and who knew what was going on inside his head. She felt sorry for him, silently hoping that whatever it was that was bothering him would right itself soon. Seeing someone, anyone really, in distress usually had that effect on her.

Instead she focused her thoughts back to the harsh voiced man who against all logic was on Euphora. If he was indeed the same man she'd heard in her dream.

Maybe it would be better to revisit the Muses and see if she could catch a glimpse of Brock in her dream. Then, if he did happen to be on Euphora, at least she'd recognize him if he approached her, and she would know to run.

That night, she had her nightmare for the first time since she'd come home.

Only this time, something was oddly different about it.

She was walking on her own in the dark courtyard, her mother nowhere in sight. Instead of being a child, she was eighteen, but this fact didn't seem to bother her as much as it probably should have.

So she kept on walking, her body draped in a long, pale blue nightgown, her hair streaming down her back in waves. Her feet were bare, and padded silently against the smooth cobblestone walkway.

The night air around her was quiet, almost eerily quiet, the absence of chirping crickets or scurrying night creatures sending off danger signals in her brain.

Moonlight cascaded through the trees, highlighting the leaves and deepening the darkest shadows beneath.

She walked cautiously, her eyes peering around, trying to distinguish something from the darkness. She hoped she would see the monsters she was sure were hiding in the shadows before they saw her. Then she might have the chance to hide herself.

Suddenly, she found herself standing in front of the jasmine, only she was too large to hide beneath its sheltering leaves this time. She knelt down anyway, reaching out to touch the gentle blossoms.

"Capri…" someone whispered suddenly from behind her. Capri jolted, startled into a standing position as she searched around wildly for the source of the voice. She found it, lying on the ground beneath her feet.

Her mother lay there, her chest smoldering as though it had been burnt, her coffee brown hair spilling over the cobblestones around her head. Her face was pale, and her brown eyes were wide and bright with shimmering tears.

"Capri…run," she said again, her voice trembling with fear.

"Mom…what?" Capri knelt down and cupped her mother's cheek in her hand. She felt tears stinging her eyes as she glanced down at the wound in her mother's chest. The fire from the demon bullet was gone, and all that was left was brutal damage.

"Hide," her mother choked out again, her eyes filled with desperation as her whole body began to shake. "*Run!*" she nearly screamed, the sound of it echoing in Capri's brain as a whistle suddenly broke the silent night. She heard the sounds of several people rushing through the front gates.

She looked up and saw the dark figures rapidly moving toward her, and the only thing she could think was that she couldn't leave her mother alone. She reached out to pull her mother with her, to escape, but the moment she touched her mother's arm, her body dissolved into smoldering ashes.

"*No!*" Capri screamed, but as she turned to run there was suddenly a man in front of her, his revolver pointed directly at her forehead, the barrel glinting in the moonlight. His face was hidden by dark shadows.

"Leave this place, and never return," he commanded cruelly, and she recognized his voice as the same one that had been haunting her since childhood. "*Now!*"

She scrambled to her feet and ran, but suddenly there was a different man following her, and he was quickly gaining speed. Fear made her run faster, as fast as she could, until she was almost to the entrance of Euphora.

She could see the meadow beyond the walls, glowing brightly in the moonlight, and the large tree she had used when she had first arrived. Frantically, she tried to remember the phrase Liam had spoken to the tree to transport them, when she suddenly realized she probably needed a different phrase to leave Euphora...

As she burst into the meadow, she kept her eyes focused on the tree, somehow feeling that she would be safe if she could at least make it there.

She could still hear the man chasing her, but she didn't look back, worried what she would see if she did. Her feet pounded the grass, and she had to lift up the skirts of her nightgown to prevent it from snagging and tripping her.

The tree was almost within reach, just a little bit further...

She stretched out her arm, her fingers spread, aching to touch the bark. Her legs began to feel sluggish and time seemed to slow, and it almost seemed as if the tree were pulling away from her, teasing her when her only desire was to reach it...

Suddenly, she felt rough hands grasp her other arm and pull her back, and she fell roughly to the ground, pain searing through her head at the contact. Her mouth opened to scream, despite knowing it was useless. She closed her eyes tightly, bracing for death.

She was caught. It was over. The demon had won.

"Wake up," someone said abruptly, their voice far away and distant. "You need to wake up now."

Her eyes flew open, but the entire world seemed to go dark as she searched for herself, trying to recover what part of her was left in this empty darkness. She felt her arms reaching out, but her mind didn't seem to process the movement. She fell on her back against the tall grass and wildflowers, her chest heaving as she gasped for air. It felt like someone else was inside her head, forcing her own brain to dullness as it took over her. She felt the sensation of choking, as though she desperately wanted to cry out but something was holding her back, clutching her throat, preventing her from making any sound.

She could feel hands shaking her roughly, trying to bring her back to reality, but she couldn't seem to escape. She was a prisoner in her own mind, shrinking away from all being, hiding out from the world in fear as someone else seemed to be controlling her body.

She felt a gurgling noise rising within her throat, and suddenly, without warning, she heard herself snarl and hiss, almost like an angry wildcat. Her hands lashed out and clawed at the air, making brutal contact with someone's face.

"Show yourself, demon!" the person shouted suddenly, and the hands that had been shaking her were now gripping her arms tightly, holding them against her body so she couldn't move. She could feel her body viciously fighting against the restraint, before going instantly slack.

Her vision cleared and she gasped for breath, her hands reaching up instinctively to her throat. She could feel the darkness that had clogged her brain recede, and with a rushing flood of relief she realized she was in control of her body once again.

The person in front of her was suddenly on their feet and ready to run when Capri reached up to touch the back of her head where she felt a throbbing pain, only to notice dark red blood on her fingertips as she pulled them away.

"I'm bleeding," she said, her vision blurring again, feeling faint.

"Damnit." The person froze mid-step and knelt in front of her, their hands gripping her shoulders more gently this time to prevent her from falling over.

She looked up wearily, blinking to clear her vision and see who was there. "Who are you?" she asked, wincing at how quiet and raspy her voice sounded.

"You remembered me before, but now you forget? I doubt your head injury is that bad." While Capri could tell the person was trying to joke, the words were dry and sober, as if it wasn't funny at all.

Recognition hit her like a brick wall.

"Rian," she murmured, her vision finally clear so she could see his face in the moonlight. He looked strained and his eyebrows were furrowed in concern, but his eyes were still sharp and focused.

"Good job," he replied. "Can you stand up?"

"I–I think so…" She glanced around, as though looking for something to hold on to while she tried to stand. That was when she realized she was in the meadow outside the front gates, and she tried to remember how she had gotten there. When she looked forward again, she noticed Rian had his hand out to help her. "T-thank you."

He pulled her to her feet, but the moment he let go her legs gave out from trembling. Her head pounded as she fell to her knees, and she reached up to the wound instinctively.

"Hold still," he instructed as he knelt beside her again, his hands on her shoulders. "Is it alright if I carry you?"

She nodded, her eyes closing against the pain as he lifted her solidly into his arms. He held her slightly away from him, as if he didn't want their bodies to touch any more than necessary, so she was forced to try and hold her head up as he began to walk.

She felt foolish, having to be carried yet again like some weak child, but the little bit of pride she had was nothing in comparison to how utterly terrified she was over what had just happened. She desperately wanted to ask him, but she could feel herself falling into darkness again, her vision blurring as the courtyard began to turn black.

She heard herself mumble, "What happened?" before she slid into unconsciousness.

The next thing Capri knew, there were hollow voices echoing in the darkness. She felt distant, disconnected from her body like she was floating. But as she focused on the voices, trying to understand what they were saying, she felt sensation return to her body, could feel herself lying in bed, and her mind abruptly registered the pain.

"How could this have happened? Right under our noses!"

"We are not even safe in our own home!"

"Someone here must have let him in."

"But who?"

"Help me," she whispered, though she was trying to shout it, her mind frantically trying to remember what had happened while the pain in her head pulsed in pounding waves.

The voices around her hushed and suddenly there were gentle, cool hands stroking her forehead gently, and others touching her hands and shoulders.

"It's okay, you're safe," one of the voices said, and Capri fought to open her eyes, fought to see who was there.

When she was able to, she saw her father's kind eyes staring back at her, worry lines creasing his forehead, his lips curved into a weak smile as his hand rested against her forehead.

"How are you feeling?" Liam was on the other side of her, smiling and holding her hand. Blythe was beside him, looking murderous.

"Well she ain't peachy keen, Liam." Blythe spat, shifting and clenching her fists impulsively like a fighter preparing for a match. "Someone is responsible for doing this to her, and when I find out who it is I'm gonna kill him."

"You're going to startle her, control yourself," Liam scolded, eyeing her intently before turning back to Capri. "You hit your head pretty hard, but you're going to be fine. A mild concussion, but no permanent damage. You just need to rest for a few days."

"But I was just dreaming," Capri replied, her brows creasing in worry. "It was just a dream…you don't get hurt from dreams."

"It may have seemed like a dream, but it wasn't," Clynn responded, his face tightening against the anger coursing through him. "You were possessed by a demon."

"What?" Her eyes widened in shock as she stared at him, trying to understand if she had heard him correctly. "How?"

"Someone let him in," a voice said from the foot of the bed, and it was then that Capri noticed that her bedroom was full of people. Thea was the one who had spoken, and she looked just as angry as Blythe, only much more controlled. Beside her were Sebastian, Rohan and Lucian, and on the other side of her were Roarke and Balgaire.

"The demon couldn't have gotten onto Euphora, much less onto the grounds, without help," Roarke said sternly, his scarred face frightening in its seriousness. She'd never before seen him look so severe, and the harsh difference between this and his usually jovial demeanor startled her.

"I think we need to focus on who had the most to gain from hurting or scaring Capri," Rohan added, glancing around at everyone present. "And if you ask me, I'd say that person would be Blythe."

"*What?*" Blythe shouted, whirling around on Rohan, her eyes fiery with rage. "Why the hell would I want to hurt her?"

"Because she has a father while you do not, and that made you jealous. Just like you have been jealous of Rhiannon for years for the same reason," Rohan countered, standing tall and sneering down at Blythe like she was a rodent needing to be exterminated. Capri had never, ever seen him act this way before, and she looked back and forth between him and Blythe, nervously waiting for fists to fly.

"Rohan, this is completely uncalled for!" Lucian cried angrily, eyeing Rohan like he had just sprouted antlers.

"Oh, that's just perfect, Rohan. Make it all about you and your precious daughter as usual. Screw you!" Blythe took off, her hands clenched into fists. She slammed the door behind her as she left.

"Do you have proof that Blythe let in the demon?" Sebastian asked Rohan, an astonished look on his face.

"No. But I wouldn't be surprised if she had. Fire is bad blood, her father couldn't be trusted, nor could his mother before him, therefore I don't trust her either."

"Rohan, as usual you are blinded by your prejudice," Thea said sternly. "Leave your personal troubles out of this."

"I know Blythe didn't do it!" Capri exclaimed, blushing as everyone turned to look at her. "She's been nothing but kind to me."

"Yeah, Blythe wouldn't do something like this," Liam agreed with a nod, turning to Thea. "She's like my sister, I know how she does things. She wouldn't do something sneaky like this, she prefers head on confrontations if she's pissed. It wasn't her."

"Capri, do you remember anything before you started having what you thought was a dream?" Clynn asked kindly.

Capri closed her eyes and thought for a moment, trying to remember anything that might help…but, once again, she was useless. "No, I just remember going to bed, and then waking up by the tree in the meadow. Rian was there…where is he?"

"He's out there currently tracking the demon," Roarke answered, pride in his voice. "Thank God he was reading next to a window and spotted you walking through the courtyard, otherwise that demon might have made off with you just like last time."

"Capri, for the demon to have been able to possess you, you would need to be in a weakened, emotional state," Clynn told her. "Has something been bothering you lately that might have caused you severe, emotional pain?"

"No," Capri answered instinctively, but then she remembered hearing the harsh voiced man in the library and how scared that had made her...but she wasn't sure she should talk about that when Rohan was standing right in front of her. Especially after the way he had treated Blythe. She was certain it would be smart to stay away from him as much as possible. "I want to speak to Rian. I need to thank him..."

"We will send him up later," Thea promised, her face relaxing. "You need your rest."

It was then that Clarity came into the room with scented herbs and flowers, and everyone else began to leave. Her father squeezed her hand in his own reassuringly.

"Thank God you're safe." He tried to smile, but it didn't quite reach his eyes. When he left, Capri was alone with Clarity.

"Relax, Capri," she said, her voice soothing and lyrical. She placed a cool compress over Capri's forehead and eyes, and began gently massaging her temples. She could smell the soothing scent of lavender and vanilla as she felt her breathing slow and her mind calm.

Within minutes she slipped into a pleasantly dreamless sleep, and all disturbing thoughts of demons began to fade away into darkness.

# Chapter Nine

*Sometime later, in* the early morning hours, Rian came into her room and stood beside her bed. She thought she remembered waking and saying something to him, but she wasn't exactly sure what it was. It was probably something along the lines of a simple thank you...and when he touched her hand and watched her in silence, she must have drifted back to sleep. When she woke hours later, she could have sworn for a moment that he was still there, holding her hand in his, reminding her that he would protect her.

But maybe she was only imagining the whole thing. After all, she had been in a very deep and heavy sleep.

"She's been out for twelve hours...shouldn't we wake her up?"

"She has a concussion, Blythe...I think we should give her as much rest as she needs."

"Right, but aren't you supposed to keep people with head injuries awake or something?"

"Are you a doctor now? I don't think so."

Capri felt her lips twitch into a smile as she listened to her friends argue quietly with each other.

"You're actually supposed to wake the person up every few hours and check on them, but seeing as its already been twelve hours I think I'm okay." Capri opened her eyes and grinned at them sleepily.

"See, I was right," Blythe replied haughtily, earning a swift punch in the shoulder from Liam.

"Shut up," he told her as he looked at Capri, a wide grin on his face. "How you feeling, champ?"

"Better." Capri yawned and stretched her arms up behind her, and when they came down she felt the bandage on the back of her head. "Oh." She pressed on it lightly, wincing at the dull pain she felt.

"Yeah, you're gonna have to wear that for a day or two until the wound heals. It's cool though, you actually look pretty badass with it on," Blythe commented, sitting down on the side of the bed and holding Capri's hand in her own, her eyes softer and more serious. "You scared us really bad, honey."

Capri sighed and leaned back against her pillows again. "I'm sorry…I guess I can't let my guard down again."

"It shouldn't be like that," Liam said irritably, sitting down opposite Blythe on the bed and taking Capri's other hand in his. "You shouldn't have to be afraid here. The Furies are going to find out who did this and then everything will be normal again, I promise."

"Okay." Capri smiled, feeling sentimental as she looked at both of them. "Thank you for being here…I really appreciate everything you both have done for me."

"We care about you," Liam replied, squeezing her hand gently.

"Yeah, so don't worry about it, okay?" Blythe agreed with a quick grin.

"Okay."

There was a sudden gentle knocking on the door and when it opened, Rhiannon peeked her head inside.

"Oh," she said, pausing when she saw Liam and Blythe sitting beside Capri, unsure what she wanted to do. "I just wanted to bring you some flowers and see how you were doing."

"Please, come in," Capri said with a kind smile as she tried to sit up. She winced at how weak she felt, but she continued to sit up anyway until she was propped up against her pillows.

"Maybe you should wait your turn," Blythe suggested, her eyes spitting fiery daggers at Rhiannon as she stepped over the threshold.

Rhiannon looked insulted and opened her mouth to retort just as Liam stepped in.

"We were actually just leaving, Rhia," he said, his eyes kind. "Come in."

He stood up, eyeing Blythe as he did so, and she rolled her eyes and stood up as well.

She looked down at Capri and smiled. "I'll come back later, 'k?" With that, she turned and headed out the door, passing by Rhiannon without another word. Liam headed out as well, but as he passed Rhiannon he stopped in front of her, and his hand came up to touch her cheek.

"Are you okay?" he asked her. Capri watched Rhiannon look at him, her eyes cold.

"I'm fine, Liam." She shifted away from him and approached Capri, standing somewhat awkwardly beside the bed.

Capri saw Liam freeze, his hand raised where it had just been touching Rhiannon's cheek, before he turned and left, shutting the door quietly behind him.

Rhiannon and Capri were both quiet for a moment, neither of them sure what to say.

"I didn't know what kind you liked, but I hope these will do." Rhiannon motioned with the vase of sunny daffodils in her arms.

"They're beautiful," Capri replied cheerfully, hoping to make Rhiannon feel more welcome.

"I'll just set them here on your nightstand."

She put the cheery blue vase down and then held out a small tin of butter cookies to Capri. Her lips curved into a smile.

"Cookies always cheer me up," Rhiannon told her as she took a seat in the wooden side chair beside the bed.

"Thank you." Capri held the tin to her chest, watching the other girl carefully.

"Are you feeling better?" Rhiannon asked, her hands folding properly in her lap and her back ruler straight. She was wearing a neat, navy blue pencil skirt and a crisp white blouse, her long coco hair pulled back into a trim ponytail.

Capri suddenly felt frumpy and disheveled compared to the pristine Rhiannon, but she had to remind herself that she had a rough night, and couldn't be expected to look exactly perfect.

"I am, actually," she replied as she smoothed out the blanket in front of her. "I slept for twelve hours apparently."

"I'm sorry this happened to you," Rhiannon said quietly, sadness in her eyes. "And with you only being home one month. I can only imagine how you must be feeling."

"I'm fine, really," Capri reassured her. "Though I suppose I should be wondering why this happened..." she added thoughtfully, feeling uneasy.

"The Furies will find out, you shouldn't worry. And until they do, you will be protected."

"That's good to know."

The two of them were quiet once again, as though each searching for what to say next. Rhiannon broke the silence first.

"I'm sorry I haven't really had time to speak with you lately... it's mostly my fault, I've been so busy," she apologized, attempting to smile.

"No, I understand. Please don't think I'm angry with you."

"Well, that's a relief," Rhiannon replied with a light laugh, relaxing. "If you like, when you feel better we can have a picnic lunch in the courtyard. It'd be fun and relaxing and I think you'd enjoy it."

"I'd love to!" Capri beamed happily. It actually was just the sort of thing she enjoyed to do, and the fact that Rhiannon invited her made it all the better.

"Good, I'm glad," Rhiannon said as she glanced down, tugging at the hem of her skirt fretfully. "Other than what happened last night, have you been enjoying Euphora?"

"Of course! I don't think I've ever been happier, really."

"We were worried you would go away after what you found out about your mother…and everyone's wondering if you will leave now because of this."

Capri stared at Rhiannon, her eyes widening in surprise. "Why would I leave because of this?"

"Aren't you frightened?"

"Well, yes, I guess I am, but I'm not going to just get up and leave because of it! This is my home…" She felt angry tears burning in her eyes, though she knew she shouldn't be upset with Rhiannon. "If it was you, would you leave?"

Rhiannon watched her quietly for a moment, forming her answer in her mind before she spoke. When she did, her face was carefully blank and her eyes were clear. "I've never known the outside world, not like you have. For all I know, I might prefer it to this prison I've lived in my entire life."

"Prison?" Capri asked, startled.

Rhiannon smiled grimly, though her eyes softened a bit. "Most of us are never given the choice of whether or not we want this life. I suppose a part of me is envious that you have been."

"I've never wanted anything more than to live here, with all of you," Capri insisted. "You can assure everyone that I will not be leaving."

Rhiannon stood up and reached for Capri's hand, gently holding it in her own. "Deep down, I think I knew you would stay. You're so strong, Capri, in ways the rest of us can only envy. Please, remember that."

With that, Rhiannon let go of her hand and left the room, leaving behind a faint scent of sage and vanilla.

Capri laid back in bed, curling up under the covers and pulling them over her head to hide the light. She wondered why everyone seemed to think she was so strong, when most of the time she felt nothing but weakness.

After two full days of bed rest, Thea finally agreed to let Capri get up and walk around on her own. She still felt shaky, though it was probably more from too much rest and not using her muscles very much for forty-eight hours than from her head injury, which seemed to be healing just fine. Her head still felt a little tender where she had hit it when she fell, but other than that she felt great.

Encouraged by her newfound freedom, she cleaned up and slipped into a pair of comfy, faded jeans and a pale yellow blouse, then headed downstairs for breakfast.

When she entered the dining hall, she immediately scanned the faces of the people who were already seated and eating, only to be disappointed. The one person she really wanted to see was nowhere to be found.

Rian had not come to visit her since the night she had been possessed, and even then she was pretty sure she had only imagined him being there. At the very least, she owed him more than the half-conscious thank you she must have given him if he had been there.

With a sigh, she sat beside her father at the dining table, who smiled happily at her.

"Good morning, darling," he greeted, reaching for the coffee pitcher to pour her a cup like he did every morning. As he started pouring, he looked up, eyeing her with concern when he noticed the look on her face. "What's wrong? Does your head still hurt?"

Capri jolted, looking flustered. "No, no I'm fine," she replied, reaching for a blueberry muffin. She picked off a small piece and stared at it for a moment before turning to her father. "Actually, have you seen Rian? I really want to speak to him."

Clynn set the coffee pitcher down and met her eyes sympathetically. "The Furies are all very busy right now, Capri, trying to figure out what happened."

"I know, but I just need to speak with him for a moment. Do you know where he is?"

"I believe he's outside in the courtyard. Most mornings he exercises there."

"Thank you." Capri kissed his cheek with a sweet smile as she stood up, handed the muffin to him, and raced out of the dining hall.

She dashed through the corridor, into the atrium and out into the morning sunshine. Glancing around, she spotted Rian off to the far right side of the courtyard, standing in front of a punching bag that was suspended from a large oak tree.

He was punching the bag rhythmically...right...left...right...left...in rapid succession, and as she approached she could hear the slaps of his knuckles against the leather bag.

He was wearing a black sleeveless shirt and basketball shorts, his feet bare.

She stopped a few feet behind him and cleared her throat, hoping he wouldn't be angry with her for intruding.

"Rian?"

When he stopped punching and turned around, she saw surprise flicker briefly over his face before it went carefully blank.

She smiled warmly at him as she stepped a little closer, her hands folded delicately in front of her.

He silently watched her, which she assumed meant he was either annoyed with her or unsure what to say.

Sincerely hoping it was the latter, she decided it was up to her to speak first.

"I wanted to thank you for saving me the other night. I'm sorry I didn't thank you earlier; I should have found a way to tell you so you wouldn't think that I was ungrateful for what you did."

"You could have died," he replied, his eyes tightening. "You don't need to be sorry about not rushing to thank me. I was only doing my job."

"Right…okay," she murmured, biting her lip and glancing down at the ground. He was always analyzing what she said in a way that made her feel like a fool, like she shouldn't feel sorry or reminiscent or worried. But she couldn't help what went on inside of her, emotions or otherwise. Maybe it was his serious nature that caused him to scrutinize everything as though it were under a microscope. He seemed like a person who didn't feel many emotions, at least not on the surface. But, despite everything, she was curious to find out more about him, even if it took a long time to crack his hard outer shell. She could be patient.

What she couldn't be patient on any longer, however, was her pursuit for understanding on why she had been targeted and attacked, and if it related in any way to the demon that had killed her mother. Knowing that Rian was ultimately going to be her best source for information on the subject, she searched for a good way to ask him about it.

"Um…so, if you're not too busy, I was hoping we could talk about what happened two nights ago."

She glanced up to look at him, and noticed he was still watching her.

"I am too busy."

"Oh, okay then…maybe another time." Capri tried to smile, hoping to hide most of her disappointment. As she began to leave, he spoke again.

"But that doesn't mean I can't spare a few minutes."

She looked at him, her eyes bright. "Really?"

His lips curved as he nodded. "Walk with me."

She fell into step beside him as they walked along the side pathway that wound through the massive gardens. His posture was rigid and flawless, and, just as before, she noticed how much he acted like a strict warrior prepared to enter battle. It was like he was groomed to be unyieldingly faultless, and one slip up could damage his reputation and his pride.

He wasn't that much taller than her, only a few inches or so, and the shirt he was wearing showed off the strength in his arms and chest. She couldn't help but wonder how often he had to use that strength against demons, and if it was common for the Furies to fight with fists versus guns.

After a moment of walking, he began to speak.

"I was reading in the library that night, facing the window. I looked up when I noticed movement outside, and it was you walking through the courtyard. I know that you don't make a habit of walking around alone at night, so I was suspicious. I caught up with you outside, and you were walking very strangely with your eyes closed. I didn't touch you at first, just in case you were only sleepwalking. But then you started speaking, and your voice was deeper than normal, throatier, and the words you said were so strange that I knew it hadn't come from you."

"What did I say?" Capri asked, alarmed.

"You said, *You will suffer as I have suffered, the outcast, disposed of like trash, not worthy of being a Dryad because of dirty blood.* You kept repeating it, over and over, until I grabbed you before you could reach the tree and then you fell to the ground and hit your head. I started shaking you to try and wake you up."

"Was it the demon saying those things?" She stopped mid-step, her eyes wide with concern. "What does it mean?"

"Yes, I believe it was the demon, though I don't know what it means," he answered, stopping and facing her. "I told Thea about it, and I think she understood it more than she let on," he paused a moment, annoyed. "I just don't know why a demon would talk about dirty blood, or about being an outcast. It just doesn't make sense. Demons have never been allowed to live on

Euphora, and I doubt they would want to anyway. They hate everything about us."

"Why do they hate us?" Capri asked, feeling sick to her stomach.

"Because we are all that's stopping them from destroying the world," he replied darkly, his eyes sparking with an excitement she'd never before seen.

So there was something he was passionate about, she thought as she watched him intently.

"I see...so what happened next?"

"When you snarled and struck out at me, it confirmed my suspicions that you were possessed, so I banished the demon from your body. I started to pursue him before he could get away, but I made the decision not to leave you alone in case there were others waiting."

"There could have been more of them?" She paled at the thought of it, her brow creasing with worry.

"Never underestimate a demon. They are smarter than we give them credit for. Fortunately, as I later discovered, there were no traces of other demons, only the one, though he was long gone before I was able to go looking for him again."

"I'm sorry...it's because of me that you weren't able to catch him." She felt horribly guilty, though she knew she should be grateful that he stayed with her, as she would have been terrified otherwise.

"Just like it's because of someone else that the demon gained access to Euphora in the first place," he countered grimly. "What we need to focus on is not who this demon is, but who let him in. Has anything strange happened to you recently, or has anyone acted suspiciously around you?"

"I..." she paused, unsure whether or not to tell him what she had witnessed in the library. It had seemed so farfetched before...but given the current circumstances, it could possibly be connected to what happened to her. "Actually, there was something...it was something Rohan said."

"Rohan?" Rian's eyes narrowed as he watched her.

"Yes…I was in the library the day I was possessed, and I overheard a conversation between Rohan and another man."

"And what did they say?"

"Rohan said something about needing the other man's word, that something would be handled…the other man just told him not to worry, that it was being taken care of," she paused, her eyes widening in shock. "Do you think Rohan might have been talking about me?"

"Anything is possible," Rian replied, looking concerned. "You didn't recognize the other voice?"

"Well, I thought I did…I mean, I know who it sounded like…but it's just not possible."

"Who did it sound like?"

Capri stared at him, shaking her head as though she didn't really believe it herself. "It sounded like Brock."

For a moment he didn't say anything, as though he was processing what she had said and was trying to make sense of it. "You've never met Brock, how do you know his voice?"

"From my dream. The man my mother trusted, the one who ordered her and I to be killed, it was his voice I heard in the library."

"Brock no longer has access to Euphora, and it is highly unlikely he was walking around the castle, much less with Rohan. Rohan is a law abiding man, he would have notified us immediately if he had seen Brock here."

"You're right…I must have misheard." Capri anxiously chewed her bottom lip. "Though, it bothered me how quickly Rohan blamed Blythe after this happened."

"Did he say why he thought she had done it?"

"All he said was that fire was bad blood, and that her father and grandmother couldn't be trusted, therefore she couldn't be trusted either. But Blythe would never do anything to hurt me. She's my friend."

"It's possible that Rohan is covering up his own tracks. Though I can't imagine him planning anything with Brock if he was so quick to accuse him of being bad blood," Rian considered, looking off across the courtyard toward the castle. "I would never assume him capable of something like this, but as I said, anything is possible."

"Why would he want to hurt me?"

"Any number of reasons, I suppose. People do brash things all the time out of desperation. But we can't start assuming it was him without proof. I will look into this; just promise me you won't tell anyone else what you just told me. Until we find out who is responsible, it's safe to say no one can be trusted."

"I trust you," Capri said before she could stop herself, blushing at the look he gave her.

"You trust too easily. You hardly know me." He met her eyes again, his expression impossible to read.

"You saved me when you didn't have to. If that isn't enough for you to earn my trust, then I don't know what is." She didn't mean to sound defensive, but she certainly felt that way.

"Well, if you insist on trusting me, then I guess I can't stop you," he said, resigned to the fact that he wasn't going to be able to convince her otherwise. "Come to me first if anything else strange happens, okay?"

"Okay." Capri smiled, feeling better. "Thank you for talking to me about this."

"Just doing my job," he said again, his mouth curving ever so slightly before he turned and walked away. She watched him go, wishing he knew how grateful she was that he had been there to protect her. If it hadn't been for him, she might very well be dead.

She stared at the daffodils on her nightstand that night, her mind numb and her body tired. Moonlight drifted in from the open window, casting a gentle blue glow around her dark room.

Never before in her life had she felt this way, as though her world was crumbling around her, falling apart at the seams despite how desperately she tried to hold on to it.

The fact remained that she was home where she truly belonged and with her family. She supposed that was at least a step in the right direction.

But then she had found out that her mother was murdered, and that her death was never solved. It shouldn't rest upon her shoulders alone to find the killer, but she couldn't just stand by and do nothing…she had spent her entire life standing by and doing nothing, and she no longer wished to continue living that way. She needed to be stronger than she felt, even if that meant putting herself in harm's way.

Which, if the events of the past few days were any indication, harm was exactly where she had put herself.

Had Rohan heard her asking questions about her mother's death? Had that sparked something within him and set him off? Had he been involved with the murder, despite the evidence pointing to Brock alone? Was that why someone had let in the demon to lead her from the safety of Euphora, so they could silence her?

Even if it wasn't Brock she heard in the library, it was still likely to be the same person who let in the demon. The two incidents were too coincidental not to be connected. But who could it be? What if the Furies didn't find out in time and the person attempted to harm her again?

Fear shivered through her as she sat on the side of her bed, and she desperately clutched her arms around herself to try and regain some sense of warmth.

She shuddered again as she recalled the helplessness of being possessed, the feeling of being trapped inside her own mind and body, fighting for release. Whoever had allowed that demon to possess her had wanted her to feel that way. They wanted her to feel powerless, weak, frightened. They wanted to take her again, only this time she was a full grown woman, capable of fighting back. And so they had resorted to possessing her, and tricking her with her own mind into walking right off Euphora and into what was surely a death trap. So who would require her silence so desperately that they were willing to surrender her to the mercy of a heartless demon?

Was it really Rohan? Could he be responsible?

Then she heard the voices. They were low at first, almost muted, but as she stood up and walked to her open window, the voices became louder and much clearer.

"I insist on accompanying you. What if you need assistance?"

It was the four Furies, all dressed in matching black uniforms, and Rohan, who looked arrogantly superior in his tailored, gunmetal gray suit. Rohan had been the one to speak, and he was looking angrier by the minute.

"What are you gonna do, Rohan, grow a plant?" Roarke laughed boisterously at his own joke, while the others around him were silent. "We have this handled, as always. It's just a lead anyway, and odds are it's not even the same demon who was here a few days ago."

Capri's stomach clenched at his words, and her eyes shifted to Rian, who was standing beside his father silently. She watched him closely, noting how he stood so dignified with his hands clasped behind his back. He had a holster around his waist with a pistol strapped to it, and she saw a strap with several dozen of the liquid nitrogen bullets on it wrapped over his shoulder.

It's like they're going into battle, she thought uneasily. Guns blazing, bullets flying, men dying…she had to bite her tongue to fight against the fear she felt just thinking about it.

"Then you should have no problem with me joining you if it is merely following up on a lead," Rohan insisted again.

Roarke paused, sighing audibly. "Fine, but you better not get in the way."

Balgaire shifted suddenly and leaned toward Roarke, quietly saying something to him so Rohan would not hear. Roarke looked at his partner questionably before turning back to Rohan.

"You better stay here, Rohan," Roarke ordered, the amusement in his voice gone. "Apparently Balgaire feels this is going to be a bit more serious than just following up on a lead. You're not trained in dealing with these demons, so you're going to have to stay behind. We'll be back in the morning."

He turned and motioned to his fellow Furies to follow him to the front gate. Rohan stood there silently while the Furies disappeared beyond the stone wall, and a few moments later Capri saw a flash of gold light announcing their departure from Euphora.

It was then that Rohan finally moved. He whirled around and stalked back to the castle. Capri hid in the shadows so he wouldn't see her if he looked up.

When he was out of sight, her heart began to pound violently. Why was Rohan so desperate to join the Furies? Was it because he knew they had the right demon and he wanted to be able to stop them somehow?

Worry tore through her as she sat on the windowsill, curling her legs up against her and resting her chin on her knees. Her heart filled with concern as she kept her eyes glued on the tree just beyond the courtyard, silently praying that nothing awful happened to the Furies while they were gone.

# Chapter Ten

*When she woke* that morning, she realized with a painful grunt that she had fallen asleep on the window-sill. Her back was sore, and her neck had a crick in it, but she managed to unfold herself and stumble into the bathroom. After filling the tub with steaming hot water and lowering herself into it, she felt the pain in her muscles easing a little.

After drying herself off and dressing, she felt almost normal again. Yawning, she headed downstairs for breakfast.

She wondered if the Furies had returned yet, but before she really had the time to think about it, she'd entered the dining hall and noticed that they were nowhere to be found.

Feeling uneasy, she sat in her usual place at the table and stared off into space, not even feeling hungry.

Her father poured her coffee as usual, though he didn't ask her what was wrong. It appeared that he was stressed out as well, and perhaps he didn't even notice that she was quieter than usual.

In fact, when she glanced around and paid attention, it seemed that everyone was more tense and quiet, as if they were all waiting for bad news. Even Blythe seemed to be lost in thought, and she was only eating half as much as she normally did every morning.

Feeling even more worried because everyone else was so nervous, Capri had to take a deep breath and try and calm herself. Everything was going to be fine, nothing to worry about...the Furies did this all the time, they would be fine.

But when the door suddenly opened with a loud bang and the four Fury men stalked into the dining hall, Capri realized that something was indeed terribly wrong.

They headed straight toward Thea— Roarke leading the way as usual with Balgaire behind him, and Rian and Brogan picking up the rear. None of them said a word nor looked at the rest of the Council...a sure sign that something was off. The four men looked disheveled, as though the night had been both long and rough. Capri particularly watched Rian and noticed that nearly all of the rounds were missing from the strap across his shoulder. She also noticed there was a deep cut across his other shoulder, where the fabric was singed and the skin beneath it blackened.

"Roarke." Thea and Sebastian both stood up, watching the Furies as avidly as everyone else. When Roarke finally reached Thea, he bowed down low to speak quietly in her ear. Capri watched her face harden in anger, and beside her Sebastian let out a startled cry.

"Thank you. You may go— rest and we will meet later to discuss this." Thea dismissed the Furies, bowing her head respectfully to them. They hastily left the room, once again not making eye contact with anyone else.

After a few moments of fearful silence, Thea took a deep breath and faced everyone at the table.

"Two Enforcers are dead," she announced, her voice solemn and her eyes full of wrath. "What was supposed to be a simple lead on the demon turned out to be an ambush. Several demons were lying in wait and attacked, and we are lucky that more were not killed, including our own Furies. Let us all have a moment of silence for the two Enforcers who gave their lives this past night."

She bowed her head and everyone around the table followed suit. Capri closed her eyes as she lowered her head, shock waves pulsing through her as she processed the news. Two Enforcers were dead. Humans who had families and friends and pets; humans who had been entrusted with the secrets of Euphora, who had taken on the duty of protecting the world from demons. All because of what? Because they were only doing their job.

It was then that she realized how easily Rian could have been killed, or his father or Balgaire or even Brogan. She had never known anyone who had died, save for her mother of course. How did it feel to lose someone you knew? Or rather, someone who you considered a friend? How would she have reacted if it had been Rian who had died? The Fury boy she had tried to befriend as a child had become a full grown man, but it didn't change how she felt. He had saved her life, and was committed to helping her in her search for the truth. She wanted to know him better, to be his friend. No matter how long it took.

When Thea sat down and continued to eat her breakfast, everyone else did the same. Capri looked down at her eggs and toast, and wasn't sure if she could eat anymore.

She turned to her father, who was glumly looking down at his own food.

"Dad…" she said quietly, nudging him as she spoke. He turned to look at her, his eyes glazed over slightly.

"Yes, darling?" he asked.

"Is it…common for Enforcers to be killed by demons?"

He shook his head. "No, it's not. The last time one was killed in action was thirteen years ago. Roarke's wife, actually. That's probably the reason he and I get along as well as we do…we've both lost loved ones to demons."

"He never said anything about it," Capri sadly realized, her eyes searching his. "I had no idea."

"He's strong, much stronger than myself, I must admit." Clynn sighed and tried to smile at her. "He handled it very well, and Rian, too."

Capri sat in silence the rest of breakfast, thinking over everything she had heard that morning. It upset her to think that this whole time she had been talking about her mother's death in front of Roarke and Rian, without any respect for their own tragedy. Granted, she hadn't known it at the time, but that didn't make her feel any less guilty.

Later that afternoon, she went for a walk with Liam and Blythe through the courtyard, hoping to take her mind off the whole situation for a little while.

They went out to the little bench on the edge of the island, where they sat together for nearly two hours, just talking, laughing, and trying to reclaim some sort of youth and innocence back from the seriousness of the morning.

In an effort to lighten the mood, Liam suggested they play a game. When Capri was about to ask if they had Monopoly or Scrabble, Blythe suddenly jumped up and quite cheerfully shot a fireball the size of a basketball out of her palm and out over the sea.

Liam, in response, stood up and caused a geyser of water to shoot up from the ocean, blocking the fireball's path and sizzling it into steam on contact.

"Is this the game?" Capri managed, looking more than a little taken aback.

"It's fun!" Blythe countered happily, motioning for Capri to stand up. "Come on, show us something good."

"Oh, well..." Capri felt her face redden in embarrassment as she stood up. "I don't know, it might take me a couple of tries."

"So what?" Liam replied with a cheerful grin. "I know you've been practicing."

"Okay, here goes." Capri smiled and lifted her right arm, aiming out over the horizon. She closed her eyes and imagined the moisture building in the atmosphere, the clouds forming and churning as the wind swirled them into a cyclone, lifting the warm air up to mix with the cold. She could hear the wind begin to roar around her, and she could feel it brushing against her skin and her hair, but she kept her eyes closed, her focus entirely on her creation.

She saw a bright flash of lightning against her eyelids and heard the echoing rumble of thunder, and her eyes flew open in astonishment.

Less than half a mile away from them was a cyclone, whirling like madness, lifting water from the sea and creating what was sure to become a hurricane within moments. Overhead, the sky was churning with dark and threatening clouds, while everywhere else the sky was clear blue.

"That is so badass!" Blythe hooted, jumping in the air excitedly. "Watch this, though!"

With a wicked gleam in her eyes, she held her palms a few inches apart and focused her energy on another fireball, which she swung over her head like a pitcher preparing to throw a baseball. She hurled it at the cyclone. When it made contact with the swirling wind, the entire mass lit on fire, forming a large, flaming tornado.

"Oh my God." Capri gasped, her eyes wide. "This is madness."

Blythe laughed and hugged Capri, her eyes glowing with power. "Isn't it magnificent? Together we are going to rule the world!"

"Not if I have anything to say about it." Liam chimed, his eyes glittering with humor as he lifted his arms. Rain suddenly began to fall from the clouds, dousing the fire at once. Capri then concentrated on ending the storm, and the cyclone died almost instantly. The clouds parted and dispersed, and within moments they were gone, as though they had never existed.

"Ruining all the fun, Liam." Blythe pouted, but her face was glowing. "God, it feels so good to let go and have a little fun, doesn't it?"

"Yeah, it does," Capri agreed, impulsively hugging Blythe. However, when she pulled away she couldn't hide the regret she felt. "I wish Rhiannon would come hang out with us."

Blythe rolled her eyes. "She's boring. We've always had more fun without her."

Capri frowned, unsure. "You don't think I'm boring, do you?"

Blythe pursed her lips and seemed to think about it for a moment, before Liam punched her playfully in the arm.

"You are not boring, Capri, and neither is Rhiannon," he reassured her before eyeing Blythe. "Contrary to what Blythe seems to think, Rhiannon is actually the furthest thing from boring."

"Yeah, well, of course you would think so," Blythe teased, her eyebrows wiggling suggestively. "Men are so pathetic."

"Oh, you are so going to get it," Liam threatened, his arms reaching out to grab Blythe around the waist. She shrieked and kicked him off of her before swiftly sprinting back into the woods. Liam grinned at Capri and motioned for her to follow before he took off running to chase after Blythe.

Amused, Capri ran after them, her feet pounding the smooth ground of the forest as she followed the path. Liam was just ahead of her and she could hear Blythe taunting from further away.

When she burst into the meadow, she let the sunlight wash over her, and couldn't help but smile. Despite everything, this one moment was perfect.

She heard Blythe shriek again over by the front gate, just before Liam tackled her to the ground and pinned her down.

"Gotcha, you little creep," he said with a laugh as he started tickling Blythe. It only took about three seconds for her to bite his hand and slip out from underneath him.

"Men think they are so smart," Blythe proclaimed as she grabbed his arm and twisted it around to his back.

"Ow! Truce! Truce!" Liam grunted in pain as Blythe let him go. She held out her hand to help him up, grinning.

"You never learn, buddy." She patted him on the back as he nursed his arm with a grimace.

"Yeah, yeah...whatever."

Capri walked forward and wrapped one arm over each of them, smiling warmly.

"You two make up?" she teased, her eyes bright.

"Yeah, we never fight for long," Blythe told her, grinning. "Let's go sit down by the pond. I wanna relax for a bit."

The trio headed back through the front gates, still arm-in-arm with each other. They stopped by the pond that Capri had seen on her second day, shaded by an ancient looking willow tree. The pond was just off the main walkway and had a cozy grass area that had become one of Capri's new favorite spots.

Just as they sat down and got settled, Capri saw Rian walk through the front gate and proceed down the path leading toward the castle. He was casually dressed in jeans and a black t-shirt, but she noticed he had a pistol strapped to his hip, the silver flashing in the sunlight.

As he approached them, Capri smiled and waved.

"Hi, Rian," she greeted politely. He slowed down when he saw her, stopping a few feet from where she was sitting. His lips twitched briefly into a smile.

"Capri." He nodded, his eyes softening as he looked at her. Shifting his gaze at Liam and Blythe, he nodded again in acknowledgement, but his face noticeably hardened.

"Were you taking a walk?" Capri asked.

He looked at her again and she could tell he was uncomfortable. "I was walking the grounds, checking to make sure we weren't followed when we returned this morning."

"Oh." Capri's eyes shifted to the pistol strapped to his waist and then back up at him questioningly. "Did you find anything?"

He had a strained look on his face as though he really didn't want to discuss anything in front of the other Dryads, and when Capri turned to look at her two friends, she noticed they were watching Rian with suspicion and distrust in their eyes.

Understanding the awkwardness he felt, Capri stood and looked at Blythe and Liam. "I'm going to head inside. I'll see you guys later."

"Seriously?" Blythe looked at her incredulously, not bothering to hide the resentment in her voice.

"It's okay, Capri. We'll see you later," Liam told Capri, his hand resting on Blythe's arm, as though reminding her not to be brash.

Capri turned to Rian and smiled. "Will you walk with me?" she asked, and again his face relaxed slightly as he looked at her.

"Of course." With that, they began to walk together, their pace slowing, as though neither of them felt the need to rush.

"How does your shoulder feel?"

He turned to look at her, taken aback that she had noticed.

"I think I'll live," he replied, humor in his eyes.

Capri smiled, but there was sadness behind it. "I was worried about you."

Again, he looked surprised, though she could tell that he was attempting to hide it. "You don't have to worry about me," he said as they approached the entrance doors. He laid his hand upon them, and when they disappeared under his touch, he stood aside to let Capri enter before him.

She walked through, stopping inside the atrium and turning to face him. He stopped beside her, watching her as the doors behind them reformed. Above, light cascaded down through the clouds, highlighting her light hair like a halo.

"What happened last night?" she asked, her eyes searching his.

For a moment he didn't speak, he just looked at her. His eyes betrayed nothing.

"We were tipped off that the demon we were looking for would be in Las Vegas. When we got there, we were immediately ambushed. The Enforcers were already dead and more showed up to help, but it took all we had to fight back the demons. By the time we'd killed a few of them, the rest ran. I would have gone after them if my father hadn't held me back and insisted we come home." His voice was noticeably bitter.

"You were hurt, of course he wanted to get you home," Capri said quietly, her eyes shifting to his shoulder.

Rian shrugged. "I don't think that's what it was."

"What do you mean?"

"He's been acting strange lately, as though he thinks he's not going to be around much longer."

"Is he planning on retiring early?"

The look in his eyes worried her. "He thinks he's going to die."

"I don't understand." She shook her head, not wanting to believe him.

"He hasn't come out and said it, but I know that's what's been bothering him lately. Ever since the demon attacked you, he's been more suspicious and secretive. I think he knows who is responsible, but he won't tell me. I'll bet he suspects that same person of organizing the ambush last night."

"Oh." Capri's hand came up to her heart, her eyes wide and anxious. "So what are we going to do?"

"You don't need to worry yourself over this. I'm handling it."

She watched him closely, wondering how he could carry so much weight on his shoulders and still seem steady as a rock. She had complete confidence in him, and she knew he would do his best to sort this out for her. She just wished he was more open to accepting her help.

Suddenly, she heard voices and footsteps approaching from the corridor ahead of them, and it didn't take long for her to register the hostility in the hushed tones.

Before she could react, Rian grabbed her and pulled her behind one of the large leafy plants in the corner of the atrium, hiding them from view. He stood protectively behind her, pinning her between the plant and his body.

Within seconds the owners of the voices were in the atrium, just beyond where they were hiding. Capri could see Roarke through the leaves of the plant, his eyes wild and his voice irritated, and Tobias, looking frightened and small beside the intimidating Fury.

"I know what's going on Tobias, you can't fool me," Roarke growled, grabbing the younger man by the shirt and yanking him roughly forward. Tobias cried out, his hands shaking.

"I don't know what you're talking about," he stammered fearfully, his eyes wide.

"I don't care what he told you, you little scumbag, but you won't get away with this. Mark my words," Roarke threatened before releasing Tobias and stalking to the front doors, which he thrust his palm against. When the door melted away, he continued out into the courtyard, looking big, burly and angry.

Tobias stood where he was for a moment, shaking uncontrollably, before taking off down the corridor, clearly eager to put as much distance between himself and Roarke as possible.

Within moments the atrium was silent once more.

Capri stood still, her mind racing. She realized she had been holding her breath, so she exhaled steadily, still trying to process what she had just seen.

She could feel Rian breathing softly, and when she turned around to face him, she couldn't help but flush at how close they were to each other.

She looked up at him, her eyes troubled.

"Tobias?" she whispered, her brows furrowing in disbelief.

He stared back at her, looking just as uncertain. "I don't know."

"Could he be responsible for everything? He's so young..." Capri murmured. Then she remembered the way he had looked at her when she'd bumped into him in the library, and how afraid of her he had seemed. Had it been his guilty conscience over what he was about to do that caused his nervousness around her? "I forgot to tell you something before because it didn't seem important, but I think you should hear it now," she began, her hands clasping together nervously. "The day I heard the voices in the library, as I was leaving I ran into Tobias and he gave me a look like he was afraid of me or something…I didn't think much of it, but what if he really is involved?"

Rian contemplated, looking disturbed. "First Rohan, now Tobias. Two of the least likely people I would ever think capable of allowing a demon onto Euphora."

"You said yourself that anything is possible, right?"

"I did." He seemed lost in thought for a moment, his eyes clouding with uncertainty as he stared at the front door where his father had just left. "Something bad is happening here. And the only connection I can make to any of it is you." His eyes shifted back to look at her.

Capri nodded in agreement. "Someone, possibly Rohan, didn't like that I was asking around about what happened the night I was taken. So this person decides to try and either kill me, or at least scare me away before more information is uncovered about that night. But, of course, you stepped in and saved me, so instead they make sure you and the other Furies are ambushed and almost killed, in an attempt to prevent the investigation from going any further."

"But we survived, and all this person did was make us even more mad," Rian added, his eyes flashing briefly with fierce anger.

"Right. So we know that your father suspects someone, possibly Tobias, of letting in the demon and staging the ambush in Vegas. But how does Tobias connect back to Rohan? It still doesn't answer the question of who the other man was that Rohan was speaking to."

"You're sure it wasn't Tobias?"

"Definitely, this was an older man. His voice was harsher, deeper than Tobias'…and if you're certain that it couldn't have been Brock, then who else could it be?"

"Maybe I'm wrong," Rian considered. "Maybe it was Brock, and he and Rohan have been working together all along, despite appearances. Why, or for what, I have no idea."

"And last night, Rohan wanted to go with you and the other Furies," Capri remembered, blushing at the look he gave her. "I was watching from my window, I saw the whole thing. It seemed very suspicious."

"It was. He's never asked to come along before. I think it's safe for us to assume that Rohan is involved somehow. And if my father is suspicious of Tobias, then more likely than not he's involved as well."

Capri couldn't help but shudder at the thought. "At least I know who to look out for..." she murmured, her eyes clouding with worry as she stared down at her clenched hands in front of her.

Rian reached out and gently grabbed her hands, prying them apart and holding them in his own. The calluses on his hands were rough against her skin, but something about the sensation was incredibly comforting to her.

"Look at me," he ordered, his voice stern but gentle.

When she met his eyes, she felt a lump form in her throat. He looked so confident, so sturdy and strong; such a contrast to how she felt.

"I'll look after you."

"Thank you," was all she could say in response. The lump in her throat seemed to expand and explode down through her chest, sending shivers through her that had nothing to do with the temperature inside the atrium. And while she had the unexpected realization that what she was starting to feel for him was more than just a desire for friendship, across the castle someone was plotting more ways to destroy her and everything she had come to love.

# Chapter Eleven

*Less than a* week later, Los Angeles received a startling surprise after weeks of sunny and warm weather: a snowstorm.

Capri stood before the globe in Air tower, her arms out as she constructed what was intended to be a light rainstorm before she became distracted and let the storm get much larger and colder than it should have been.

It took her father's sudden frantic outburst to bring her back to reality.

"Capri!"

She stared in disbelief at the storm, her mind freezing as she completely forgot what she was supposed to do if something like this happened. Thankfully, Clynn nudged her out of the way and proceeded to fix the storm himself, his hands lifting and skillfully altering the temperature in the atmosphere to swiftly change snow into rain.

"I'm so sorry." She backed away, rubbing her face with her hands. "I wasn't paying attention."

"It's alright, it's fixed." He walked over to her and pulled her into a hug. With a deep sigh, he looked down at her sympathetically. She was still covering her face with her hands. "Are you feeling ill?"

Capri's hands fell away from her face as she looked up at him. "No, I'm fine. I just got distracted...it won't happen again."

"Don't worry about it so much," he told her reassuringly. "What's on your mind that's distracting you?"

She had to try incredibly hard not to laugh. If only he knew everything that had been on her mind all week. Then he would probably understand completely why she had zoned out; why she had been struggling to concentrate on her work for the past few days. But she knew she was better off not sharing all of the details with him because it would only upset and worry him. As long as she and Rian could figure everything out on their own, then there would be no need to bring the adults into it.

Even Blythe and Liam had noticed her increasing unease as the days passed, though she refused to explain anything to either of them. She knew it was unfair, since in her heart she knew that the two of them could be trusted. But she had given Rian her word that she wouldn't discuss the situation with anyone else, just to be safe.

"It's nothing," she lied, trying to smile.

"Is it about the demon?" Clynn cupped her chin in his hand, watching her carefully.

Capri shook her head, feeling horrible. She didn't like lying to him, but she knew she had to. "No, it's really nothing."

"Okay then." He kissed her forehead, content. "Let's get back to work."

"Okay."

Just then, there was a steady knock on the door. Clynn walked over to open it, and when he did, Capri saw Rian standing just outside.

"Rian!" Clynn said with a smile, shaking the younger man's hand. "What brings you over here today?"

"I'd like to speak with Capri, sir," Rian replied, his voice polite.

"Oh." Taken aback, Clynn turned to look at his daughter, who immediately flushed with embarrassment. "Well, I suppose we can wrap this up later."

"I'll be right back." Capri laid a hand on her father's arm, but her attention was already focused on Rian, who was waiting patiently just outside the door.

She closed the door behind her, leaned against it, and looked at him, her lips curving in a warm smile. "Hi."

"Hi." He tried to return her smile, but she could tell there was something on his mind.

"Is everything alright?"

He sighed and shook his head, averting his eyes from hers to stone floor. "No, I don't think it is."

"What happened?" Worry tore through her, rapid and swift, and she had to fight back the urge to reach out and comfort him. He looked more troubled and restless than she had ever seen him look before.

"I asked you awhile ago to visit the Muses again to see if you could remember any more of your dream. Have you done it yet?" He glanced up to watch her again, and she was reminded of how he had looked at her when she first met him, like he was measuring her every move. It was as though he already knew the answer, and just wanted to make sure she didn't lie to him.

"No, I haven't." She blushed, feeling guilty. "I guess I got distracted with everything else that happened and I forgot about it."

"Please come with me right now to see them. It's important that we find out if there's anything you remember after the demon took you away from Euphora."

"Oh, okay." She hadn't been prepared for this, but the urgency in his tone beneath his usual seriousness confirmed that he wouldn't be asking if it wasn't of utmost importance.

He led the way down the stairs and out into the corridor without saying anything else. She wished he would say something, anything, to distract her in some way, because the idea of reliving her dream was starting to alarm her. She wasn't sure she was ready to go through that again, and she hadn't even had time to prepare herself for what was sure to be another onslaught of fear, misery, and regret.

"Rian?" she managed, reaching out for his arm, slowing him down to a stop.

"What is it?"

She saw the flicker of annoyance in his eyes, and she felt completely foolish for hesitating. She wrapped her arms over her chest protectively as she took a deep breath, unable to look at him again.

"I'm sorry...I'm just scared." She choked out a half laugh, disgusted with herself. "I'm so pathetic. Scared of a stupid dream..."

"I understand." He reached out and laid a comforting hand on her shoulder. When she glanced up, his eyes were kind. "I know this is hard for you. And I'm not just saying that to be nice, because I really do know how you feel." He paused, his face tightening slightly as his own memories flashed inside of him. "I lost my mother to a demon when I was ten years old. I didn't witness it, but my father did. And he told me about it so I would respect how she had died, and what she had died for. And hearing it from him, like he was reading about the weather, so factual and cold, was one of the hardest things I've ever gone through. So believe me when I say I understand, because I do. And I would never ask this of you if it wasn't extremely important."

Her chest felt heavy, so much so that breathing was becoming increasingly difficult. Knowing his story, sharing his pain, humbled her more than she could have imagined. And knowing that he was willing to share that dark part of himself with her, that he trusted her with his feelings, shook her to the core.

"I'm so sorry," she said as she stepped forward, wrapping her arms around him without hesitation, her chin resting on his shoulder as silent tears streamed down her cheeks. He seemed taken aback at first, but within seconds his arms came around her and held on tightly. For a brief moment, she felt like they were children again, and she regretted that she hadn't been there to comfort him when it had happened all those years ago. Would it have made a difference to him if she had?

"I'm ready to go." She pulled away from him, her eyes clear and steady.

"Then let's go." He looked calm on the surface, but she could tell more was going on inside him. Pulling her with him, he led the way to the Muses' tower.

"Can you tell me why this is so urgent?" she asked as he held open the door for her, following her in and leading the way to the staircase that led up to the tower.

When they stopped just outside the Muses' door, he turned to her, his face strained.

"My father and Balgaire left for Richmond this morning and refused to take Brogan and me with them. I don't think this is a coincidence. I think the demon that possessed you is the same demon who murdered your mother and kidnapped you, and I'm sure they know it. I need to know everything you see in your dream, and then I'm going after them."

Capri looked worried, but didn't have a chance to comment since Rian pushed open the door and ushered her inside. To her surprise, the Muses were already expecting them. Apparently Rian had not intended on anything other than Capri's full cooperation.

Once again, she had to lie back in the leather recliner. Only this time, Rian sat beside her in a wooden chair, holding her hand in his. If the Muses noticed the intimacy of the touch, they didn't say anything. Instead they proceeded to guide Capri into a deep sleep, and slowly but surely she fell into the darkness.

The Muses had been instructed to speed her through the beginning of the dream, and to focus on the last part. Because of this, Capri experienced only a clipped version of what she had experienced before.

When her vision cleared and the blurry images became solid, she realized she was in her mother's arms, being carried through the courtyard. Only this time, the world around her slid into darkness, only to reappear again, and without warning she was several steps further than before, as if time had been sped up. Again, the world went dark, and when it reappeared, her mother was sliding her into the jasmine, telling her to be quiet. Before Capri could do more than register the worry on her mother's face, the world went dark again. When it rematerialized, she heard her mother's scream, saw the flash of fire, and felt the rough hands lift her from the safety of the jasmine.

She fought to look at the man who held her, who began to run with her, but all she could see was fire. Again darkness swallowed her surroundings, and when it appeared again, the demon was running through the meadow toward the tree, his pace swift and direct as he carried her. When the dream slowed, she managed to focus on what was around her.

The moonlight glinted on the grasses in the meadow, highlighting it with its pale, blue glow. She could see the wall surrounding Euphora, and the wrought iron gate that had reformed after they ran through it. She saw the castle looming in the distance, glowing orange with the fires raging below. The trees captured the eerie glow as well, and seemed to pulse with the brutal heat.

The man who held her was breathing quickly and efficiently, as though no stranger to physical exertion. She turned her head and saw his hair was long and black, pulled back into a tail at the nape of his neck. His skin was tanned, but youthful and wrinkle free.

Before she could catch a glimpse of his face, he slapped his hand on the trunk of the tree and muttered words she could barely hear over the sudden shouts and screams coming from beyond the courtyard walls.

And, within seconds, the meadow and trees around her melted away in a ghostly haze, and the tree glowed with vivid gold light. She had to close her eyes against the brightness of it, but she could see it glowing beyond her closed lids.

When it faded to black, the darkness gave her an odd sense of relief. Until she opened her eyes, and the fear set in once more.

Where was she? Where was her mother? Her father? The others? Were they looking for her?

Her heart began to beat frantically in her tiny chest, and even though the grown woman behind the dream knew the horrifying answers to all of her questions, the doubting child refused to believe the reality of them. To her, the fear was real and gripping in its stranglehold on her heart.

She let out a frightened cry, finding no other solution to her panic. The man who held her shifted her roughly.

"Shut up," he scolded, his voice unmerciful as he began to walk away from a small park. He stalked through the shadows, the streets around them lit dimly by streetlights and the buildings dark and empty.

The sidewalk beneath them was broken, cracked with age and neglect, with weeds sprouting up desperate for release from their cement prison. There were few cars along the nearly empty street, and the ones that were there looked as decrepit as the sidewalk.

Suddenly, he made a quick turn down a narrow alleyway, lit only from the hazy moonlight above. Clotheslines were strung from one building to the next, the garments hanging from them as still as the quiet night. She could see the brick on the walls, worn and blackened with time, anciently urban. It was a vivid contrast to the elegant stone castle she called home, and this fact had her clenching her tiny hands on her captor's shirt, sorrow rapidly mixing with the fear she felt. All she wanted was to go home…

Tears began to spill from her eyes and fall down her cheeks, but she kept silent. Her parents would want her to be strong and not to cry. She wouldn't be a little baby…she would be tough.

When the man stopped, Capri shifted to look up at him, hoping to see his face. Who was he?

His eyes were set ahead, but she studied his profile. He had an angular face with high cheekbones and a firm mouth. His nose was hooked and slanted, as though it had been broken more than once in his lifetime. The eyes housed beneath dark brows were sharp and focused, and were the color of molten amber.

"It's done," he spoke, his mouth shifting and forming the words delicately, as if to a lover.

Capri twisted in his arms, searching to see who he spoke to. She saw her, a short, shifty woman of about fifty years of age with fiery red hair in wild spirals circling a sharp and bitter looking face.

"What have you done? Who is this?" The woman appeared irritated and flustered, her eyes darting from the man to Capri in rapid succession.

"This is Clynn's daughter. Her mother made the unfortunate mistake of getting in the way of our plan. I've been instructed to dispose of her."

"Why the hell did you bring her here? To me? Did you think about how this would affect me?" the woman spat, her eyes flaring up viciously. "But no, you don't think, do you?"

"Damnit, I didn't have any other choice! I had to get the hell out of there!" the man retorted heatedly. He set Capri on the ground then, and with the skill and speed of a man accustomed to doing such things, he pulled out his pistol and aimed.

"*Wait!*" the woman screamed, and Capri looked up from the polished barrel of the gun to see the woman's anguished face. "Let's just leave her here. They'll never find her anyway; she'll be as good as dead to them. Just don't make me watch you kill her, not when my own flesh and blood is her age. I can't bear it! I just can't bear it!"

"Fine," the man muttered through gritted teeth as he sheathed his weapon. "Let's go."

With one last disdainful look at Capri, which allowed her to see his face fully, he took off down the alleyway to the street. The woman knelt down beside Capri, her hand resting on her Capri's head briefly, before she suddenly took off after him, the skirts of her plain cotton dress billowing behind her.

The world around her shuddered into darkness, and Capri felt herself rising out of the dream. Her eyes flew open and she exhaled shakily, her heart pounding. She tried to continue to breathe, but her throat felt blocked, and it was then that she realized her face was wet with tears. Closing her eyes again, she tried to quiet her racing heart. She felt a gentle squeeze on her right hand, and when she opened her eyes and turned her head to the side, she met Rian's gaze.

He was pale, but he was steady. "Are you okay?"

She nodded, and as she did another tear slid down her cheek. Without saying a word, she sat up and reached out to him, needing the comfort more than she could say. He held her, stroking her hair in an instinctual act to soothe as she fought for calm after the storm.

When she pulled away from him, she remembered the Muses, who were standing around them, looking both concerned and amused.

Capri looked up at Serendipity, and she managed a weak smile. "Thank you, I think I've seen enough for today."

With that, she stood up, fighting against the impulse to crumble to pieces. Rian followed her as she led the way out of the tower. When they emerged out into the corridor, she instinctually went straight for the library. Rian didn't object, instead he just followed her, knowing that the library was where she would feel most comfortable.

When they reached it, she walked right in and settled none too steadily upon one of the many sofas, her hands clasped together and her eyes brightly clear.

"Now that we're alone," Capri began, watching him as he took a seat beside her on the sofa. "Let me tell you what I saw."

She launched into a full description of her dream, sparing no details as she relived it once more in her mind. Rian let her speak, studying her silently as he mentally filed away everything she said. When she was finished, he nodded and stood up to pace.

"It's going to be hard for us to determine who the demon is based upon a physical description alone, seeing as he was possessing a human and could have upgraded since then, but at least we have something. Tell me more about the woman."

"She had curly red hair, and she was small, petite, but older, maybe fifty or so…she looked worn out, stressed, bitter…" Capri paused, trying to hone in on the image of the woman in her mind. "I've never seen her before, but something about her was familiar. And she saved my life. She stopped him from killing me right then and there. Whoever she is, I owe her my life."

"I think I know who she is." Rian stopped pacing and faced her, his eyes sharpening with focus and understanding.

"You do?" Capri looked at him with wide eyes.

"Yes, and it only confirms everything I've already assumed." He looked nervous, anxious almost, as he started pacing again. "I think that the woman you saw was Brock's mother, Blythe's grandmother."

Capri couldn't hide her shock and disbelief. "You're sure?"

"It makes sense. We know Brock was working with the demon, and Brock's mother was banished from Euphora years before either you or I were born, though they've never told me why. Maybe she was involved in the raid and she was the demon's contact in Richmond. And if Brock's mother was living in Richmond at the time, then it's possible that when Brock himself was banished, he might very well have gone to Richmond, too."

"And you think he may still be there?"

"If he is, then my father and Balgaire are most certainly heading into a trap."

Capri stared at him with sudden and brutal comprehension, fear skittering down her spine.

"I have to go, I have to help them." He clutched his head with his hands in anguish as he continued to pace, and Capri watched worriedly as he stopped and faced her, his hands dropping to his sides. "I can't waste any more time. I appreciate your help, but I have to go."

"I understand," she managed, unable to do more than watch as he left the room. Within moments the library was silent, and Capri was left with nothing except fear and a deep regret that she was unable to do more.

She returned to continue work with her father, and while she explained to him that she had been to see the Muses, she refused to elaborate on what she had seen, claiming it wasn't anything important. She didn't want to trouble him, as he had already made it clear to her that he preferred to leave the past in the past. She had no problem honoring his request.

Around one o'clock in the afternoon, Capri headed to the dining hall for lunch, only to run into Rhiannon in the corridor.

"Capri, I'm glad I caught you." Rhiannon smiled warmly, a large wicker basket cradled in her arms. "I was hoping we could have that picnic today."

"Oh," Capri paused, her mind focusing away from the earlier events and to the present. "Yeah, sure, that sounds wonderful." She felt her lips curve in a smile, but she couldn't muster up the heart to make it into anything more than just a smoke signal. Inside, she was nothing but frantic nerves and emotions.

"Great! I think you'll enjoy what I packed for us." Rhiannon winked as she led the way out into the courtyard, where the sun, as always, was shining mistily through the morning haze. Capri tried to keep pace with Rhiannon's efficient walk, amazed that the basket didn't seem to hinder the other girl. She still walked with elegance and poise, like she was on a runway versus outside in a garden. Even the clothes she wore were classy and stylish, from her suede pumps the color of ripe plums to her flowery skirt and matching plum blouse. Rhiannon was like a picture out of a high end fashion magazine. Capri wondered briefly if it took her any effort at all to look that way, or if it just came by her naturally.

"This is a good spot," Rhiannon said cheerfully as they came to a stop in the middle of a small meadow within the court-yard, shaded by trees with dappled sunlight peeking through. Wildflowers sprouted from the yielding grasses, adding bursts of fragrant color. She set the basket on the ground and lifted out a linen blanket, which she spread out for them to sit upon.

Capri helped straighten the blanket before sitting down, feeling plain in her faded jeans and simple light blue t-shirt. Maybe if she had known Rhiannon wanted to have the picnic today, she could have dressed up a little, she thought miserably. Although, why were outfits important when much more serious events were happening at that very moment?

"Here you go." Rhiannon handed her a plate and napkin, which Capri numbly took.

What was she doing? How could she pretend to have a good time when so much was going on? She couldn't possibly focus and give Rhiannon the attention she deserved when chaos was literally erupting within her, clawing its way through her stom-ach and up into her throat. But she knew she had no excuse to give, nothing she could say with honesty in her eyes that would forgive cancelling the picnic when Rhiannon had obviously worked so hard to put it together. She was just going to have to suck it up, and push all thoughts and fears about Rian and the other Furies out of her mind.

"This is lovely," Capri heard herself say as Rhiannon began opening several containers housing various types of picnic food. Though, it wasn't the typical picnic food Capri would normally associate with outside dining.

There were tiny slices of toasted French bread that Rhiannon skillfully topped with a roasted tomato and fresh basil mixture, which looked like something out of a home and garden magazine, along with brie cheese nestled on fine peppered crackers with sprigs of sage as garnish and crab stuffed pea pods– and those were just the appetizers.

Rhiannon promised more surprises for the main course before shutting the basket and nibbling a bite of brie cheese.

"How has your work with your father been going?" Rhiannon asked politely, gently wiping her lips with a cheerful yellow napkin.

"Fine," Capri replied, swallowing a mouthful of bruschetta. "I mean, it's been great. It's a lot of fun so I'm enjoying it a lot."

"That's good to hear." Rhiannon reached for a pea pod and took a bite. "You'll have to come by and see me work sometime; I think you'd find it interesting."

"I saw the greenhouse when I first arrived, it's beautiful," Capri complimented, remembering the lush indoor garden with glass walls and sparkling sapphire pond that served as a window to the outside world, much as the birdbath did for her and her father. "What kinds of things do you do?"

"We regulate animal populations, plant and tree cycles, changes in the Earth's crust, including the occasional necessary earthquake." She grinned at Capri. "It's a lot of work, but it's very rewarding. It takes skill and precision, and a great attention to detail. I'm sure you've found that your work requires the same."

Capri guiltily remembered her earlier mistake with the snowstorm. "Yeah, it does."

"You know, when we were little, they would let all of us out to play at the same time, kind of like recess in a human school. You probably don't remember this, but we used to play that spin and fall down game, you know the one where you hold hands and spin? Right on this very spot."

Capri smiled and glanced around her. "I wish I did remember; I bet it was a lot of fun."

"It was! This one time, Blythe and I tried to encourage the Fury boys to play with us because we wanted to have an even bigger circle of people. They refused, naturally, but we tried." She smiled, amused at the memory.

Capri's brows knit together sadly. "You guys never played with them as kids?"

Rhiannon shrugged. "They always made it very clear that they wanted nothing to do with us. The Furies and Fates are raised in a much stricter environment than the Dryads and Muses. I don't know why, but that's the way it's always been. Very rarely do the Furies and Dryads mix, or the Muses and Fates. It just isn't done." She laughed lightly, rolling her eyes. "Though we were just kids, what did we know?"

Capri couldn't help feeling sad at hearing this. "I see…"

"Don't get me wrong, I admire the work the Furies and Fates do, I just can't see anything more than a casual friendship being possible. Brogan and I have sat down and had a conversation a few times, and I find him perfectly agreeable."

"I've never really spoken to him," Capri told her, her interest piqued. "What is he like?"

"Much like you'd expect, I suppose." Rhiannon pursed her lips, thinking how to put it. "He's quiet, and very serious, very dedicated to his work. I suppose that's what I like about him. And he's polite, well mannered, well bred. His mother is a very well respected professor at Oxford University."

When Capri stared at her blankly, Rhiannon elaborated. "After Brogan was born and she found out what Balgaire was, she chose not to live this life, and so her memory was erased. She doesn't know Brogan exists."

"That's terrible." Capri's eyes filled at the thought of how horrible Balgaire must have felt at being rejected just because of who he was.

"It is. But Brogan doesn't let it get to him; he's always very courteous to me and everyone else." Her eyes drifted toward the castle, the rich sage changing to a deeper jade and her lips curving into a slow, considering smile.

"Do you like him?" Capri asked with a grin, her feminine curiosity peeked.

"I always have," Rhiannon murmured, her eyes focused over Capri's shoulder. Confused, Capri turned and saw Liam and Blythe taking a walk down the cobblestone pathway. She watched as Liam spotted them and smiled at the cheerful wave he sent their way. Beside him, Blythe locked bored and irritated, her arms crossed tightly over her chest and her eyes locked on the tops of the trees.

Capri quickly glanced back at Rhiannon, who was watching the pair. Her face that had been so openly beautiful just seconds ago had become guarded and cold.

Understanding washed over her as she watched her earthly friend, noting the contrast between the longing that had been in her eyes seconds before and the polite indifference that had replaced it.

"Anyway, let me show you what we have for the main course." Rhiannon smiled coolly, her mask carefully replaced.

It was then that Capri understood that there were some things that were much too complex for her to ever fully understand, including the strange, albeit intricate, art of love.

That night, dinner was as sullen and tense as it had been the last time the Furies had been gone. Capri felt like her entire body was taut and strung like a wire, capable of springing loose and destroying everything around her.

She kept her eye on both Rohan and Tobias, hoping they would give something away that might hint at their involvement. But, throughout dinner, they both looked just as nervous and stressed as everyone else. There was nothing to hint at either of them being involved in anything of a dark and sinister nature, despite how badly Capri wanted to see it. It would just further prove to her that she and Rian were right.

When she went to bed that night, sleep cruelly evaded her. What was happening at that moment? Were they okay? Had they been ambushed again? All of her worst fears plagued her while she tossed and turned, restless and afraid.

Sometime after three in the morning, she tumbled into an equally restless sleep, more from sheer mental exhaustion than anything.

She had no way of knowing that within hours, everything that had come to fruition during her time on Euphora would take a drastic and deadly turn for the worst.

## Chapter Twelve

*She awoke hours* later to a scream so anguished, so hysterical, that she thought for a split second that the world was crumbling around her.

But when her eyes flew open and she sat up in bed, her heart racing and her mind still foggy from poor sleep, the only thing she could think was no... no...no...

She tossed the blankets aside and stumbled out of bed, racing to her open bedroom window. She pushed aside the sheer drapes and looked straight below into the courtyard, blinking to clear her vision.

The three Fate women were huddled together, holding each other, sobbing uncontrollably. One of them, Nyxa, tilted her head back and screamed again, the sound shrill and deafening, but so filled with sorrow and devastation that Capri felt chills greedily chase up and down her spine.

Her heart racing, she watched as Lucian and Rohan suddenly appeared, running toward the Fates, shouting in question at their sudden outburst. She saw Rohan grab a hold of Nyxa, pulling her away, grabbing her shoulders roughly and shaking her, his voice demanding as he repeatedly asked her what happened. Lucian was busy comforting the other two Fates, who were holding each other and sobbing.

Capri could barely hear what Rohan was saying, but when Nyxa suddenly cried out, her voice tortured with misery, Capri heard her loud and clear.

"*The Fury is dead. He is dead!*" Her head fell back and Rohan nearly dropped her as she suddenly went limp, fainting in his arms.

He said nothing as he looked up at Lucian. Stunned disbelief filled the faces of both men.

Capri felt her heart stop beating. It stopped beating for what must have been five full seconds. Her entire body felt numb, her ears buzzing, her vision tunneling, and she suddenly realized she was going to faint if she didn't pull herself together.

Shaking her head to clear it, she steeled herself of all emotion and raced to pull on something other than her nightgown. After shrugging into yesterday's jeans and a t-shirt, she all but ran out her bedroom door, racing down the stairs and bursting through the door that led to the corridor. All she could think was that it couldn't be him, it just couldn't be, there must be a mistake, he had to be alive. She couldn't lose him, not yet. Not like this.

She didn't even realize she was barefoot as she broke into a full run through the corridor, out into the atrium. She thrust her palm against the entrance doors, impatient as they melted away beneath her touch.

When she fell out into the hazy morning sunlight, its rays shining down against her face, she felt she was almost at wits end. She would break, any moment, if she didn't find out the truth.

When she lifted her eyes to where the Fates were huddled together on the cobblestone pathway, she saw a group of men emerge through the front gates.

At first she couldn't make out who they were, but she searched for Rian amongst the sea of faces.

And when she saw him, alive..whole...safe, she fell instantly to her knees.

The Fates, Rohan, and Lucian stepped aside to let the convoy of men through, none of them saying a word. At the lead was Balgaire, his face stonily furious. Brogan walked beside him, his dark eyes wide with shock and his face pale.

And then there was Rian, numb denial in his eyes and his mouth set in a firm line.

Behind them were four men, all wearing matching gray uniforms, carrying a body wrapped in a black cloth.

While Capri watched the group approach her, she kept her eyes on Rian, the numbness she felt beginning to ebb into a completely different emotion, something shamefully mixed between grateful relief and desolate misery.

She stayed where she was, crumbled to her knees just outside the front doors, as they passed her. Rian met her eyes just briefly, and she saw the grief flash in them before he looked away and headed inside. Unable to do more, she broke down and wept.

It was quite obvious to her that Roarke was dead.

The worst had indeed occurred.

Capri stayed where she was for awhile, leaning against the wall of the castle just outside the entrance doors, hugging her knees to her chest. She stared blankly ahead, not seeing anything but the grief that had been in Rian's eyes. It kept repeating, over and over, the scene of him walking with the surviving Furies and the Enforcers carrying the body. And, as with pretty much everything bad that had been happening in her life, she once again felt helpless to do anything.

Eventually the Fates and the two Dryad men had returned to the castle in their haste to find out what happened, but none of them paid any attention to her. For this she was thankful, as she wanted to do nothing more than privately grieve.

When her father found her some time later, he pulled her into his arms and she wept again. He patted her back and held on, his own face streaked with tears.

He pulled away from her after some time, and cupped her face in his hands, studying her closely, a strange mix of emotions in his eyes.

"Capri, I want you to hear this from me, because you have a right to know." He hesitated, his hands shaking as they fell away from her face. "Balgaire explained the details of what happened, and it has come out that Roarke was the one responsible for letting in the demon who possessed you, and for staging the ambush that lead to the Enforcers being killed. He also assisted Brock in executing the raid all those years ago."

She stared at him for a moment, digesting what he told her. When she spoke, her voice was shaky with disbelief. "But…why? How do they know it was him?"

His lips tightened as anger flashed in his red rimmed and tired eyes. "Apparently he confessed to everything in front of the other Furies and the Enforcers, before attempting to shoot Balgaire. Thankfully, Balgaire dodged the bullet, but after the shot was fired the Enforcers, as trained, shot Roarke and he was mortally wounded. He was alive through the night, unresponsive, but this morning he passed away."

Her hand shot up to cover her mouth, her eyes wide with shock. She didn't know what to say. A part of her accepted that if Roarke had confessed, then surely he must have been responsible, meaning that she and Rian had been gravely mistaken in their assumptions. But another part of her rejected the explanation completely. There was no way Roarke was responsible. It didn't make sense. But she had no evidence to back up her belief in his innocence. And, in contrast, the evidence of his guilt was a confession witnessed by several credible people.

"Come inside, darling." Clynn rose and pulled her with him, his arm still around her in support. "This is unsettling news for all of us."

Later that evening, Thea gathered everyone for dinner, and she explained everything Balgaire had told her. The adults had all heard it, of course, but this was so their children could hear and understand.

Her message was simple: Roarke had betrayed the people of Euphora, most notably her and Sebastian, and had committed horrible crimes. She commended Balgaire on securing a resolution to those crimes by way of the confession, and added that she hoped he was coping with his partner's unexpected betrayal. With that, she led a toast to the Furies and the Enforcers, and afterwards everyone began to eat dinner in silence.

When dinner was over and everyone poured out into the parlor or went up to their rooms, Capri searched for Rian amongst the crowd. She hadn't seen him all day until dinner, and even then he sat several seats away, his gaze focused on nothing but the plate in front of him. She didn't even see him eat; he just sat there in silence.

She didn't see him enter the parlor, so she headed away from the majority of the crowd and out into the corridor. Just as she walked through the door, someone grabbed her hand and pulled her to the side.

"Rian." She wrapped her arms around him the moment she saw his face. He held her back tightly, unsure what it was about her that comforted him. He only knew he needed it.

When she pulled away, she had tears in her eyes.

"I'm so sorry," she mumbled, shaking her head, sorrow so clearly written on her face.

"I am too," he said in return, reaching out to hold her hand, to have some kind of contact with her so he wouldn't lose control. His face was strained, as though he was trying to contain the rage he felt. "I know my father is not guilty of doing those things. Confession or not, it isn't true. You must believe me."

"I do," she said immediately. "It doesn't make sense."

He seemed to relax a little, relief coursing through him. "You weren't there, you didn't see it happen. But I did." His face hardened at the memory. "And I can tell you, something was wrong with him, he wasn't himself, it wasn't him talking. I knew him better than anyone except Balgaire, and something was off about the whole thing. My father was a good man; he would never have done those things."

"So what do you think happened?"

"I'm not sure." He took a deep breath, steadying himself. "But I'm going to find out."

"I want to help you." She blushed, diverting her eyes at the look he gave her. "That is, if you want me to."

"Of course I want you to," he replied, and when their eyes met she recognized that he needed her now just as badly as she had needed him before.

Before she could respond, Balgaire emerged from the dining hall and approached them, his face set in stern lines, his dark eyes cold. Capri watched him as he walked straight to Rian, leaning in to murmur something in his ear. Rian's brows knit in concern as he listened silently, nodding as Balgaire walked away.

Balgaire eyed Capri grimly, but didn't say anything as he turned and stalked off down the corridor.

"Why does he always do that?" Capri wondered as she watched Balgaire's retreating figure disappear through one of the doors.

"Do what?" Rian asked as she turned back around to face him.

"He mumbles, he never says a word out loud. He must be the shyest person I've ever met if he's afraid to speak in front of people." She looked slightly hurt at the idea that he was afraid of her, something that Rian found briefly amusing.

"I don't know what you're talking about, he speaks out loud all of the time. Maybe you just catch him at moments where he feels the need to be discreet."

"Like just then?"

He nodded. "Yes. Though all he told me was that he wants to speak with Brogan and me first thing tomorrow morning regarding my new obligations as lead Fury." He sighed, shifting uncomfortably. "I'm stepping into my father's place much earlier than expected, but I have no other choice."

"You'll be great." She squeezed the hand she held, smiling at him. "I know it's hard, but you're one of the strongest people I know. If anyone can get through this, it's you."

"Your faith in me is astounding," he chuckled, causing her face to redden slightly.

"All I know is that I wish I had even half of your strength." She bit her lip and glanced at the floor, fighting against embarrassment. "I know that sounds cheesy, but it's true."

"Thank you."

She looked up at him and he was smiling at her. She realized it was the first time she had seen a true smile on his face, and it comforted her to know that he felt at ease with her to let his guard down.

"So what do we do now?"

"I don't know." His smile faded and he looked troubled. "No one else seems suspicious about all of this, but I know better." He paused for a moment, deep in thought. "Meet me in the courtyard tomorrow night after dinner, and bring a list of every detail you think is significant from your dream. There has to be something we've missed, some piece that can explain what is really going on here."

"I'll start working on it right away," Capri assured him. "We should probably—"

"Capri?" Clynn stood just outside the dining hall doors, his eyes narrowing suspiciously at seeing his daughter standing in the darkened corridor with Rian. "Is everything alright?"

"Y-yes, everything's fine." Capri's hands fell away from Rian's awkwardly, and she sent him one last knowing look before walking to her father who led her back into the dining hall. Rian didn't follow, instead heading to his room.

"What were you and Rian talking about?" Clynn asked her quietly as he led the way to the parlor, where everyone was sitting around talking.

"I was just giving him my condolences," she replied, hoping there was enough truth in the statement to convince him.

He nudged her down onto one of the many plush sofas and sat beside her, watching her closely.

"He is going through a tough time; he might prefer some time alone to grieve," he told her, reaching for her hand.

She looked up at him. "Are you telling me I shouldn't talk to him?"

"No, not at all," he defended, looking sheepish. "I just think that maybe you should give him time. I know he's been helping you figure out who the demon is that kidnapped you." He chuckled at the surprised look on her face. "I'm not blind, Capri, nor am I oblivious to the passion you have for finding this demon. But keep in mind that Rian currently has other things on his mind, and he may not have as much time to devote to helping you as he had before."

Capri considered his words for a moment, feeling guilty that she was not going to be able to follow his suggestion. She knew the last thing Rian wanted was for her to leave him alone. And regardless of what her father seemed to want, she was going to continue helping him, just as he was going to continue helping her. They now had a common goal, and even loyalty to her father couldn't keep her away from pursuing it.

"Okay, I won't bother him for awhile," Capri told him, mentally crossing her fingers to offset the lie.

Clynn patted her knee, smiling. "Good girl."

She smiled back at him, though it most certainly didn't reach her eyes. He didn't seem to notice, however, as he turned and began a conversation with Lucian about some storm in Russia that needed attention.

Capri looked around the room at the few remaining people who had yet to retire upstairs, and noticed that no one really seemed angry or upset anymore. On the contrary, it appeared that most of the people seemed to believe that the recent events involving Roarke were enough to conclude their fears about everything that had been happening on Euphora. They were all content with the explanation that he had confessed to everything, and since he was dead then justice had been served. Case closed. How they could hide their heads in the sand and believe something so honestly unbelievable was beyond her.

Even Blythe, Liam, and Rhiannon seemed unperturbed by the news, and were acting as though everything was fine.

Was that really how the people of Euphora dealt with murder and scandal? Just accepting the first valid explanation as complete and utter truth? Why was there no doubt in anyone's mind that Roarke might not have been guilty? Sure, she supposed that in most of their eyes a confession was the end all be all of an investigation, but why didn't anyone look to Roarke's character and the years of faithful service he had given to them? The protection he had offered all of Euphora in times of crisis didn't seem to mean anything. It shamed her to think that his memory was tarnished by what she knew was an outright lie.

And if they so easily condemned Roarke and dismissed his entire reputation because it was easier to accept that he had been guilty, then it raised doubts in her mind about Brock. What if Brock hadn't actually been guilty either? What if he had been framed, used as a scapegoat for a crime someone else had committed? And what if that same person had now done the same thing to Roarke?

Uneasy, she pressed her hand to her stomach, feeling suddenly sick. No, Brock must have been guilty; his own mother was there with the demon the night she had been kidnapped. Why would she be involved if it weren't to help him?

She took a steadying breath, trying to calm herself. Rian would help her figure this all out, and then the truth would be discovered and everything would be fine. Until then, all she could do was compile that list of details from her dream before she met with him the following night.

She said goodnight to her father and the others, feeling numb and exhausted. It had certainly been a long and trying day, but she couldn't go to sleep yet. She had to write that list.

Rising from the sofa, she slipped out through the parlor doors into the dining hall, and then out into the corridor.

Back in the parlor, one of the Fates watched her leave, his gypsy eyes carefully blank despite his broken heart.

List in hand, Capri snuck through the atrium the following night and out into the courtyard, grateful for the darkness outside. She had complained of a headache and gone to bed just after dinner, only to sneak back down moments later, accompanied by the list she had spent the better part of the night before compiling.

The pale, blue moonlight illuminated the courtyard and deepened the shadows cast down by the trees. Capri glanced around, searching for Rian, wondering if she had arrived before him. As she walked along the pathway, her eyes scanning around her, she saw him appear from the shadows to her right.

She walked over to him, her lips curving into a smile.

"Hi," she greeted, keeping her voice low in case someone had a window open above.

"Let's walk." He cupped his hand under her elbow gently before leading her swiftly down the walkway to the front gates. They walked in silence, neither really knowing what to say, but each comforted by the other's presence.

When they reached the gate, he placed his hand upon the wrought iron, which melted away beneath his touch. He led the way through the meadow and down the same pathway Liam and Blythe had taken her, the path that led toward the bench on the edge of the island.

Under the cover of the forest, the moonlight did little to help light the way. She wanted to ask him if he had a flashlight, as she hadn't even thought to bring one, but he seemed to know the way well enough in the dark.

She could see the open sky through a break in the trees just ahead, the stars exploding against the deep velvet blue of night. When they left the forest behind them and were out in the open meadow, facing the edge of the island that dropped off dramatically to the sea, Capri felt momentarily mystified.

If she had thought this place to be beautiful in the daytime, it was nothing compared to what it looked like at night.

The stars were so bright and illuminated that they seemed to be alive and glittering, and the moon above them was crisp and clear, its body surrounded by a glowing blue ring. Everything was reflected in the ocean below, making it seem as though there was no break between sky and sea, but instead in an all-encompassing universe, and she was standing right on the edge of the planet.

In the open moonlight, she could see the grasses swaying slightly in the gentle and cool breeze, and when Rian gestured for her to sit on the bench she sat and reached down instinctively to pick a dandelion growing up from the ground in front of her. Twirling it between her fingertips, she did what she always did with such things: she made a wish.

When she suddenly blew at the dandelion, sending the tiny seeds bursting into the air to be carried by the breeze, she heard Rian chuckle beside her. Blushing, she tossed away the stem and turned to him, grinning.

"What was that for?" he asked, the amusement clear on his face.

"I was making a wish," she defended good-naturedly. "Haven't you ever done that before? I used to always do it when I was little."

"Can't say that I have," he shrugged. "What did you wish for?"

"I can't tell you or it won't come true." She smiled again, relaxing, her gaze drifting out toward the sea. "It's so beautiful here. I should come and sit on this bench every night."

"It's quiet." Rian leaned back against the bench, relaxing as well. "I can think clearly when I'm out here."

"That's good because we have a lot of thinking to do," Capri reminded him, holding out her list for him to look at. "That's everything. Most of it we have already talked about, but it helped to put it down on paper."

He took the list from her and looked it over in silence. When he was done reading, he set it down in his lap and turned to her.

"The only thing I can't seem to figure out is who the second man was in the library." His brows furrowed as he looked at her. "We know Rohan is most likely involved, and my father was suspicious of Tobias, so he's involved somehow. And Brock is also most likely part of this since we assume he has been residing in Richmond which was where my father and Balgaire went last. But none of this answers who the voice was that you heard. That is the missing piece."

"I swear the voice sounded exactly like the man from my dream, the man who by all accounts was Brock." Capri chewed her bottom lip in thought. "But I'm probably wrong, as there is no way he could have gotten onto Euphora undetected, especially during the day. Maybe it was one of the Enforcers? Though I don't know what they would have against me."

Rian shook his head. "They could have just been hired by Rohan to do the dirty work, though I doubt it. They rarely come to Euphora, and if one was here someone would have said something to us. And Rohan has little to no weight when it comes to the Enforcers. They strictly work for Thea and the Furies."

"Right…" Puzzled, Capri continued running names through her head. "We can exclude my father, and Lucian, too, as he has no reason to do any of this, and Tobias and Alastor are too young, so really that just leaves…" she paused, her eyes widening as they met his. "Rian, I don't mean to insult you, but do you think it might have been Balgaire?"

"I've thought about it," he admitted, watching her, his face unreadable. "I just can't see him doing it. He was like a brother to my father, and he's like a second father to me. I don't know what his motivation would be for hurting us this way, much less you and your father."

"Okay..." Though she chewed on the idea a little bit more, unsure whether he was right or not.

A noise from behind them had her turning around curiously. Rian was already on his feet, his hand on the pistol at his hip. His eyes scanned the dark trees, looking for the source of the sound.

"Who's there?" he asked, his voice stern and intimidating. She realized just how much he looked like his father when he was in protective mode, and the fact that she felt no fear when she was with him had her heart skipping a beat. There was nothing to worry about when he was around. A giant, man-eating bear could come charging out of the forest at that very moment and she would feel absolutely no fear.

"Hello, Rian...Capri." The youngest Fate, Alastor, appeared from within the forest, his hands held up, spread in an expression of peace. "I'm sorry to bother you both."

Capri saw Rian's eyes narrow in suspicion, his hand not leaving his pistol. "It's late. You should be in bed, Alastor."

"I know, but I saw you both walk out here, and I wanted to talk to you about your father." Alastor moved closer, his hands still raised, his gypsy eyes on Rian.

Capri rose to stand beside Rian, watching Alastor intently. The boy was barely fourteen years old, and small for his age at that. He had luscious black hair that curled around his thin face, and dark eyes surrounded by heavy lashes set against dusky, olive-toned skin. He really was the image of a gypsy, suited to the exotic faraway lands in the east.

"What about my father?" Rian asked.

"Look, you may not believe me when I tell you this, but Roarke was like a father to me," Alastor began. His voice was quiet and shy, still in the awkward stages of adolescence, but there was a certain otherworldly intelligence in his eyes that Capri would have called an *old soul*.

"My father was a human, and my mother has never contacted him about me. He doesn't know I exist." Alastor shrugged, as though pretending it didn't bother him. "I'm not the first member of Euphora to go through that, so I know I shouldn't feel too sorry for myself. But Roarke was always willing to listen to me when I had a problem, and I suppose he filled that void in me. I don't believe he confessed of his own free will. In fact, I know he didn't."

"I know he didn't either, but that doesn't solve the issue of what happened," Rian countered coldly. Capri glanced at him, unsure why he was still being so hostile. If anything, Alastor was being complimentary to their cause and offering his support.

"No, you don't understand. I know he didn't do those things," Alastor repeated, eyeing Rian intently. When Rian didn't seem to understand, Alastor elaborated. "Male Fates have powers that the female Fates do not, an anomaly that we've yet to discover the reason for. However, what it means is that I can see things and sense things that the others cannot."

"Go on." Rian still sounded suspicious, but his curiosity was evidently peaked.

Capri was nearly bouncing with excitement. Her father had told her about how Alastor was supposed to develop some kind of strange powers, though she had never found out what it would be. Now, it seemed, she was finally going to get the answer.

"Since it is my duty to spin the thread of life, in a sense I touch every soul that enters this world. Because of this, I am in a way connected to every soul on this planet because they have passed through the spindle that I am bonded to by blood. So when I touch a person, I can see whether their soul is pure, or if it has been touched by another—usually evil—being."

"In layman's terms, please," Rian said impatiently.

"By touching someone, I can tell whether they have been possessed or not. I can also tell if two or more people have been possessed by the same demon, because of the signature that is left behind on the soul."

For a moment the three of them were silent. Capri could hear the sounds of night creatures in the forest, could hear her own heart beat. She could also, quite definitely, feel the chill that ran across her spine as understanding reached her.

"Roarke was possessed by a demon," she murmured, her eyes wide as she stared at Alastor. He shifted and met her gaze as he nodded.

"And I believe the demon left his body the moment before he was shot, thereby only killing Roarke and not himself," Alastor added, anger and sorrow flashing in his sober eyes. "I can only hope that Roarke was too disoriented to realize what was happening, and that he didn't suffer while he lay there dying through the night."

"And you think that the demon who possessed my father might be the same one who possessed Capri?"

"Actually, I do, which is why I wanted to come and see you," Alastor replied, his eyes still on Capri. "Will you let me touch you? Just on the arm is fine, but this way I can do what little I can to help you both find those responsible for killing off the only father I ever knew."

"Of course." Capri nodded as Alastor walked around the bench toward her. Rian watched him over Capri's shoulder, a clear warning in his eyes.

"Is this going to hurt her?" Rian asked before Alastor could touch her.

"No, she won't feel a thing," Alastor reassured him. He reached out and lightly laid his hand on Capri's right forearm, and closed his eyes. His hand felt cool against her skin, and she could feel a light tingling sensation as he seemed to penetrate through to her soul.

He took a deep breath, and moments later his eyes flew open. "The signature is the same." He withdrew his hand, watching them both. "There is something else you should know."

"What is it?" Capri asked, rubbing her arm where he had touched it.

"The signature that both you and Roarke have on your souls…it's not only a demon signature."

"What do you mean?" Rian rested his hand on Capri's shoulder protectively, drawing himself closer to her.

"Well, and I honestly don't know how this is possible, but the signature is both demon and Dryad."

"Excuse me?" Capri's breath caught in her throat as she tried to process what he had said.

"Demons have been known to have very strange powers, and I wouldn't be surprised if they knew how to jointly possess someone, but I've never heard of it so I can't be sure. And if that's not what it is, then maybe we're dealing with some kind of demon/Dryad hybrid being."

"That isn't possible," Rian countered, bristling behind Capri. "You must be mistaken."

Alastor shrugged. "Do what you will with the information. I just wanted to tell you both before I go to Thea tomorrow and let her know. If she orders me to be silent about it, then I will have already told you."

With that, he nodded at the two of them and turned, heading back into the dark forest. When he was gone, Capri turned around to face Rian.

"So your father really is innocent." Her hands twisted in front of her anxiously, understanding in her eyes as she felt more pieces of the puzzle fall into place. "I have a new theory."

"Let's hear it." Rian's voice had a slightly dangerous edge to it, and she could tell he was attempting to curb the anger he felt.

"I think that Brock was framed. That would explain why the voice from my dream matches the voice of the man from the library that we are almost positive couldn't have been Brock. I also think that the person who framed Brock has done the same thing to your father. Whoever it is, they are behind everything, but they made scapegoats out of both your father and Brock."

Rian's eyes sharpened as his jaw clenched, and he turned away from her to begin pacing. He was silent a moment, clearly thinking over her new theory, working out the angles for himself. When he stopped and faced her again, he looked suspicious.

"Even if we assume there is someone on Euphora framing decent men for crimes they didn't commit, that doesn't explain why Brock's mother was in your dream."

"Unless she wanted revenge for him for staying behind on Euphora while she was banished," Capri added.

"It's possible," Rian agreed thoughtfully, running a hand through his hair restlessly. "But the Dryad signature on your soul? I just can't wrap my mind around that, there's just no way."

"Alastor said that demons have been known to have strange powers. Maybe the one we're dealing with has the ability to bring someone else with them when they possess someone."

"That part I could maybe understand, though I still think it's highly unlikely. I've been studying demons my entire life and I have never heard of anything like that," Rian told her, pacing again. "But the part that I really cannot believe is that there is some half demon, half Dryad running around."

"Because we are forbidden to have children with demons, right?" Capri asked, remembering what Blythe and Liam had told her.

"Exactly." Rian stopped and sat down on the bench, gesturing for her to sit beside him. When she did, he turned to her. "Apparently this is a lot bigger than I originally thought," he admitted, frustration on his face. "I will leave telling Thea about this to Alastor, and hopefully we can be sure it's not Sebastian who's behind it all. I want to tell Balgaire, but it could just as easily be him. It could even be Lucian, or Rohan, or any of them. I just don't know anymore, and the not knowing is really starting to get to me."

"It's getting to me too," Capri agreed, reaching out for his hand. "Maybe we should take some time away from this, clear our heads a bit. And as we do so, we will watch and observe. Eventually this person is going to slip up somehow, or more information will come out, and then we will know. And once we know, then we can figure out what we're going to do about it."

Rian watched her quietly, his blue eyes as serious and steady as always, but she could feel his adrenaline and emotions pumping from his hand to hers.

After a moment, he finally spoke, his voice lower and more level than before. "I have never needed a friend, Capri," he told her, "until now."

She squeezed his hand, her lips curving. "Do you think if I hadn't been taken that we would have been friends growing up?"

His lips twitched into a cynical smile. "I don't know. I don't think so."

"I think we would have found a way." She watched him thoughtfully as she shifted closer, leaning against him. She rested her head on his shoulder, and kept her hand linked with his between them. She felt his head turn and his cheek lightly brush against her hair, sending welcomed shivers down her spine.

They sat together in silence, hands joined, neither exactly sure where their feelings for each other fit in with the madness that threatened to consume their world.

## Chapter Thirteen

*Thousands of years* in existence was bound to give a person insight into the nature of things. For example, it only took one or two bloody and vicious wars to see the fundamental cause and effect, and to see the signs when another one was brewing in the hearts and minds of men. History was always bound to repeat itself, unless it was tactfully and dutifully observed. Even in the case of vast, powerful empires, it was always obvious that they couldn't possibly stay in control for long. They always crumbled, often costing thousands of lives, because of undeniable greed and an unholy sense of human superiority.

It was because of her uncanny sense of predicting outcomes that Thea mentally patted herself on the back over her latest prediction. From the moment she had seen Capri again, spoken with her, acknowledged her wants and needs, and she had recognized another who would ultimately need her just as badly as she would need him.

And so, as she strolled along the cobblestone pathway in the courtyard, morning sunlight highlighting the rich chocolate in her hair, she spotted the two of them, and the sight of it warmed her heart.

She had never considered herself a hopeless romantic. Being an immortal and living for as long as she had thus far had long since dried out her inner sense of romance. But she could appreciate the image of young love as well as the next person. She certainly wasn't heartless, after all. She loved Sebastian with a deep, powerful devotion that could never be comprehended by anyone other than him, and him alone. Their love went beyond the normal, and he was as much a part of her as her own eyes, ears, and mouth.

But in the case of her youngest Dryad and her most promising Fury, it appeared that she had been spot on in encouraging that they get to know each other. It had all started when she had asked Rian to bring Capri down to dinner the night after she had first relived her dream. She had noticed the hesitation in his eyes, but he had followed her orders obediently regardless, and look at how happy they both were. She was always right in her predictions. Well, almost always.

They were currently sitting beneath one of the largest and oldest trees in the courtyard, seated on the supple, green grass at its base. Rian was leaning against the tree, his legs folded casually, his arms resting on his knees. He looked more relaxed than Thea had ever seen him before, and it only made her more sure that this was good for him. The boy needed to lighten up, especially since things were only going to get harder for him. He had always been a serious child, never playing with the other children, keeping to himself, following his father around like a faithful, obedient puppy. Perhaps Roarke had been too hard on his son, encouraging him to work all hours of the day, and rarely giving him a chance to experience the innocence of youth. But no one could question just how much he loved his son, and how much his son loved him. It was sheer and unshakable devotion on both sides, and Thea had to admire the two of them for that.

Capri sat across from him, little brown birds fluttering all around her, chirping cheerfully as they fed on grain from her open palm. She was laughing, her smile lovely and bright, and the sound like the gentle chime of bells. Thea watched as Capri encouraged one of the birds to land in Rian's hand, and she smiled at the startled look on his face as the bird began to dance in his open palm.

Yes, they gave something to each other that wouldn't have been found elsewhere, Thea concluded, feeling content. Capri needed his stability, his cool, clear mind and unshakable strength. And Rian needed her innocence, her easy humor and her open heart.

As she approached them, Rian turned and watched her warily, his eyes suddenly guarded. Capri looked startled and unsure, and in her confusion the birds scattered, making their hasty escape into the trees.

"Rian...Capri." Thea nodded at the two of them, her smile warm. Rian nodded in return, his face carefully blank, but Capri smiled sweetly, glowing with happiness.

"Good afternoon, Thea." Capri brushed the seeds from her palm into the grass, then made to stand up before Thea stopped her.

"No need to get up. In fact, I think I'll just have a seat myself. It's been too long since I've sat in the courtyard," Thea told them as she sat gracefully on the grass, tucking the long skirt of her jade colored dress underneath her and shaking back her long dark hair. When she was seated comfortably, she turned to both of them, smiling. "I suppose I should just cut to the chase and bring up what it is I have to say." She sighed, and her warm smile faded as the seriousness of the situation returned to her mind. For a moment, she had let herself forget just how bad things were. She could only hope that these two were as strong as she thought, and that they could survive what was sure to befall both of them very soon.

"Alastor came to me this morning and told me about Roarke being possessed. Naturally, he also told me that he had told you two about it before he came to me." Amusement flickered briefly across her face as she turned to Capri. "As you know, you and Roarke were both possessed by the same demon. I feel it is necessary that we keep this information to ourselves for the time being. I have my own suspicions, which I will not share with you at this time, but I do want to ask both of you to put this to rest for the moment. This is a very dangerous situation, and we must be careful who we trust with this information. Someone, most likely one of those amongst us, is responsible for this, and therefore it is of the utmost importance that we not speak of it just yet."

Rian looked irritated, but Capri nodded. "We wouldn't have said anything anyway."

Thea's lips curved slightly. "Good. But please promise me that you both will discontinue your efforts in investigating this." Her gaze flicked to Rian and she watched him very closely, aiming her words at him. "I'm warning you now that this is quite possibly the most dangerous threat Euphora has ever faced, and I am ashamed to say that I, for once, did not see this coming."

"So you expect us to just sit by and twiddle our thumbs?" Rian said, barely controlling the anger in his voice. He wanted to show respect to Thea, but her request was taking things a bit too far. "My father is dead and you expect me to do nothing?"

"Yes, because I cannot afford to lose another Fury," Thea responded, her eyes sharpening. "And I certainly do not want to lose my Air Dryad now that she has so recently returned to me."

"Thea…if I may, there is a lot at stake here for both Rian and myself, and I promise we won't do anything brash or dangerous…but please, don't ask us to stop trying to figure this all out."

Thea looked at Capri. "Trust me, this goes beyond what either of you can even imagine. I'm ordering the two of you to drop the subject completely. I will take over the investigation from here, utilizing outside sources, and we will get to the bottom of this.

I need you both to stay alert and focused, but do not go looking for trouble. The last thing I need is to bury another member of my family because of this asshole, whoever he is."

Tears threatened her eyes as she thought of Roarke, but she willed them away. Crying never solved anything, even when emotions were running high. She stood up swiftly and carefully brushed at the grass on her skirt before facing them again.

"I'm in the mood for a good rainstorm today," she stated with a smile as she turned away, her head tilting to look up at the sunny sky. Suddenly, clouds appeared out of nowhere and steady rain began to shimmer to the ground.

Capri stared after Thea's retreating figure as she got to her feet, grateful the tree protected them momentarily from the rain. When she turned to Rian, she saw him stand and shrug out of his t-shirt.

He held up the shirt, holding it over her head like a make-shift umbrella. "Let's get inside before you get too wet."

She tried to hide the embarrassment she felt at unexpectedly seeing him shirtless, and raced beside him as they headed back to the castle. Once inside the atrium, he pulled the soaking wet shirt back over himself, and she couldn't help but grin, humor in her eyes.

He looked at her as he ran a hand through his damp hair, arching an eyebrow and smirking. "What?"

"It's just that no one's ever gone shirtless just so my hair wouldn't get wet before." She bit her lip, trying not to laugh. "It was very...chivalrous of you."

He dug his hands into the pockets of his jeans, trying not to be amused. "Would you prefer if I let you catch a cold?"

"Of course not!" Her eyes lit up as she smiled again, enjoying herself. "It's just that you made me feel like I was a princess or something...it was nice."

"I see..." he murmured, watching her carefully. "I'm certainly no prince charming."

She shook her head, smiling as she stepped closer to him, amazed at her own daring. "To me you are."

She tilted her head up just slightly, her eyes focused on his. So serious, so steady. Unshakable.

Perhaps it was that the moment presented itself, because under normal circumstances she knew she would never have the courage to do what she was about to do.

But seeing him, wet from the rain, his serious blue eyes intent on hers, knowing everything they had gone through together in such a short amount of time, she found no other suitable course of action but to kiss him.

And kiss him she did. Shyly, at first, her lips barely teasing his, her eyes open and gauging his reaction. But when he grabbed her waist and pulled her closer, deepening the kiss, she closed her eyes and let go.

Joy burst through her stomach, mixing with nerves and anticipation. Shimmering waves ran through her as her arms wound around his neck, her hands diving into his wet hair. Her heart shuddered and stumbled, and her mind cleared of everything but him.

She gradually pulled away, biting her lip in an attempt to curb the smile she knew had come across her face. His hands were still around her waist, and somehow she felt protected.

They were only a few inches apart, and when his hand came up to cup her cheek, sliding gently down to her neck, she shivered despite not feeling even the slightest bit cold.

"Again," he murmured, his mouth seeking hers. His hand wound its way into her hair as his other hand trailed to her lower back, holding her closer against him.

The kiss was gentle, yet eager, and the warmth she felt from him surprised and comforted her. She hadn't known it could be like this...especially from someone like him. He, who always projected so much strength and strict discipline. Who, at first glance, appeared so hard, so callous and cold. But he wasn't... there was so much more to him than she had ever imagined.

This time he pulled away, his eyes searching hers, his hand still cupped behind her neck. He didn't say anything, just watched her, until she felt compelled to speak.

"That was…nice." She blushed at the look he gave her.

"Nice?" He smirked as he let go of her, distancing himself. "I suppose I should be flattered?"

She crossed her arms over herself protectively, feeling foolish. "What I meant was, it was nice to finally do what I've wanted to do ever since you saved me from that demon. I never did properly thank you." She looked up at him, smiling again. "Consider yourself thanked."

There was humor in his eyes as he continued to watch her. "I can't think of a better way to say thank you than that."

"Good." She let her arms fall to her sides as her grin faded, the memory of what Thea had told them returning to her. "I suppose we have to do what Thea said."

His face hardened, the bitterness evident in his eyes. "I don't see a way around it. It's too hard to hide anything from her."

"Well, maybe this is a good thing," Capri suggested, gauging his reaction. "We were at a dead end anyway, and Thea was right, it would be foolish for us to put ourselves in harm's way." She reached for his hands, holding them in her own. "Your father wouldn't have wanted you to hurt yourself over this. He would have wanted you to continue your work, to make him proud."

"When I find out who did this, I might just have to kill them. I think he'd respect that."

"Oh, no, don't say that." Capri looked startled, her eyes wide. "You have to let Thea deal with it."

"You don't understand." Anger flashed in his eyes, but his voice remained steady as he continued. "Actually, I would think you would, because this bastard is responsible for your mother's death as well. We both lost parents because of him, and you don't feel any anger?"

"Of course I do!" Capri managed, unnerved by his words. "But I believe in justice, and I believe that once he is uncovered, Thea will punish him justly."

"Sometimes justice takes too long," he murmured, and she could tell there was misery behind his anger.

"Rian…" She reached up to touch his face, hoping to comfort him. "I know this is hard, but—"

A sudden noise behind them had her turning just in time to see her father, Liam, and Lucian turn the corner and walk down the corridor, heading right toward them. The men were talking and laughing, but the moment they saw Capri and Rian, they quieted, concern on their faces.

Capri's hand dropped from Rian's face as she stepped back slightly, shifting to face her father and the others as they stopped a few feet away. She tried to smile, but it scarcely hid her embarrassment.

"Did you guys come down to see the rain?" she asked, motioning to the entrance doors. The sound of the pattering rain could be heard beyond the castle walls.

"Looks like you've already seen it," Liam commented, eyeing Rian's wet shirt and hair, eyebrows raised. He smiled just slightly, but it barely concealed his suspicion and disapproval.

"Capri, you shouldn't stand out in the rain without an umbrella, you'll catch a cold," Clynn scolded, though he could see very well that her hair was not wet at all. He looked at Rian, who was standing so still he could have been a statue.

"I wasn't standing in the rain…I ran into Rian in the courtyard and he used his shirt to cover me so I wouldn't get wet."

The alarmed look in her father's eyes and Liam's snort of disapproval had Capri wincing at her choice of words. She saw Rian shift uncomfortably out of the corner of her eye, and she wished desperately for an amicable way out of the situation.

"Well, perhaps we should head outside for a stroll before Thea decides rain is no longer in style," Lucian said suddenly with a bright smile, lifting up his large blue and white striped umbrella. Clynn nodded, still looking apprehensive.

"Capri, would you like to join us?" he asked. "There's room enough for one more under the umbrella."

"Um…" she hesitated, her eyes shifting to Rian. He nodded just slightly. "Okay."

"Excellent!" Lucian beamed, obviously trying to smooth out the awkwardness of the situation as he stepped forward to open the entrance doors. He popped open the large umbrella, then stood beneath it as he stepped outside, looking cheerful as the rain showered around him.

Clynn pulled Capri along with him, nodding politely to Rian as they passed. Liam was the last to leave, and as he walked past Rian he sent him a warning look, as if to say, *I saw that, and I don't like it. Back off.*

Before she knew it, three weeks had flown by as if time was on fast forward. Capri had been working nearly every day, longer hours than before, due to what her father termed as *end of spring, early summer storm season*. Because of this, she was waking earlier and finishing later, exhausted from hours of creating and managing storm systems.

On top of work, her father began to teach her the different types of clouds, how they were formed, how smog and pollution affected the atmosphere, etc. He had given her stacks of books on the subject, and insisted she read them and take a quiz nearly every day. She understood his insistence that she learn as much as she could, but it was like he was literally cramming fifteen years worth of lessons into several weeks. And if that wasn't enough, she had a sneaking suspicion that his ulterior motive behind this was because he wanted her to see as little of Rian as possible. The reason, as of yet, was a complete mystery to her.

Despite him not even once mentioning the incident in the atrium just weeks earlier, she could tell it was constantly on his mind. Whenever they would go down to lunch, he would make sure it was always after Rian normally ate. Even at dinner, he would engage her in conversation with the Dryads so she wouldn't have time to speak with the Furies.

She figured he thought he was being sneaky with all of his careful planning and precautions...but she was on to him.

And she didn't appreciate any of it, not one bit.

She was never one to question the authority of adults, much less her own parent now that she had one. But there was something about the fact that she was eighteen, a full grown adult capable of making her own choices that fueled her desire to want to break the rules for once.

Not to mention the fact that she was sure Rian thought she was avoiding him on purpose. The very thought of it bothered her so greatly that she kept trying to think of ways to get past her father's protective grasp and talk to Rian alone. But, in the span of three whole weeks, she had yet to be successful in any of her attempts.

Twice her father had thwarted her suggestion to retrieve more books from the library by insisting on accompanying her, saying that he knew all the best books and it would take her much too long to locate them. Another time he had called her bluff about having a headache, insisting instead on her taking an aspirin and sitting down to rest beside him while he continued to work.

It was becoming increasingly obvious that it was going to take a miracle for her to be able to break free from him.

It was surprising that he would react this way about her and Rian, even though she had never told him about her feelings for him. She had been under the impression that he liked Rian and respected him, based upon how she had seen him act around the Furies before. Maybe his distrust over the situation was merely a father being protective of his only daughter, and wanting her all to himself. It made sense that her father didn't want her to spend time with another male, especially when he had barely spent much time with her himself. They had been apart from each other for fifteen years, after all, and any father in that situation would probably be defensive over letting his daughter date anyone.

But it worried her that maybe it was more than that. Maybe the prejudice that Liam and Blythe had against the Furies was something that her father believed as well. How all of them thought the Furies were cold and merciless was beyond her. She could see how Balgaire and Brogan could be taken that way, but Rian? He was intelligent, brave, considerate and selfless. He made her feel safe, protected, and secure, something she had never realized she so desperately wanted.

Thea had not mentioned anything about Roarke in weeks, not to the Council or to Capri. Instead, she pretended that nothing out of the ordinary was happening, and that all was well. It was only when Capri saw the worried crease between Thea's eyebrows every once in awhile at dinner that she knew Mother Earth was lost in thought about the subject. It troubled her that it hadn't been solved yet, but she had promised Thea that she wouldn't worry herself over it, and so she tried to push it to the back of her mind.

Roarke's body had been cremated, his ashes spread over the cliffs' edge and out to sea. By the time Capri had found out about it, Thea, Rian, and Alastor had already quietly completed the task. It bothered her that her father had failed to mention it, claiming it had apparently slipped his mind. This, perhaps more than anything else, caused a rift between their normally amiable and loving relationship.

She wasn't good at confronting others or speaking her mind when something bothered her, so instead she resorted to showing her irritation through silence. She barely spoke to him, and when she did, it was passive and curt. She knew he could tell something was wrong, but she refused to explain when he asked.

In her mind, he should know exactly why she was upset with him, and she shouldn't need to explain.

And so, after another long work day with her dutifully giving him the silent treatment, she slipped down to dinner, exhausted and miserable, and tried, as always, to look better than she felt.

Of course, she was no actress, nor was she good at hiding her emotions, and so it took mere seconds for Blythe to comment.

"You look awful."

Capri couldn't help the annoyed look that crossed her face, cocking one eyebrow and pursing her lips as she turned to stare at her friend.

When Blythe started laughing, Capri felt even more irritated.

"Shut up," she spat, turning back to her food, her rarely used temper flashing like lightning bolts around her. Blythe's laughter immediately died, and her own temper, much too readily used, flared up.

"Sheesh, what's your problem?" she countered, turning in her seat to face Capri. "You've been acting this way for weeks, what the hell is going on with you?"

"It's nothing," Capri began to cut viciously into the chicken breast on her plate, her hands shaking. "Absolutely nothing."

Liam, who was sitting across the table from her, watched her knowingly. "I think the problem is that you're overworked."

"Tip of the iceberg," Capri muttered, feeling her visage of indifference come crashing down. Tears welled in her eyes and she cursed herself for being an emotional wreck. "I'm not even hungry."

She pushed her plate away and began to stand up, only to have Blythe pull her back down.

"I've never seen you act like this." Blythe's temper cooled as concern deftly replaced it. "Maybe you need a break, honey."

Capri pouted, feeling resigned. "I need more than a break, I need a therapist."

Blythe's face flashed with a grin as she patted Capri on the back. "I've got something better." She leaned over the table toward Liam, covertly glancing around to make sure none of the adults were listening. "Liam, go down to the wine cellar and get us a couple of bottles. Meet me and Capri outside in the court-yard in twenty minutes."

Liam nodded with a grin. "Aye, aye, captain." He stood up and excused himself, winking at Capri and Blythe as he left the dining hall.

Capri turned to Blythe, her eyes wide. "We're stealing wine?"

"It's not really stealing…I mean, it's there for everyone to drink, so what's the big deal if we take a few bottles?"

"I suppose…" Capri bit her lip, worried what would happen if they were caught. Then she realized that this was exactly the kind of rebellion she needed to feel free again. "Alright, what are we waiting for?"

"Absolutely nothing." Blythe grinned wickedly as she rose from her chair, politely excusing herself. She practically skipped out of the dining hall, her fiery hair bouncing as she walked.

Capri turned to her father and, with the most innocent look-ing expression she could muster, explained that she was going outside with Blythe and Liam. He beamed at her, clearly excited that she had spoken more than two words to him and that she seemed happier. He waved her off, obviously content that Rian would not be welcome if Liam was involved. She stood up and was about to leave the dining hall when she spotted Rhiannon pretending not to watch her as she added salt to the potatoes on her plate.

Feeling impulsive, Capri leaned down next to Rhiannon to whisper in her ear.

"Liam, Blythe and I are having a little party out in the court-yard, will you come with us?"

Rhiannon looked up at her, startled, and for a moment seemed to consider all angles of the request before answering. "I'll think about it."

Capri tried to hide her disappointment, but she knew she should have expected hesitation from Rhiannon. After all, it was no secret that Blythe and Rhiannon did not get along. Capri just felt that maybe it was time that she tried to bring them back together again, to see if there was any way to bridge the gap between them.

She nodded and smiled as she pulled away and left the dining hall, closing the door behind her with a quiet click. The corridor was dimly lit by lanterns on the walls, and was eerily silent. Feeling energized and devious, she made her way to the atrium, where Blythe was waiting for her.

"Come on!" Blythe whispered, her amber eyes glittering with excitement in the firelight.

The two of them headed out into the courtyard, Blythe leading the way down the cobblestone path. They walked all the way to the far left corner, where, up against the stone wall, a small square of grass roughly eight feet across was hidden from view by tall, leafy plants. Blythe pushed aside a large branch so Capri could enter, and immediately she proceeded to create a fire pit.

"I didn't know this place was here." Capri glanced around as Blythe knelt down in front of the pit she had created and cupped her hands, forming a ball of fire which she then released into it. It hovered just above the dirt, the flames licking at the night air.

"Actually, you *used* to know this place was here," Blythe told her as she plopped down on the grass, grinning. "All four of us used to come here when we were really little. It used to freak our parents out since they had no idea where we were, but we got a kick out of it."

"Yet another thing that I wish I could remember," Capri mused, nestling down in the grass beside Blythe. She turned to her friend and reached out for her hand, holding it in her own. "I'm sorry I snapped at you earlier."

Blythe laughed, the husky sound of it echoing off the stone wall. "Are you kidding? I've been waiting for you to crack ever since you got here. You're always so nice; you're entitled to a moment of bitchiness once in a while."

Capri snorted, her lips curving. "I suppose I am, aren't I?"

"Damn straight."

Just then, Liam appeared through the plants, a couple of bags in his arms. A grin flashed over his face as he spotted the two of them.

"Ladies…." He set the bags down and sat across from them, reaching in to dig out the contents. "As your humble servant, I bring alcohol, s'mores and cheese!"

"Really, Liam? Cheese?" Blythe snickered, reaching for the wine bottle he handed to her.

"What is wine without cheese?" He winked at Capri, passing her a wine glass.

Capri held the glass as Blythe uncorked a bottle of pinot noir and poured generously for her. She eyed the wine before taking a tentative sip, the velvet tartness of it smooth on her tongue.

"Here's to breaking the rules and having fun while we do it!" Blythe held her full glass up in a toast, her face glowing from the fire, split in a mischievous grin.

Capri and Liam held their glasses up, clinking them against Blythe's before they all took a deep sip.

Just then, a rustling sound came from the plants, and seconds later Rhiannon appeared, gently pushing aside the branches and entering their secret hideout.

Capri saw surprise flash over Liam's face and irritation over Blythe's, and took the split second to not only lay a warning hand over Blythe's arm, but to also smile warmly at Rhiannon.

"I'm glad you came. Please, sit down." Capri turned to Liam and Blythe, trying to keep the situation light. "I invited Rhiannon; I thought it would be nice for all of the Dryads to be together tonight."

"Good idea." Liam smiled as Rhiannon sat beside him, tucking the skirt of her sapphire blue dress beneath her. She eyed him warily before turning to Capri, her lips curving in a tiny smile.

"I wasn't going to come, but I knew it would make you happy if I did."

Capri felt Blythe bristle beside her, but she kept her hand firm on the other girl's arm.

"It makes me very happy." She also saw that Liam looked noticeably perked up as well, which only made her more sure that it had been right to invite Rhiannon. Turning to Blythe, Capri put on her best peacemaker's smile. "I was hoping we could all put aside our differences for the evening, and be together, just this once. You're my family…my sisters, my brother…I want to be here with all of you, to remember what it felt like…before."

Blythe pursed her lips, but nodded, and Capri could tell she understood. She let go of her arm and reached for her glass.

"Liam, do we have an extra glass?" she asked. Liam reached into the bag and pulled out another one.

"I'm always prepared for the unexpected," he said, passing the glass to Rhiannon, his smile kind. Rhiannon accepted the glass, watching carefully as he filled it.

"Thank you," she murmured, lifting the glass to her lips to sample the wine.

It bothered Capri how awkward the atmosphere had suddenly become, so she took another healthy swig of wine and turned to Liam. "So, what did we use this little hideout for when we were little?"

"Well, we used to pretend that we were fugitives on the run from our evil parents who wanted to imprison us and force us to eat vegetables and study, and this was our lair." He laughed at the memory, and how silly it sounded now that he was an adult.

"It's still kind of like that, isn't it?" Capri glanced around at the three of them, blushing at the confused looks they gave her. "I mean, I feel the need to hide from my dad right now…he's been driving me crazy."

"He has been working you pretty hard lately, hasn't he?" Blythe asked, sipping her wine. "I'm lucky; I don't have anyone to boss me around."

"Don't get me wrong, I love him, but he's been piling on more and more work and studying, on top of watching me like a hawk everywhere I go. It's been like that ever since..." She stopped herself, her eyes flicking instantly to Liam as she realized she had said too much. He paused midway at sipping his wine as his eyes narrowed.

"Since what?" Blythe asked curiously. Capri cursed herself for setting herself up for this dangerous trap.

"Um...since he decided I needed to brush up on more of the basics," she lied, knowing full well that she probably looked like she was hiding something.

"Maybe it's a good thing he's keeping you busy. He doesn't want you making any...mistakes," Liam told her seriously.

"Nah, I think he's working her too hard." Blythe pursed her lips as she noticed the hard look on his face. "Capri deserves time off, and as for mistakes, she hasn't made any yet."

He chuckled darkly, shaking his head. Rhiannon was looking at him with wide eyes, obviously unsure why he was acting so strangely. Even Blythe had one eyebrow cocked in confusion as she watched him.

"What's the deal, Liam?" Blythe shifted closer to Capri in a protective move that made Capri feel incredibly guilty. If Blythe knew the reason Liam was acting the way he was, then she would surely be on his side, not hers.

"It's not for me to say," Liam said, reaching for a slice of cheese from a plate he'd unearthed from one of the bags. He bit into it, smiling. "So, who wants to hear a scary story?"

## Chapter Fourteen

_And just like_ that, the subject was dropped. Capri was grateful that Liam didn't feel the need to divulge the information to the others. Despite how he may feel on the subject, he was still considerate enough to keep it to himself.

An hour and three exceptionally frightening ghost stories later, Capri felt incredibly cheerful and a little light headed. Blythe opened a third bottle of wine, and the happy popping sound of the cork was drowned out by laughter.

Liam, being naturally funny, had turned from scary stories to jokes in the blink of an eye, and unexpectedly had all three of them laughing. Capri didn't think she had ever laughed so much in her entire life, though she had to credit the wine for part of it, as she was feeling delightfully tipsy.

Against all odds, their little party had turned into quite the reunion that all of them had so desperately needed. Capri watched Rhiannon open up in a way she hadn't expected, and what she saw was fascinating. Who knew the highly polished and formal Rhiannon could be so...free? When she was enjoying herself, actually enjoying herself, she was positively wonderful to be around. Even Blythe seemed to notice the difference, and even though the two of them still held a certain amount of reserve with each other, they were at least communicating and laughing together. It warmed Capri's heart to see it, and to know that maybe all they had needed was someone neutral to come along and push them.

"Here." Blythe suddenly reached over to refill Capri's glass, and she winced at the amount of red liquid sloshing around in her glass.

"Oh, no, I shouldn't…" Capri bit her lip, contemplating as she watched the glow of the firelight through the deep red of the wine.

"Why not?" Blythe asked, sipping more herself and grinning. "You're rebelling, remember? Enjoy it."

"You know what? You're right." She held out the glass, clinking it with Blythe's, nearly spilling out the contents as she pulled it back to drink. She took a big gulp, and then covered her mouth as she started hiccupping. "Oh, shoot."

The others laughed, and Blythe patted Capri on the back sympathetically. "Hold your breath, honey."

Capri did as she was told, and after a few tries the hiccups subsided. She exhaled in relief, smiling again.

"I wish we had some music," she mused, sipping more wine.

"Actually, we used to keep a guitar out here just for times like this," Liam replied as he jumped up and immediately began rustling through one of the nearby shrubs, unearthing a natural wood acoustic guitar. He inspected it for a moment, checking the strings and fishing out a few leaves from its hollow core. "It got a bit wet from the rain a couple weeks ago, but I think it'll still work."

He sat back down beside Rhiannon and held the guitar in his lap, his fingers fine tuning the strings. He tested out the sound and, deeming it suitable, looked to Rhiannon with a grin.

"What song should I play, Rhia?" he asked her, his charming blue eyes watching her intently.

She paused, wondering whether she should suggest something. "I've always liked *Tiny Dancer.*"

"*Tiny Dancer* it is, then.'" He winked as he began to strum the guitar, mimicking the crisp, expressive sound of the piano from the original song. When he began to sing, his voice was smooth and poignant, and hit all the right notes.

Capri realized at that moment that despite all the bad things that had happened since she had come home to Euphora, she still had this. She had them. Her family, her friends...because of them, she knew her life was complete. She only hoped that sometime in the near future, she could bring Rian into this circle, and they could all be together.

Feeling sentimental, she pulled Blythe into a hug and swayed, her eyes welling with tears that had nothing to do with sadness.

When Rhiannon suddenly began to sing, picking up the next verse in the song without missing a beat, Capri watched her with a shocked smile. Her voice was lovely, lilting, and the smile she wore as she met Liam's eyes and sang was nothing short of mesmerizing.

Capri nodded to Blythe as the chorus began, and the two of them cheerfully joined in.

The following morning was not really what Capri would call the happiest morning of her life. It actually ranked pretty low on the scale of mornings, at least in regard to her overall physical wellbeing. Apparently, something about the combination of wine, singing, and laughing gave a person a miserable headache the next day. But, given the choice to do it differently, she would have changed nothing. In fact, she wouldn't have traded it for the world.

Relaxing and having fun with all three of her fellow Dryads had opened something up inside of her, a missing link that hadn't fallen into place until they were all brought together again. It was like the deep bond that connected them together had surfaced for one night, and they had for once experienced what it would be like if life were much simpler, and if circumstance hadn't driven them all apart.

And if experiencing that meant she had to suffer from a mild hangover the next day, then so be it. However, it wouldn't have been nearly as bad if Thea hadn't dutifully noticed it within moments of the four of them sitting down for breakfast.

"You four look a little worse for wear this morning," Thea commented, her lips curving into a smile as she buttered a piece of whole wheat toast. "I hope you had fun."

Capri flushed, then winced as her head pounded mercilessly. She tried to hide her reaction by gulping down hot, over sugared coffee.

Rhiannon had liberally applied makeup to her face that morning to cover up most of the puffiness around her eyes, but to Thea's well trained eye there was no disguising it. Blythe had taken less care in hiding how she felt, and instead was more bleary eyed and short-tempered than usual. Liam looked a little tired and disheveled, but obviously his duet with Rhiannon the night before had done wonders for his spiritual wellbeing. He seemed happy as a clam.

"I'll apologize in advance, Thea. This one talked us all into it." He pointed his thumb at Blythe, who immediately stepped on his foot.

"You were all too willing," Blythe muttered, forking up a bite of scrambled egg doused in ketchup.

"Yes, but it was your idea," he reminded her, gulping down nearly his entire glass of water.

"Regardless, it's nice that the four of you spent some time together," Thea put in. She smiled warmly at Capri. "It's been, what, fifteen years since it last happened?"

Capri nodded, blushing again under Thea's gaze.

"I could use a night of fun," Sebastian pouted a bit, winking at Liam as he nudged Thea gently in the arm.

Thea eyed him knowingly, her lips curving. "I suppose we could all stand to loosen up a little bit," she mused. "It's settled. Tonight, we shall have a formal event in the court-yard. Champagne, music, dancing..."

"Romance..." Sebastian supplied, leaning in and eyeing her suggestively.

"Yes," Thea replied, her eyes flicking to Capri and her smile widening. "We could all use a little bit of that, too."

At first, the idea of another party was not in any way appealing to Capri. She lay on her bed, her arm draped over her face, willing her headache away. But when her father came into her room, knocking politely, and she noticed what he held in his arms, her mood dramatically improved.

"This was your mother's," he told her, holding out the long, tea green dress for her to take. She sat up, reaching for it eagerly.

"It's beautiful," she murmured as she stared at the gown, taking in the single shoulder strap adorned with a blooming flower and the heart shaped neckline. The chiffon fabric layered over itself at the bodice, wrapping around to the low backline before dropping away into a long, smooth skirt.

"I know you've been...unhappy with me lately. I hoped we could make amends." He watched her closely, and the guilt and misery in his voice humbled her.

She sighed, setting the dress aside on the bed. Her hands twisted together in her lap as she tried to find the right words to say. "I just...don't understand why you don't want me to see Rian."

Blushing, she chanced a look at him, gauging his reaction.

"I just don't think he is right for you, Capri." He moved to sit down beside her, patting her back. "And, to be honest, I suppose I wanted you all to myself for awhile."

"I know you do…but I'm eighteen, and I can decide by myself who's right for me. I like him, and I don't want to stop seeing him just because you don't approve."

He inhaled deeply, regret clear on his face. "I've lived without you for so long, and when you came back to me, I suppose I expected you to need me more than you actually do. I never expected you to be a grownup, capable of making your own decisions, but you most certainly are."

"Of course I need you." She reached out for his hand, squeezing it gently. When he turned to look at her, she smiled. "I just need him, too."

"I guess part of me was hoping that you and Liam would hit it off…in that way," he admitted, smiling sheepishly at her.

Capri smirked at the idea, remembering how she had felt when she had first met Liam. He had been like a noble prince, rescuing her and bringing her home. "I guess from the moment I met him I thought of him as my brother. It just seemed that was the way it was meant to be between us."

Clynn sighed again, though this time his eyes were bright with amusement. "I guess Lucian and I won't get to share grandchildren like we always wanted."

Capri snorted. "You guys are already talking about grandchildren? Does Liam know this?"

"Of course he does. We bring up the topic as often as possible around him, trying to get him to make a move."

He's making moves, just not at me, Capri thought, remembering the night before and Liam and Rhiannon's duet.

"So, you'll wear the dress tonight?"

Capri nodded. "Yes, definitely."

"Will you let me escort you? I can come by at eight, after you've had time to get ready."

"That would be lovely." She leaned in and gave him a tender kiss on the cheek, feeling remarkably better about pretty much everything.

After dinner, Capri rushed upstairs with Blythe and Rhiannon to get ready. The three of them congregated in Capri's room, changing clothes and fussing with hair and makeup. It was like prom all over again, Capri mused, noting the gorgeous dresses both Blythe and Rhiannon had chosen to wear.

Blythe's dress was cut above knee-length and was a bold, electric blue, with no straps and a skirt that clung to every curve.

Contrasting in nearly every way other than impact, Rhiannon's dress was long and elegant, the color of molten steel, with thin straps lined with glittering jewels, crystal clear like diamonds. There was a slit up the right side, opening up the dress so she could walk, and showing off her long, slender legs.

While they certainly weren't "buddy buddy" with each other, Capri was pleased to see Blythe and Rhiannon being cordial, even helping zip up each other's dresses. It showed that they were both making a conscious effort to try and get along, no matter how hard it might be.

When Capri slipped into her own dress, she stepped in front of the mirror, and stared at her reflection for a full minute.

When Blythe and Rhiannon noticed, they both sighed in envy.

"You look so beautiful," Rhiannon told her, laying her hands gently on Capri's shoulders and smiling. "It's like it was made for you."

"See, I could never pull off a dress like that. Way too feminine for me," Blythe said, eyeing the dress thoughtfully. "But it suits you perfectly."

"Thanks." Capri bit her lip as she ran her hand down the light green fabric, seduced by how lovely it was. And knowing her mother had worn it, had loved it just as much as she loved it now, made it even more special.

"Let's do something fun with your hair, Capri. You always wear it down." Rhiannon lifted Capri's long, blonde hair up, piling it on top of her head, positioning it so a few tendrils fell down by her face. "See...an updo would show off your slender neck, and make you look taller, more sophisticated."

"That's good, right?" Capri asked, feeling giddy as she looked at herself in the mirror. She felt like a different person in this dress, more confident and elegant. In fact, she imagined she felt like Rhiannon did every day.

Rhiannon grinned at her. "Let me work my magic with you, and they won't even know what hit them."

She certainly didn't care about everyone else, but she wanted Rian to notice her. And as she walked arm-in-arm with her father out into the courtyard, where most of the people were already dancing and popping champagne, she saw him sitting at one of the many tables. When her eyes met his, she saw that Rhiannon had indeed been right. He looked absolutely and positively stunned.

She watched him start to stand up, but before he could do so, her father led her onto the dance floor and into a dance. She glanced over her father's shoulder, watching as Rian sat back down and sipped his champagne thoughtfully.

She smiled at him, hoping he noticed, but before she could make sure, she was engulfed by more people dancing and lost sight of him.

Focusing back on her father, she rested her head on his shoulder. "Do I look alright in the dress?"

"You look magnificent. Your mother would have loved to see you wear it," he replied, holding her tightly.

She felt sadness wash over her, missing the mother she had never really known, and she embraced it, knowing it didn't make her weak. It was just one of the many things that defined her.

As before, glowing balls of muted golden light hung in the air over the dance floor, and the music wafted in from seemingly nowhere. It was a slow, bluesy song, the female singer belting out about Memphis on a steamy, summer's night.

Enchanted, Capri felt herself let go, enjoying the moment, a serene feeling of contentment growing in her heart. While her fear and anxiety still rested at the back of her mind, she felt entitled to push it a bit deeper, just for the night, because at this very moment it seemed as though everything was finally right in the world.

She and her father were speaking to each other again, and he seemed to be warming to the idea of her seeing Rian. Blythe and Rhiannon were more or less on speaking terms, a big improvement over their normal hostility. Capri knew they were mostly doing it for her benefit, but that fact didn't bother her. Wasn't that what Rhiannon had said in the beginning? It had been losing Capri that had driven them apart. Well, now it would be she who would bring them together again.

When the song came to an end, her father pulled away from her, a slow smile crossing his face.

"I think there's someone who would like to dance with you, darling," he said, motioning over to where Rian was rising from his seat and approaching them.

Capri blushed, her heart aflutter as she watched him. He was wearing a three piece gunmetal gray suit with a black tie and shoes, and as usual he walked purposefully, his back straight and his eyes focused intently on her.

She tried to act casual, as though she did this every day. If only he knew how rapidly her pulse was skittering under her skin, and how fast her heart beat just looking at him.

Her father bowed his head just slightly at Rian when he reached them, and then left the dance floor, leaving the two of them alone.

"Would you like to dance?" Rian asked, holding out his hand to her.

"Okay." She took his hand and rested her other on his shoulder as he placed his on her waist. It was much more formal than she was used to when dancing with either her father or Liam, but she figured Rian was a more formal person, and he probably understood that everyone would be watching them very closely.

They turned in a slow circle on the dance floor, neither of them being very proficient dancers, though Capri couldn't care less about appearances. She was just delighted to be there.

"I'm sorry I haven't been able to talk to you for awhile...I hope you don't think it's because I didn't want to."

"We've both been busy," he stated, his lips curving slightly. "And I imagine certain outside forces may have had a role."

She sighed, feeling foolish. "Over protective fathers and brother-types are very hard to fool. And I'm already a horrible liar."

When he laughed, she blinked, startled at the sound of it. Had he ever really laughed around her before?

"I've missed you," he said, his eyes softening. Her heart fluttered even more, and she was pretty much certain he could feel her pulse quickening beneath his hand.

"I've missed you, too." She smiled warmly, instinctively shifting closer to him, until their bodies were touching just slightly.

She felt the hand on her waist pull her in even closer, until she had to tilt her head up to look at him. Her eyes were on his, and for a few moments, neither of them felt the need to speak. Music wafted lazily on the air as Ben E. King let them know he wouldn't be afraid, as long as they stood by him.

Perhaps it was the mood of the moment, or maybe the lyrics of the song, but she found herself engulfed in an emotion she had never before felt. She felt safe, whole, and above all, she felt wanted. Not just needed, in the way that the people of Euphora needed her for *what* she was. But wanted, because of *who* she was. It both thrilled and unnerved her to see it so clearly in his eyes that he wanted her.

As the song came to a close, she exhaled, not realizing she had been holding her breath. He pulled away from her, but kept his hand over hers.

When a new song started up, this time a fast paced, rock and roll beat, Capri bit her lip against a sheepish smile.

"I don't really know how to dance to something like this."

He glanced around at the people who were still dancing. They heard Blythe cheer excitedly as she pulled Lucian out to dance, the two of them once again showing off to the less talented dancers.

"Me neither. Want to go for a walk?"

"Sure."

They left the dance floor, still hand in hand, and headed out into the darkened courtyard, over to a small bench hidden from view by a large tree. They were still within earshot of the party, but far enough away to not be heard or seen.

Capri sat down, brushing at the skirt of her dress, nerves eating away at what was left of her stomach. She watched him sit beside her, noting how he scanned around them, seemingly out of habit, ensuring they were alone.

She reached out for his hand, hoping to relax him.

Around them, fireflies were hovering in the still, night air and she could hear crickets chirping musically from the nearby flowery plants. Moonlight shone from overhead, cascading through the branches of the tree above them to highlight the grass at their feet. In the distance, she could still hear the music, and the buzzing conversation of those seated at the tables.

They were silent for awhile, both unsure what to say. It was the first time they had really been alone in weeks, and Capri couldn't seem to remember any of the things she had wanted to say to him. Except, of course, for one.

"I'm sorry I wasn't there when you spread your father's ashes." She watched him turn to face her, his expression hard to read. "I should have been there for you."

"It's alright," he told her, misery flashing in his eyes momentarily as the memory resurfaced. That final moment of accepting his father's death and letting go had been the hardest thing he had ever gone through. And it had troubled him that it had hurt even more because she hadn't been there, that he had needed her to be. It was a feeling he needed to get used to. "Thea said that your father would have been suspicious if you had come."

"Maybe, but when I found out he had *forgotten* to tell me, I didn't speak more than two words to him for almost three weeks." She smiled faintly, shrugging her shoulders. "But we're past that. I don't think he'll get in the way again."

"I don't blame him for not encouraging this. I'm not what most fathers would consider best for their daughters," he paused. "I have a very…dangerous line of work. I'm sure he would prefer you with the Water Dryad."

Capri pursed her lips as she stared at him, indignation rising within her. "I don't care what he thinks, and I don't care what everyone else thinks. I want you and that's all that matters." Her cheeks flushed at the look he gave her, his eyebrows raised and his serious eyes filled with humor. "That is, as long as you want me…"

He chuckled, amused by her. "I've never understood why you are so unsure of yourself." He reached over to cup his hand below her cheek, leaning toward her. "You're beautiful, kind, smart… how could anyone not want you?"

"They never have before," she faltered, her heart racing again as he leaned in, his lips teasing hers. Her eyes fluttered closed as her breath caught in her throat, the thrill and anticipation washing over her in glorious waves. She leaned into him instinctively, her hands trailing up his chest.

"Lucky for me, then," he whispered, kissing her fully. She felt her heart do one slow, easy tumble. "By the way, you look stunning in that dress."

Her lips curved against his as she smiled. "Thanks. You don't look half bad yourself."

"Mmm." He deepened the kiss, both hands cupping her face, reveling in the feel of her soft skin and the warmth of her quiet sigh as she yielded to him, as caught up in the moment as he was.

Her hands clutched his jacket, holding him to her as her mind went blissfully blank.

A sudden scream from behind broke them apart, and they turned in the direction of the party. Capri's eyes were wide as she tried to see what was happening, and she felt Rian stand up beside her, one hand protectively resting on her shoulder.

She could see people crowding around one of the tables and several of them were shouting. When the crowd parted, Capri saw that Rohan had Blythe by the hair and had dragged her to the floor.

"*You are nothing but trash!*" Rohan shouted, his face red, madness in his eyes.

"Screw you!" Blythe swung out with her free arm and cold cocked Rohan in the jaw, causing him to howl in pain and release her. She would have stood and taken another swing at him if Liam and Lucian hadn't held her back, both crouching beside her, holding her arms.

"Oh my God," Capri whispered, her eyes wide with shock. "Blythe." She got to her feet and began to run to her friend, worry and fear racing through her. Rian grabbed her arm, however, slowing her down.

"She's fine. I don't want you going near Rohan," he said firmly.

"No, I need to go to her." She pulled her arm from his grasp and despite his hesitation, she lifted her skirt and raced to the dance floor, where Blythe was still being restrained by the others.

She heard Rian behind her, but she didn't stop, her complete focus on Blythe. When she reached her, she knelt down beside her friend, worry in her eyes. "Are you okay?" Capri asked, reaching to touch Blythe's shoulder.

"I'm fine. Back the hell off," Blythe spat, her temper at a vicious boiling point. She swatted Capri's hand away as she stood, her legs shaking from rage. Without saying a word, she shook Liam and Lucian off of her and stormed off to the castle.

Capri, pale with shock, watched her leave. When she felt Rian lay his hands on her shoulders, she jolted at his touch.

"Rohan!" Thea's voice thundered over the music as she approached, fury on her face. "Your conduct is outrageous! How dare you disrespect another member of the Council in this manner?"

"I–I apologize, Thea," Rohan stammered, his face no longer red. Instead it was ghostly pale. "I don't know what came over me."

Beside him, his wife, Serendipity, was holding his arm, distress and anger on her beautiful face. In the distance, Capri spotted Rhiannon, who looked numb, her face blank and her eyes glassy.

"Get inside and cool off. I expect you to apologize to Blythe first thing in the morning," Thea ordered, inhaling deeply to calm herself. Sebastian stood behind her, his expression livid.

Rohan immediately did as instructed and went back to the castle with his wife in tow. Capri watched Liam start to walk over to Rhiannon to offer comfort, however, she took off before he could reach her, racing after her parents.

Deeply troubled, Capri turned to Rian.

"She didn't need me, I guess," she mumbled, tears forming in her eyes.

"No." He lifted her chin up, making sure she looked at him. "She doesn't need you right now. But she will need you tomorrow. Give her time to cool down."

"I just hate feeling so helpless," she told him, worry creasing her forehead. "How could Rohan try and hurt her like that?"

"Hate causes even great men to do terrible things." He watched her closely, hating the sadness in her eyes. "I'd be interested to know what she said to set him off like that."

Capri couldn't help the small smile that crossed her lips. "She can be…sassy, sometimes."

He smirked, pleased to see her lighten up. "Yes, she can."

"Capri!" Clynn appeared suddenly, looking distraught. He stopped in front of them and tried to catch his breath, bottles in his arms. "I was inside getting more champagne and I heard shouting. Are you alright?"

"I'm fine," she reassured him. "It was Rohan, he attacked Blythe. She's okay, though. She just went up to bed."

"Dear God…why did he attack her?"

"I'm not really sure." She stared at the castle, silently hoping her assumption about Blythe being okay was correct.

"Well, it looks like the party is over," Clynn commented as he glanced around. Most of the people were heading inside, heads together, buzzing with gossip. "Just as well, there's plenty of work to be done tomorrow. We should get some sleep. Shall we go inside, Capri?"

"Alright." She turned to Rian, trying to smile. "Goodnight."

"Goodnight." He nodded to her, and based on the way they acted no one would guess they had been exchanging kisses just minutes before.

Capri noticed her father smile and nod at Rian, though it was not entirely friendly. There was still uncertainty there, and it pained her to see it. He wrapped his free arm around her, leading her back to the castle.

She sighed, resigned with the knowledge that her brief night of peace had come crashing down in glorious flames.

## Chapter Fifteen

*When Capri awoke* the next morning, she lay silent for a long while, her mind filled with worry and her heart heavy with emotion. Morning sunlight filtered in through her gauzy canopy, and through her open window she could hear birds happily chirping. Her chest rose and fell evenly, her eyes staring blankly above as she lost herself in thought.

Her mother's dress lay on the wooden chair beside the bed, and when she looked at it, her eyes filled with unexpected tears. She shut them resentfully, feeling the tears fall down her cheeks as she rolled over, covering herself with her blankets.

In the darkness under the covers, she could hear her own heart beat, feel her breath warm on her arm. All it did was remind her that she was alive, while two other people were not...her mother and Rian's father. Both had died at the hands of the same person and she was powerless to do anything about it.

Seeing Rohan's outburst against Blythe the night before had shocked awareness back into her. There was a real and imminent danger on Euphora, and if Rohan was involved, he might very well target

Blythe, or Rian, or Liam. Capri knew she couldn't stand by and let any of them be harmed. If it was Rohan who was responsible, then Rhiannon was most likely safe, but even then, who knew how deep his madness went. Maybe he would even target his own daughter.

Shivering at the thought, she took a deep breath, trying to calm herself. Nothing was solved by hiding away, she told herself as she tossed the covers off and sat up in bed. Everything was solved by action. And her first course of action was to make sure Blythe was alright. Then she would find Thea and talk to her personally about the status of the investigation, namely Rohan's likely involvement in everything.

She stood up and got ready, taking a quick bath and getting dressed. She hoped to catch Blythe before she went down to breakfast, so she headed out into the hallway just outside her bedroom, shutting the door quietly behind her. A few doors down was Blythe's room, and when she reached it she knocked lightly on the door.

Hearing a grunt in response, she opened the door. Blythe sat in bed, still in her pajamas, throwing darts made out of fire at a board across the room. Capri watched as she threw one expertly, hitting the bull's eye dead on. The dart was destroyed in a puff of smoke, leaving behind a black burn mark.

"How are you?" Capri tentatively asked, shutting the door behind her. Blythe grunted again, her face tight with anger as she threw another dart.

"I've been better," Blythe said suddenly, inhaling sharply as she threw another dart. This time she missed the mark completely and burnt a hole in the wall. "Damnit!"

Capri jumped at her outburst, but she didn't move. When Blythe noticed the shock in her friend's eyes, she sighed.

"I'm sorry, Capri, come here," she said, holding out her hand and motioning for Capri to join her.

Capri sat, her hand in Blythe's, and watched her carefully. "I can come back later if this is a bad time."

"No, it's not. I'm just…pissed." Blythe chuckled darkly, shaking her head. "That bastard drives me crazy."

"Rohan?"

"Yeah. He's always had a problem with me, just because of who I am. It's bullshit, really, but there's nothing I can do about it."

Capri's brows furrowed in confusion as she continued to watch her friend. "I don't understand."

Blythe shifted, curling her legs underneath her. "It's really stupid and pathetic." She pursed her lips, her anger rising again. "He hates me because he hated my dad."

When Capri didn't say anything, Blythe continued.

"When our parents were our age, my dad was dating Serendipity, Rhiannon's mom. They were an item for a long time, and everyone thought they were gonna get married. But then, for some reason, Serendipity left my dad and married Rohan instead. Up until that time, Rohan and my dad were best friends, and this obviously destroyed their friendship. Anyway, ever since then Rohan always suspected that Serendipity was cheating on him with my dad, even though he had married my mother and had started his own family. They didn't speak one word to each other for years, and when the raid happened and my dad was banished, Rohan was one of the people who helped prove his guilt."

"And he hates you because of association?" Capri asked, her eyes wide.

"Pretty much." Blythe shrugged. "Though I've been told I act a lot like my dad, so I bet it's hard for him. Personally, I enjoy thinking that I bother him. Sometimes I even go out of my way to annoy him just to see him get all flustered." She grinned, quick and mischievous.

"Is that what happened last night?"

Her grin faded to disgust. "No. He started *that* little fight." She ran a hand through her red curls, combing through them with her fingers. "I caught him talking crap, saying how I was bound to go down the same path as my dad and my grandmother, and that I would end up banished because it's in my nature to break the rules. Naturally, I confronted him about it, and because he hates being confronted, he grabbed me and threw me to the ground. He's such a goddamn coward." She sneered, her fist clenching. "At least I got a punch in. Bastard's lucky Liam held me back, because I would have done much worse."

"I'm sure you would have." Capri nodded seriously, causing Blythe to laugh as her lips curved into a sad smile.

"I'm sorry if I snarled at you last night. I was seeing red, and I didn't want to take it out on any of you. When I get like that, I pretty much have to leave or I might do something I'll regret later."

Capri tried to smile, squeezing her friend's hand. "I understand."

"Anyway, I think Rohan's been on edge lately," Blythe began. "He's never gotten violent like that with me, so I think the stress has gotten to him."

"Why do you think he's stressed?" Capri's heart began to beat faster, her mind racing with the possible reasons.

"Well, he's convinced himself that my father is involved in what's been happening lately and Roarke's confession only fueled his theory further. You saw him try and blame me after you were possessed. He's convinced I'm working with my dad to hurt you and that Roarke took the fall for us. It's utterly ridiculous, but I can tell it's been eating away at him lately. The last thing he wants is for my dad to somehow get back to Euphora."

"Because he wants to protect Rhiannon," Capri said thoughtfully.

"That and he wants to keep my dad away from his wife."

"But why is he so paranoid about Serendipity when she chose him over Brock to begin with?"

Blythe smirked, her expression dark. "Let's just say he's a very jealous and possessive man. I think he figures my dad would somehow seduce Serendipity away from him if he made it back to Euphora. It's how his twisted mind works, which is why he's been acting so crazy lately."

Capri bit her lip, wishing she could tell Blythe everything that she knew. Instead, she played on what little information she knew she could discuss.

"So Rohan is not satisfied with Roarke's confession?"

"Nope. Until the day he dies he's gonna blame me or my father in some way for every little thing that happens here. I hope you believe me when I say that I didn't have anything to do with any of this. I hardly ever spoke to Roarke and I haven't seen or heard from my father since he was banished." Her eyes flashed with anger for a moment, though it was obvious she was fighting to control it as she continued. "I would never, ever hurt you."

Capri nodded. "I know you wouldn't." She leaned in and hugged Blythe tightly, hoping to comfort her in some way. When she pulled away, she smiled. "Other than the obvious, last night was a lot of fun."

Blythe grinned, her eyebrows wiggling suggestively. "I bet you had a good time." She winked, causing Capri to violently blush.

"Oh, well…sure I did," she managed, turning shyly away to hide her face. Blythe reached over and turned her head back, her eyes alight with humor.

"I thought I told you to stay away from the Furies, honey?"

Capri bit her lip, trying not to smile. "I guess I didn't follow your advice."

"Well, if it's any consolation, I think Rian's alright."

Capri's eyes widened in honest surprise. "You do?"

Blythe laughed again, wrapping her arm over Capri's shoulders. "Honey, the way that boy looks at you, I don't think any of us have anything to worry about. I've known him my whole life, not very well mind you, but enough to gauge his personality. He's always been way too serious, way too quiet, and seldom happy. But when he's around you…he smiles. It freaked me out the first time I saw it, but then I realized why he was so happy. It's all because of you."

Capri's eyes went dreamy, staring off into space, reminiscing about the look in his eyes when he had told her he missed her. He *had* looked happy. Was it really all because of her?

"Oh, boy." Blythe snorted, rolling her eyes. "You're gone over for him, aren't you?"

"What?" Capri blinked, her mouth opening slightly as she tried to find the right words to say. "No, no...well, yes...okay, maybe a little..."

"It's okay if you are, you don't have to worry about me," Blythe told her. "As for the others...I could tell there was something bothering Liam, this must be what it was."

"Oh, I hate to upset him...I know he's just trying to look out for me." Capri chewed her bottom lip fretfully, a worried crease forming between her brows.

Blythe waved the thought away. "He'll come around. It looks like your dad is alright with it. I saw him hand you off to Rian on the dance floor last night."

"It's because I told him I didn't care what he thought about Rian and me." Capri blushed at the look Blythe gave her.

"You talked back to him?" she asked, her eyebrows raised incredulously.

"Well, no...I just...yeah, I guess I sorta did."

"This is a week of firsts for you, isn't it?" Blythe looked extremely amused, but also proud. "First you talk back to me, then your father, then you run off with your boyfriend, not giving a damn about anybody else." She paused a moment. "I think I'm rubbing off on you."

"He's not my boyfriend." Capri blushed again, feeling awkward.

"Then what is he?" Blythe grinned mischievously. "Your... lover?"

"Oh, no, we haven't...it's not like...that." Capri slapped a hand against her forehead and laughed despite herself. "I don't know what we are. It's complicated but pathetically simple at the same time. But...I do think I might be...falling in love with him."

"No shit?" Blythe hooted out a laugh, hugging Capri. "Good for you, honey. You deserve a little romance after all you've been through. And if he's the one you want, then don't let anyone tell you otherwise."

"Thanks." Capri felt her eyes welling with grateful tears as she pulled away, wiping at them with her hand.

"Oh, don't cry. You're gonna get me started too." Blythe sniffled and hugged Capri again. Then the two of them proceeded to cry anyway.

When Capri left Blythe's room a while later, she felt much better than she had when she first arrived. Not only was Blythe doing fine in regards to the confrontation the night before, but she also approved of Rian. Not to mention that talking about Rian and admitting her feelings out loud had done something amazing to her wellbeing. She felt like she was walking on a cloud, drifting along, butterflies in her stomach and warmth in her heart.

She almost wanted to go out into the courtyard to find him, to sit and watch him as he went through his daily workout routine, but she had promised herself to visit Thea first. But right after, she would look for him, and maybe she would tell him how she felt.

She had to pause halfway down the staircase that lead to the main corridor and take a deep breath, biting her lip against the smile that wouldn't seem to leave her face. Would he be happy to know that she thought herself in love with him? She hoped so. She hugged herself, needing a moment to suppress the giddy excitement she felt.

Still smiling, she continued down the staircase, imagining his face when she told him. Would his eyes darken to that deep, cornflower blue and his mouth curve into that cynical smirk? She couldn't wait to find out.

Reaching for the handle of the door, she paused, hearing voices on the other side. Her smile faltered as she recognized Tobias' voice. He sounded as distressed as he did the day she saw him with Roarke.

She hesitated, pressing her ear up against the door. Her body froze in shock as she heard the conversation, her heart skipping frantically with sudden terror.

"It wasn't supposed to be this way. You never told me you were planning on getting Roarke killed! You said you just wanted him to confess and then that would be it!" Tobias whined, hysteria in his voice.

"My reasons for disposing of Roarke do not concern you." A second harsher and much older voice said. Capri felt chills shiver through her as she realized she knew that voice. Oh, yes, she knew that voice *very* well…it was the voice that haunted her dreams and tainted her memories. The only thing she didn't know was who it belonged to…

"All I wanted was for Capri to be gone. I didn't want any of this. I only helped you because you said the demon would lead her away from Euphora, and then everything would go back to the way it was before. And I only helped you with Roarke because you said he would take the fall for us. I never wanted him dead!" Beneath the fear, there was bitterness and resentment in Tobias' voice.

"Do you think I ever gave a damn about your feelings, boy? This is serious! The girl is on to us; we must get rid of her."

"I don't want to do this anymore!" Tobias whispered hastily.

"You're in too deep, Tobias. She knows you're involved. We need to act tonight. We'll make it look like she ran away, and then you can erase her memory so she won't be any the wiser. She won't be dead, Tobias, just lost again. Isn't that what you wanted?"

There was a brief moment of silence, and for a second Capri wondered if they had walked away, but then Tobias spoke, his voice even quieter than before.

"Fine. I'll do it." Suddenly, Capri noticed the knob on the door in front of her begin to turn, and she realized with a jolt that Tobias was going to come upstairs. Thinking fast, she backed up a step and tried to look blankly surprised when Tobias opened the door.

He stopped dead, his green eyes huge with shock and panic, his mouth open in surprise.

Capri tried to smile, pretending she had heard nothing.

"Hi, Tobias," she greeted, grateful her voice didn't tremble as she spoke. She continued down the last step as Tobias backed away, giving her room to pass. As she emerged into the corridor, she turned her head to finally identify the man who had successfully eluded her for months.

When she saw him, she knew that her poor acting skills were going to be the end of her. She could feel her face drain of all color and her eyes widen. Her lips parted in honest surprise and she felt her knees begin to give way.

She attempted to pull herself together, but she knew she had fooled no one. Especially not him. He, who never spoke out loud in front of her. He, who she had thought to be shy and something of a hero for battling the demons during the raid. He, who Rian considered a second father, and who Roarke had considered a brother.

It had been him, all along. And now that she knew, she wondered how she had ever missed it.

Balgaire stared back at her, his dark eyes menacing and his mouth set in a stern line. His harsh face looked particularly threatening compared to when she had seen him before, and the sheer hatred she saw in his eyes sent fear racing down her spine.

She tried to smile again, knowing that if she acted casual enough, she could walk away out the front doors and find Rian. Or she could go to Thea and reveal everything. Besides, it was the middle of the day, what could Balgaire possibly do to her? There were other people that would surely be walking around at some point who would notice if he tried to hurt her, right?

There was no way he would take that kind of risk, especially since he had no idea if she had even heard their conversation. Feigning ignorance was the only thing that was going to save her.

She continued to walk past him, averting her eyes, trying to act as nonchalant as she could. Just when she thought she had cleared him completely and that he was going to let her go, she felt his hand close over her arm.

She braced herself to scream, but within seconds his other hand was clamped over her mouth.

Fear bolted through her like lightning, and she saw shock and disbelief cross over Tobias' face as he watched Balgaire struggle to hold her.

"What the hell are you doing?" Tobias asked, his voice shaky and his eyes wild with fear.

"Doing what needs to be done," Balgaire replied darkly, sneering as he continued to struggle with Capri, who was kicking wildly and clawing at the hand that covered her mouth. He turned to Tobias, looking furious. "Say anything and I will tell everyone what you have done. They will take my word over yours, and I will see to it that you are banished, or worse. I am the law around here, boy. Don't forget that."

Suddenly, he began walking with her, and despite her struggles she was no match against his strength. She had never realized how strong he was, but now that she knew, it only made her more afraid. He was going to kill her, all because she knew his secret.

Clinging to hope that she could get away, she opened her mouth and managed to bite down hard onto one of his fingers. She heard him snarl quietly but he didn't move his hand. Instead, he pressed it harder against her mouth, making it hard to breathe.

He continued to drag her quickly down the corridor, and when he stopped in front of the door leading to the Furies' chambers, she prayed that Rian would somehow be there, even though she knew he was most likely still outside.

Balgaire opened the door and dragged her inside, shutting the door behind him. She continued to struggle, and this time she managed to kick back with her right foot and hit him hard against the knee. He faltered, releasing her, but as she tried to run past him for the door, he grabbed her and rammed her head hard against the stone wall.

The whole world shot instantly into darkness.

The first thing she felt when she came to was blinding, red hot pain. It pulsated at her left temple, beating in time with the heart she knew still lived in her chest. She wasn't yet dead, which was a plus. But she certainly didn't appreciate being alive at that moment, either.

She struggled to open her eyes, wincing against the throbbing pain. Groaning, she blinked to try and clear her vision, hoping to figure out where she was.

Gray stone walls surrounded her on all sides, two torches lighting the tiny room. It was hardly larger than a walk in closet, with one door and no windows.

She was sitting on a metal chair, her hands tied behind her with thick metal chains. Her mouth was gagged by a cloth, and her eyes watered against the heat she felt coming from the door.

When her eyes adjusted to the darkness of the room, she saw what was projecting the heat. It prowled and paced in front of the door, its throat grumbling with a menacing growl.

It was a rather large, dog-like creature with jet black fur and glowing red eyes. When it opened its mouth and bared its teeth at her, she saw molten fire burning in its throat.

When she realized it was chained to the wall beside the door, she felt mild relief. At least it wasn't going to attack her...yet.

She desperately tried to slip her hands free of the chains that bound her, only to cut and bruise herself. Tears welled in her eyes as she glanced around for something, anything that would help free her so she could escape.

Even if she could free herself from the chains, she still had to get past the dog. And she had never been very good with dogs, much less fire breathing ones...

If only she could get the gag away from her mouth, maybe she could scream for help. She tried to scream against the gag, but the muffled sound made the dog growl loudly, so she stopped out of fear. She didn't want to provoke an attack, despite it being chained near the door.

Helplessness coursed through her as she realized all of her options were exhausted. Balgaire was going to come back and kill her, either by setting the dog loose or by shooting her with one of the many weapons she knew he had access to. She only prayed it would be quick.

She thought of her mother, and then of her father, and tears began to fall freely down her cheeks. What would her father do when he found out? Would he think that she had run away? Or would Balgaire leave her body for them to find, maybe framing Tobias for her murder?

And Rian. She sobbed hard against the gag as she thought of him, and how worried he would be. It was all useless...all of it. She should have never returned to Euphora. All it had done was spark a madman to wreak havoc on those she loved. And they would suffer further because of him, and in a way, because of her. It would have been better if she had just stayed in Virginia, away from all of this. Then Roarke and the two Enforcers would still be alive, and Rian would eventually find someone else to love him. The very thought of it sent a vicious pain through her chest, like arrows to the heart. Balgaire would probably target Rian next and then his blood would also be on her hands. It was all because of her.

Gritting her teeth against the gag, she struggled against the chains again, fury pulsing through her. She had to protect him, and the others, against this madman. Somehow, she had to do something. Anything.

All she did was hurt her wrists more so she settled down, trying to breathe deeply and calm herself. She had to clear her head and think.

As she tried hard to concentrate, her breathing became shallow, and her vision blurred. Her head wound viciously pulsed and after a few moments she felt herself fade back into unconsciousness.

"*What!*" Thea thundered, looking particularly distraught as she immediately stopped pacing. She stood amongst her many exotic plants and animals, her dark hair frazzled and her eyes sharp as poisoned daggers. Beside her, Sebastian looked equally stressed, his long blonde hair unkempt and shadows under his eyes.

Tobias tried to swallow the lump in his throat as he bit down hard on his tongue, tasting blood. He was so scared that he was trembling, and the dark circles under his eyes spoke of little sleep. When he spoke again, his voice was small and weak.

"I know who took Capri," he repeated, his eyes fixed to the floor, too worried to see the look on Thea's face.

It had been nearly twenty-four hours since anyone had seen Capri, and the search had been frantic and unsuccessful. The last person to report seeing her was Blythe, who said Capri had left her room around ten in the morning. Past that point, she had quite literally disappeared into thin air.

Until now.

"Well...who did it? Where is she?" Thea shouted, her temper boiling. She kept the fear and dread at bay by focusing solely on her anger. It was much easier to act when angry then it was when you were scared. And underneath it all, she was terrified over what might have happened to her young Air Dryad.

Tobias winced at the fury in her voice, but he forced himself to be strong. Ever since he had seen Balgaire haul Capri away, he had been fighting with himself over whether or not he should say something. He was just young enough to believe Balgaire when he said that no one would believe him. But at the same time, he was scared of what Balgaire might do to Capri, and the only thing he knew was that he didn't want another person to die because of him.

"Balgaire took her. I saw them go into the Furies' chambers, but I don't know where they went from there."

Without saying anything, Thea suddenly swept past him and headed for the door, Sebastian in her wake.

"Wait!" Tobias shouted, his face anguished.

Thea whirled around, furious. "Time is of the essence, Tobias. She could be dead as we speak because you waited so long to tell us. We can't wait any longer."

"Please, send the others to find her, but I need to speak to you. I need to tell you the whole story…"

Maybe it was the pleading look in his eyes, or her desire to know the truth that had her turning to Sebastian, fighting to keep her voice steady.

"Sebastian, take Rian, Clynn and Lucian with you and go to the Furies' chambers immediately. Have Rohan and Liam locate Balgaire, and when they find him, hold him until I can speak to him."

Sebastian nodded and raced out of the room.

"Alright, Tobias." Thea took a deep breath and turned to him, her arms crossing over her chest. "What is it you have to tell me?"

Tobias straightened, biting back the fear, knowing the trouble he was in. But he wasn't a coward. No. He was going to take responsibility for his actions like a man.

"It all started when Capri came home," he began, his voice shaky but his eyes clear. "You probably didn't know this, but I've hated her my whole life. I didn't think it was fair that she disappeared and that her mother died on my birthday. Why couldn't it have happened on another day? You probably think it's stupid, and maybe it is, but my whole life I've never had a fun birthday because everyone was always moping around about it. I never even knew her or her mother, but I hated them anyway." His lips pouted slightly, the old feelings resurfacing despite how the growing adult inside of him tried to beat them away.

"When she returned, I was unhappy. Here she was to steal the attention all over again. Balgaire approached me one day, told me he understood how I felt. He said he didn't like her either, and that if I helped him, he could make her go away. He told me that if I used my powers to open her mind, he could let a demon onto the grounds who would possess her, and then force her to leave Euphora. He said he would see to it that she didn't return. I didn't really ask what he was planning on doing to her, or why he wanted her gone, I just knew what I wanted, and that was all that mattered." He paused for a moment, bracing for what was next. "So on the night she was possessed, I went up to her room and quietly slipped inside. She was sleeping, so I stood over her and concentrated on opening her mind. It only took a few minutes; she was already emotionally vulnerable which made it much easier. After I was done, I backed out of the room, and just as I shut the door behind me, Roarke was there doing patrol. He saw me right outside of her room, and I panicked. I ran past him without saying anything, hoping he would just think I was taking a walk or something. But he knew. He didn't say anything to me for awhile, so I thought I was in the clear. But then after those Enforcers were killed, he must have known that the demon involved was the same demon Balgaire had let in to possess Capri, only he thought that I had let in the demon. He confronted me about it, said how it didn't matter what the demon had told me, that I wasn't going to get away with it. I got scared and I told Balgaire, and he suggested that the only thing left to do was to frame Roarke for everything, that way it wouldn't come back to us. I didn't see another way out, so I did what he told me to. We went to Richmond, and I hid in the shadows with the demon while Balgaire brought Roarke into the warehouse. Balgaire hit Roarke over the head and knocked him out, and I opened his mind to let the demon in, and then I left. I didn't know they planned on getting him killed…I just thought he would confess and that would be it, he'd be banished just like Brock was. I honestly didn't know he was going to die."

He choked on a sob, his voice strained and his eyes watering. Thea was watching him with a stone cold look on her face, but he was at least grateful that she wasn't screaming at him anymore.

"When I found out Roarke had been killed, I didn't sleep for days. I thought he was haunting me, blaming me for his death. I felt horrible, but again I was too scared to do anything. I hoped it was all over and that it would just go away. I didn't even really care about Capri anymore. I just wanted to forget about everything. But Balgaire wouldn't let it go. I avoided him for weeks, but then yesterday he came to me and said that we had to get rid of her, that she was on to us. He said he wanted me to open her mind again that night, and he would let the demon in again, and he would lead her away from Euphora, make it look like she ran away. He told me that I should erase her memory so that she would get to live; she would just be lost again. It sounded fine, really, and I was happy she wasn't going to die. So I agreed. But she caught us. She was right there behind the door, listening to us, and when Balgaire saw her he grabbed her. He told me that if I told anyone anything, that they wouldn't believe me, and that they would take his word over mine. And so I didn't say anything. But seeing him at dinner last night, pretending to look worried about her, disgusted me. I don't know if he's hurt her…" He grimaced, sick to his stomach. "I'm sorry, Thea. I made a huge mistake."

Thea pursed her lips, eyeing him. "I'm torn, Tobias," she began, her eyes meeting his. "Torn between banishing you for being a selfish, little crybaby, endangering the life of my Air Dryad, and assisting in the murder of my top Fury…and thanking you for manning up and coming to me, hopefully before it's too late."

"I don't deserve it, but I am asking for your mercy, Thea," he pleaded, his eyes glassy and huge.

"I will only forgive you if Capri is still alive," Thea decided. "Now, I have a very important question for you."

"Anything."

"Do you know the identity of the demon Balgaire used to possess Capri and Roarke?"

"I never learned his name. But I saw him."

"Can you describe what he looked like?"

Tobias looked confused for a moment, but he tried to picture the demon in his head. "He was tall, thin, tanned skin, in his thirties, maybe. Long, dark hair pulled back. Funny looking nose, kind of hooked and broken looking. And he had weird eyes, they were like, gold, or something."

"Did they look similar to Blythe's eyes?" Thea asked, her body tensing.

His own eyes lit up. "Yeah, actually, they looked just like hers. Kind of an amber color."

"Anything else you remember about him?"

"Yeah. He didn't speak a lot, but he kept glaring at me, like he hated me or something. And I mean *hated*. I was glad to get away from him."

"One more question." Thea braced herself, already sure she knew his answer. "When you saw him possess Roarke, what happened to his other host body? Did Balgaire hide the body somewhere so the Enforcers wouldn't see it?"

Tobias looked extremely confused. "I don't...that is...I don't think he really left the human body. He just...morphed, I guess... into a shadowy snake form. There wasn't a body left for us to hide." He frowned. "I've never seen a demon other than him. Is that how it normally happens?"

"No, it's not." Thea's eyes burned with dread. "A demon can only possess one person at a time, and must leave one body in order to possess another."

"So…what does that mean?" Tobias asked, frightened.

"It means we are all in very great danger," Thea told him, dismissing him with a wave as she turned to stare out the windows. "Please, leave me. I need some time to think."

She felt a new emotion rise within her as she heard Tobias shut the door behind him. It was battling its way through her stomach and beating against her chest, pounding in her head and thundering through her blood.

It wasn't just rage and fear she felt; it was something much more akin to revulsion.

Her greatest fears had come true. He was back.

## Chapter Sixteen

*She didn't know* how long she waited in the chamber. It could have been hours, days, weeks...she had no concept of time. She drifted in and out of consciousness, weak from hunger and worn out from fear.

She had resigned herself to die of dehydration, knowing that he had left her there. So she did the only thing she could do: sleep and wait for death.

She awoke to the sound of a latch being opened on the other side of the door. Her eyes flew open, imagining Rian or her father or Thea, only to fall upon Balgaire as he pushed through the door, shutting it promptly behind him.

The dog growled, but Balgaire threw down a large, meaty bone. Within seconds the dog was gnawing on it, satisfied.

Balgaire trudged into the room, approaching Capri. His face was cold and unreadable, his eyes calculating. He roughly removed her gag, and she took a brief moment to readjust her sore jaw. He had a glass bottle in his hand filled with water, and she nearly wept when he put it to her lips and poured some into her mouth. She swallowed thankfully, feeling her parched throat absorb the moisture.

"No one will hear you down here, anyway." Balgaire told her, tossing the gag and the empty glass aside. He crossed his arms as he stood in front of her. When she looked up at him, she felt chills shiver down her back. She had been right in her original impression of him when she had first come to Euphora. He was downright cold, and his harsh face mirrored the cruel person beneath. "You think you're so smart, don't you?"

Capri shook her head, strands of her light hair falling into her eyes. "No, no I don't."

He sneered. "You just couldn't leave it alone, could you? You had to know who was behind your kidnapping. I will never forgive that bastard for not killing you when he had the chance fifteen years ago."

"Who? The demon?" Capri asked timidly, her curiosity getting the better of her.

"The identity of my associate does not concern you," he hastily replied, looking impatient. "I would kill you myself, but it looks like I'm going to need you to get out of here. That brat Tobias went to Thea and ratted me out. Lucky for us, Brogan overheard their conversation and came to me before the others even knew where to start. Everyone in the castle is looking, but they won't find us in here. No one knows that this room exists, except Roarke of course, but he's dead." He laughed, that crazy, maniacal laugh that had haunted her dreams since childhood. She shuddered involuntarily, wincing from the sound of it. It brought back the memory of him standing over her mother's burning body, his brutal laughter ringing out into the dead night.

"Of course, framing Brock and Roarke for everything was a brilliant idea, and it would have worked perfectly if you hadn't gotten in the way, yet again," he snarled, beginning to pace. "That was the one thing we hadn't planned on: you returning to Euphora and figuring out the truth."

"Do whatever you want to me, but please, don't hurt anyone else," Capri pleaded weakly, pain coursing through her head.

"There won't be any need to as long as you do as I say," he told her, smiling darkly. "Listen to me carefully. I want you to create a diversion so that we can escape the grounds and make it to the tree outside the front gate. When we get there, you'll come with me and then I will decide whether or not to let you go."

"How do I know you won't just kill me when we get there?" Capri asked.

"You don't. But I should tell you that there is another chamber, just like this one, nearby. I am holding Rian in there. Like I said, no one else knows these chambers are here. If you cooperate, I will leave behind a note letting the others know where to find him. If not, then I leave you both to rot."

Uncertainty warred with the fear she felt. She wasn't sure she believed he actually had Rian locked up. But there was no way she could take the chance. If he really was in danger, she needed to do whatever she could to save him.

"Okay. What do you want me to do?"

"I need you to create a storm," he began, his eyes glinting with barely contained madness. "Thunder, lightning…tornado. Specifically a tornado in the far east side of the grounds. I want everyone to be distracted and head over there, thinking you are signaling for help. Then we will sneak out of the castle through the front doors, and out of the courtyard."

"I–I don't know if I can do that, from in here…" Capri stammered, uncertainty in her eyes. "I won't be able to see what I'm doing."

"Figure it out, or I find another way out and leave you here," he threatened, his voice dangerous.

For a moment, Capri was silent, a flood of emotions running through her. This time, anger prevailed over everything else.

"So once again, you're going to let someone else take the fall for you?" she said suddenly, fury rising within her. "First Brock, then Roarke, now Rohan?"

"Rohan?" He looked amused as he watched her. "You think Rohan is capable of pulling off something like this?"

"I heard you!" Capri cried out angrily. "I heard you talking to Rohan in the library, talking about getting rid of me!"

Balgaire chuckled darkly. "Have you and Rian been looking at Rohan this entire time? That fool didn't have anything to do with this; he was only worried about himself and what would happen if Brock returned to Euphora. Not that Brock has been any the wiser to what's been going on. I imagine he's still rotting away in a gambling hall in Vegas somewhere. Good riddance."

"So that's why he wanted to go with you and the other Furies to Las Vegas? He thought Brock was planning an ambush?"

"Yes. And I let him think that. I also let him think that I would do my best to keep an eye on Brock, ensuring he had no opportunity to return. Rohan is easily fooled."

"And Tobias? You fooled him as well?"

"He hates you. He always has. It wasn't hard to convince him to help me," Balgaire smirked, his eyes flashing with delight. "Apparently, you being kidnapped on the day he was born has always put a damper on his birthday. Everybody moping around, mourning you and your mother, not giving him any attention. Pathetic, really, and childish. But useful enough for me."

"I never knew he felt that way," Capri murmured sadly, wishing there was some way she could talk to him, to let him know that she knew how he felt. As an orphan, her birthdays had never been very special, either. "You manipulated him. You used his insecurities against him."

"He's ultimately getting what he wanted, so what does it matter? And if he hadn't gone to Thea, I would have no need to flee Euphora. No matter, though. I have ways to take care of him once I'm gone."

Capri felt shock waves pulse through her at his words. "Please don't hurt him. He's just a kid."

"He betrayed me. He has to face the consequences," Balgaire coldly declared. "Enough talking. Get working on that storm. Once it's started, we'll head out."

Capri bit her lip as he moved behind her to unlock the chains binding her wrists. When he lifted them away, she tenderly rubbed her raw and bloody skin.

"By the way, did you enjoy having my demon hound as company? He was a gift from my associate." He chuckled as the dog opened its mouth to yawn a few feet away from them. Fire glowed brightly from deep within its throat like molten hot lava.

Capri didn't say anything, but closed her eyes, focusing her thoughts away from the dog and away from Balgaire. Instead she thought of Rian, and how if he was indeed alone in a chamber nearby, he would soon be safe. Even if Balgaire killed her after they got away, at least Rian would be alive.

Fighting back a sob, she cleared her mind and tried to picture the eastern part of the grounds near the back of the castle in her mind. She had rarely been back there, so it was difficult, but once she had it, she held her arms out and began to imagine clouds forming.

She could feel it in her arms as the clouds were building across the grounds, and in her mind's eye she could see them forming, shifting and growing more and more violent. The first rumble of thunder could be heard from somewhere far away, and she knew she was making progress. Balgaire stayed silent, but she could still sense his presence. He was clearly listening for the telltale sounds of the tornado once it began.

She imagined the warm and cold air mixing together, swirling to create a funnel out of the clouds. She encouraged the wind to pick up, swirling through the mass of the darkening storm. She felt it when the cyclone began to form, and when it made its descent near land. Her arms vibrated with energy, and she could feel the wrath of the tornado as it made contact with the ground, kicking up grass and dirt. Exhaling sharply, she released herself from the storm, tears in her eyes as she lowered her arms. It was done.

Balgaire reached out and grabbed her, pulling her roughly to her feet. "Let's go."

He pushed past the dog and opened the door, glancing briefly around to make sure no one was there. They were in a narrow hallway, which had a staircase at one end and rows of doors along the way. He roughly dragged her along to the staircase, swiftly pulling her up. They reached another door, which he gradually opened. Again he checked to be sure they were alone. This door led to a dungeon, much like the one Blythe worked out of. Capri glanced around, but nothing looked familiar to her.

When they walked through yet another, much smaller door, she realized where they were. They were beneath Air tower and they had emerged into the atrium. The room she was held in must connect the Furies' chambers to it. Balgaire pushed aside the plants hiding the door and yanked Capri out, his hand clamped tightly on her wrist so she couldn't run.

She briefly thought about screaming, but she didn't know what would happen if Balgaire killed her right then and there. Rian might never be found. Instead, she kept silent and followed him as he led her out the front doors and through the courtyard. No one was in sight.

Up above them, the storm raged mercilessly. The clouds churned and writhed like a living being, shades of gray swirling together. A crackling bolt of lightning broke out against the sky, spider-webbing greedily through the dense air. As if answering its call, thunder boomed around them, so loud it vibrated the ground at their feet. She could feel the wind, and hear it howling around her, and when she quickly turned her head, she saw the tornado in the distance, black and ominous. Knowing she had created such a monster struck fear into her heart, violently stabbing like a knife.

Balgaire started running, almost too fast for her to keep up. Her head pounded in pain from all the sudden movement, and when she suddenly tripped over the cobblestone walkway and tumbled to the ground, Balgaire cursed and tried to pull her to her feet.

"You stupid bitch," he muttered furiously, dragging her up. But fear made her legs go limp and as her dazed eyes met his, she heard a resounding voice behind them.

"Stop right there."

She turned and saw Rian, pistol in hand, pointed directly at Balgaire. She felt numb with relief at seeing him, knowing he was not locked up after all, but terror ripped through her when Balgaire pulled out his own weapon and aimed it at Rian.

"No!" she screamed as Balgaire fired, the demon fire bullet just barely missing Rian as he ducked out of the way. It hit a nearby tree and burst into flames.

Rian was about to fire back, but Balgaire grabbed Capri and shielded himself with her.

"Shoot me and you shoot her, boy." Balgaire had one arm over her chest, pressing her against him, and his other arm held his weapon, still aimed at Rian.

"Let her go, this is between you and me," Rian said, his voice cold and fury in his eyes.

"Is it now?" Balgaire chuckled darkly. "Then you won't mind if I take her out of the picture."

He turned the gun, pressed it firmly against the side of Capri's head, and cocked it.

The steel tip of the revolver pressed into her aching temple, right below where she had hit her head. The world seemed to slow down in front of her, nothing making sense except the brutal understanding that she was quite possibly about to die.

A steady buzzing sound of white noise began to echo inside her head, numbing her and draining everything else out. She saw Rian's lips move, the brief flash of panic cross his face, but she couldn't hear anything.

All she knew was that a gun was pressed against her head, and she was a trigger's pull away from death.

She could feel pressure on her chest where Balgaire's arm held her, and she could feel his breath on the nape of her neck, but the words he uttered she couldn't understand.

What would happen when he finally pulled the trigger? Would it hurt? Or would everything just go black like in the movies? Would he point the gun at Rian and kill him too?

Her fear brought her back to reality, pushing past the numbness and the shock. The terror of what was about to happen enabled her to focus on what was being said between the two Furies, and process the weight behind the words.

"He trusted you. We all trusted you, Balgaire," Rian was saying, his voice strained but steady.

"Roarke never trusted me," Balgaire spat, resentment in his eyes. "He never thought I was as good a Fury as he was, and he always treated me as though I were beneath him. But not anymore! It was much too convenient to use him for my own means, with the added bonus of the Enforcers killing him. A bit ironic, don't you think?"

"He was a good man, he thought of you like a brother." Rian's voice remained calm, but Capri could sense his anger sparking in the air. "Is this why you betrayed us? You were jealous of him?"

Capri could tell that Rian was trying to keep Balgaire talking, playing against his ego in the hopes of distracting him from killing her. She wondered where the others were, if they were still investigating the tornado, wondering where it came from. She hoped they would think, as Rian must have, that Balgaire would try and make a run for it out the front gates.

Above them the storm raged on, the clouds swirling like madness. Lightning crackled again, illuminating the darkened courtyard. In the light, Capri saw several birds diving for the cover of a nearby tree, frightened by the deadly electricity in the air. It was then that the idea hit her.

"I was never jealous of him!" Balgaire shouted angrily, causing Capri to shudder at the sound. She could feel the revolver shaking in his hand as the rage pulsed through him, even as she slowly reached out her own hand ever so slightly, concentrating on the birds she knew were hiding in the tree. "I despised him, I always have. Ever since we were boys he and everyone else left me to rot in his shadow of superiority. And then I watched him do the same with my son and you. That, above all else, crossed the line, and made it all too enticing to destroy him the moment I had the opportunity."

"So what about Brogan, Balgaire?" Rian asked. "You say you care so much about your son, that you worried he would end up in my shadow, always second best, just like you did. What do you think all of this is going to do to him? He looks up to you, and now you're nothing but a murderer. What is he going to do when you're gone?"

For a moment Balgaire didn't say anything. Capri could feel him breathing heavily, and the hand that held the revolver to her head still shook. But she didn't think it shook from fury any longer. Instead, she had a feeling it shook with fearful uncertainty. Rian had apparently hit the mark.

"My son will be fine," Balgaire managed, his voice rough as his anger returned. "I can't say the same for you."

Capri felt the revolver leave the side of her head right as she beckoned the birds to dive at her and Balgaire. The diversion was enough to startle him as the birds zoomed through the air and began to attack his face.

Capri ducked out of his grasp as he fought against the attack, and she urged her legs to not give out as she stumbled to Rian.

A shot rang out into the air, and Capri felt the demon bullet whiz by her shoulder, grazing her skin as it continued on its path, hitting the stone wall of the castle with an instantaneous explosion of fire.

She fell into Rian's arms, and he immediately pulled her behind him, his gun still pointed at Balgaire. She pressed herself against the back of his shirt, her eyes shut tight as fear tore through her. She shivered as she heard Balgaire howling in pain.

Just then, she heard footsteps running to them, voices calling out in confusion and fright. She couldn't bear to open her eyes, however, and instead remained clutched against Rian as he turned to see the others approach.

"There they are!" Liam's voice rang out over the howling wind and rumbling thunder. "Over here!"

"Capri," she heard Rian say, one of his arms gently wrapping around her. "You need to call off the storm, baby."

She opened her eyes, still frightened by what was happening. But she nodded as her eyes met his, acknowledging his words. She closed her eyes again and imagined the entire storm dissipating, and as she did, she could feel the wind die down and the clouds disappear, revealing the glorious morning sun above.

When she once again opened her eyes, her father was running to her, along with the other members of the Council. They immediately surrounded Balgaire, who was still swatting at the birds that continued to assault him. His pistol had fallen to the ground, useless against them.

Liam and Blythe were tailing her father, worry on their faces. Behind them, Brogan ran toward the circle of people surrounding his father, his eyes huge and his face drained of all color. He stopped several feet away and stood as still as a statue, unable to do more than watch.

"Capri!" Clynn rushed up to her, grabbing her and holding her tightly. He pressed his face into her hair, his chest heaving and his entire body shaking. "Are you hurt?"

"No." Her voice trembled as she spoke, but when she looked up at him, she managed a small smile. "I'm fine."

Thea pushed her way through the crowd , waving her arms to call off the birds. Balgaire fell to the ground, gasping for air and clutching his head in pain. Hundreds of small cuts and scratches covered his face and neck where the birds had ruthlessly attacked him.

"*How dare you!*" Thea roared, her voice echoing throughout the courtyard. She kicked his gun aside and stood in front of him, glaring down at him with rage in her eyes. Sebastian stood beside her, looking equally as furious. The gun came to a skidding halt in front of the Fates, who stared down at it curiously.

"I am so disgusted, I can't even *begin* to decide what to do with you." Thea's eyes darkened nearly to black and her entire body trembled with unspeakable power. When Balgaire looked at her, there was fear in his eyes.

"It's all lies," he choked out, rubbing his hands over his face as if he could still feel the birds.

"Is that so?" Thea tilted her head and stared down her nose at him. "I find that very hard to believe."

"I'm being framed!"

"By who? A fifteen year old?" Thea smirked, though she was hardly amused. "You must think I'm an idiot, Balgaire."

"No...no..." He looked up at her, agony in his dark eyes.

"I already knew that Roarke was innocent, I didn't need Tobias to tell me that. He was forced to confess to something he had nothing to do with by a demon who possessed him, a demon who vacated his body seconds before he was shot and killed."

There was a collective gasp throughout the crowd. Capri glanced over at Rian, who still had his pistol pointed at Balgaire, watching the other man's every move, disgust in his eyes. She felt her father hold her closer as the pain of knowing his old friend had been framed coursed through him.

"I also knew that the demon who possessed Roarke is the same demon who possessed Capri. The demon *you* let onto the grounds." Thea heard murmured whispers amongst the others, and she reveled in knowing the secret was out. "You see, the only thing I didn't know, Balgaire, was that it was you, all along. But even without Tobias confessing about helping you, my Enforcers would have uncovered the truth in time."

Capri watched the fear fade away from Balgaire's face, and the fury replace it. His hands clenched at his sides as he continued to crouch on the ground.

Feeling inspired, Capri eased away from her father, clearing her throat before she spoke. "There's more, Thea."

Thea whirled around, her eyes flashing to Capri. She looked rather frightening, but Capri could tell that she was trying to reign in her temper.

"Yes, Capri?"

"Balgaire was responsible for the raid, not Brock."

Once again, everyone around them gasped, including her own father. Rian looked at her, understanding dawning in his eyes.

"How do you know?" Thea paled slightly, her temper evaporating.

Capri flushed, feeling everyone's eyes on her. She could sense Balgaire watching her as well, and she tried to ignore his heated stare. "When I went to the Muses to relive my dream, I heard his voice, not Brock's, order my mother and me to die. I just never realized it was him because he never spoke out loud in front of me, I assume because he suspected that I would realize it had been him. That was why he let in the demon in an attempt to get rid of me. And when Roarke was on to him, he framed him for everything and ultimately got him killed."

"But now that you've heard his voice, you can say with assurance that it was indeed him, and not Brock?"

"Balgaire told me he had framed Brock. But even still I knew his voice the moment I heard it. It was never Brock; he had nothing to do with it. Just like Roarke had nothing to do with it. It was Balgaire all along." She felt powerful uttering the words out loud, especially knowing that both Brock and Roarke would finally have their names cleared, even though only one of them was alive to see it.

Thea watched Capri for a moment, reflecting on what she had just heard. It certainly filled in the gaping hole in Tobias' story about why Balgaire wanted Capri gone in the first place.

He knew she would eventually uncover the truth if she stayed on Euphora.

The crowd was buzzing with murmured whispers, everyone astonished by the news.

When Thea turned around, she glared down at Balgaire once more. "Is this true?"

He licked his lips, obviously warring between his safety and his pride. He suddenly bared his teeth in a sneer, his eyes filled with hatred. "It is."

With one fluid swipe, Thea slapped him hard across the face. His head whipped viciously to the side, but he remained kneeling. He swiped at the blood dripping from his lip with the back of his hand, bitterness in his eyes.

Everyone was silent, too stunned to move or say anything. Capri noticed Rian watching Brogan, a mix between pity and uncertainty on his face. When she looked at Brogan herself, she realized why Rian looked so uneasy. Brogan wasn't moving; it looked like he was hardly breathing. Instead he stood resolutely still, even his dark eyes unblinking. It was like he was frozen from both shock and disbelief. She felt sorry for him, and hoped that once everything was over that she could find some way to comfort him, even if it was just a little.

Rohan stood beside Brogan, looking mortified, clutching both his wife and his daughter protectively. His wife was quietly sobbing into his shoulder, and Rhiannon was shooting nervous glances at Brogan, as if she expected him to break down or explode at any moment.

"Why, Balgaire? Why did you frame Brock?" Thea was trembling still, mostly with remorse and regret for her Fire Dryad who had been an innocent man all along.

Balgaire glanced over at his wife, Nyxa, who was staring at him with wide eyes and a slightly manic expression. He kept his eyes on her as he spoke.

"Because he was a scoundrel and a womanizer, and he didn't deserve anything he got. He had you, Nyxa, while I could never seem to impress you, and he was never faithful. And so I made him go away. I let the demons onto the grounds, and made sure Brock was busy in the dungeon so he would have no alibi. When he came out, he saw the flames in the courtyard and naturally he tried to fight off the demons. But none of that mattered, because I had instructed one of the demons to surrender, and to name Brock as the man who had let them onto Euphora. It was all too easy, especially because Rohan was more than eager to believe Brock was guilty, and coupled with my own testimony, Brock didn't stand a chance."

"And so I banished him, completely trusting you, never thinking for one moment that you were capable of doing something this despicable." Thea looked incensed, her eyes on fire. "And I suppose it's safe for me to assume that you have been looking for a good way to get rid of Roarke for years, and this was just too perfect to pass up, am I right?"

Balgaire nodded, looking eerily triumphant. "It was the perfect plan. Except for the one last loose end, the end that should have been destroyed fifteen years ago."

"And how unfortunate for you that she was not destroyed," Thea spat, her eyes dangerous. "One last thing, Balgaire, before I make up my mind on what I should do with you."

She knelt down in front of him, meeting him eye to eye. Sebastian kept one hand on her shoulder protectively, though she knew it was more for a show of support than anything else. She, above all the people of Euphora, could take care of herself.

For a moment she didn't say anything, she searched the face of the man she'd known his whole life. She'd been present at his birth, witnessed his first scraped knees and his eager first attempts at demon hunting. She'd seen him get married, have children of his own, and serve her as an excellent Fury. When and where had everything changed? Where had it all gone wrong?

"Tell me who the demon was, Balgaire," she said finally, her voice deadly quiet. "I've had a hunch for awhile, but I want to hear you say it. Who is the demon you've been working with? Or should I say, Dryad?"

Capri felt her father bristle beside her, even as her own breath caught in her lungs. Did Thea know the identity of the demon who had possessed her and Roarke? The demon, who according to Alastor, had left behind a partial Dryad signature?

Balgaire grinned wickedly, his lip still bloody, cruelty in his dark eyes. When he spoke, his voice trembled with the excitement of a man sharing his most lucrative secret.

"*Dante.*"

The crowd exploded in a sudden eruption of noise. The adults were shouting in alarm and hysteria, while their sons and daughters were looking at each other, wide-eyed, wondering who in the world Dante was, and why his name sent everyone into a panicked frenzy.

Capri looked at her father, who had gone ghostly pale. His mouth was open slightly, his eyes wide in astonished disbelief. She squeezed his hand, but he didn't move. Alarmed, she shook him, frightened at the blank look he gave her.

"Who is Dante?" she asked him, shaking her head in confusion.

"I can't believe..." he mumbled, looking more than a little nauseous. "It's not possible..."

"What's not?"

Before he could answer her, a loud shriek echoed over the din of the crowd.

"*You bastard!*" Nyxa screamed, Balgaire's revolver in her shaking hands, pointed directly at him.

"Oh, God. No." Capri started forward, only to stop mid-step as the shot rang out into the air. She winced at the sound of it, and felt her legs go numb as she watched Balgaire become instantly consumed by fire.

Sebastian grabbed Thea and dragged her away, shielding her from the flames that were erupting out of Balgaire's chest. Within moments, both Lucian and Liam were dousing

Balgaire's lifeless body with water that jetted out of their open palms. Apparently Dryad water could extinguish demon flames as well as milk could...

Rian reached for Capri as her legs gave out from under her, her eyes locked on what was left of Balgaire.

"Look away," he ordered her, pulling her against his chest and holding her tight. "Don't think about it."

She felt bile rising in her throat and despite how tightly she shut her eyes, the image of him burning wouldn't go away. She didn't think she would ever forget it.

She heard shouting and screaming, but she didn't feel she had the strength to move. It was over. The truth was out, and Balgaire was dead.

Rian held her tightly, and for that she was grateful. She needed something solid, something steady, to keep her from crumbling. He had his face pressed into her hair, and when he shifted, his lips caressed her forehead lightly.

"It's okay, baby," he told her, his voice gentle. "It's over now."

## Chapter Seventeen

~

*"I'm fine, really."* Capri protested as Rian lifted her up into his arms and began walking toward the castle.

"You have dried blood and a bruise the size of a baseball on your head, which tells me that took a nasty blow at some point," he began, his voice stern. "You were locked up God knows where for nearly twenty-four hours, I assume without food and water. You have a burn on your shoulder from the demon fire bullet that needs to be treated. And, to top it all off, you just witnessed a man burn to death. I think we need to be honest here and acknowledge that you're a little less than fine."

Capri pouted, realizing that her shoulder did in fact hurt and she was pretty weak from not eating. Regardless, she felt like she could at least walk on her own two feet...

Her father raced beside them, his face strained.

"He's right, Capri, we need to get you inside, away from all of this. You've had a rough past couple days," Clynn told her, oddly not bothered by Rian's insistence on carrying his daughter.

"But what if Thea has more questions for me, or if she needs me to help, or something?" Capri questioned, shaking her head at Rian. "There's too much going on, I want to help."

In response he merely shook his head and continued into the castle and through the corridor, leading the way up to her room. When they got there, he set her carefully down on the bed as if she were a porcelain doll about to shatter, and turned to Clynn.

"We should get her something to eat and drink, and some salve for that burn."

Clynn nodded, still looking stressed. "Right. I'll go get everything." He began to leave, only to stop and eye Rian with a curious expression on his face. "Thank you for saving her—again. I can tell that you care about her...and, well...I suppose that's what matters most."

With that, he nodded again and left the room, quietly closing the door behind him.

Rian stood unmoving for a moment, until Capri nudged him with her foot, startling him out of his reverie.

"Maybe you're the one who needs to lie down," she joked, hoping to lighten the mood. He looked more than a little taken aback, and it amused her. "I told you he wasn't going to stand in the way anymore."

"Right..." he murmured, still lost in thought. However, when he turned back to look at her, his eyes sharpened once again with purpose. "Get under the blankets. Let me get a washcloth to clean the blood off your face."

She did as she was told, sliding comfily into her bed, gently exhaling as she did. It felt amazing to finally lie down after so many hours of sitting in that horrible metal chair. Her back was screaming and her head still pounding, but at least she could finally relax.

Rian returned from the bathroom, a small cloth and a bowl of water in his hands. He sat on the wooden chair beside her bed, and proceeded to dab the cloth on her head wound. She winced in pain, but grinned anyway at how cute he looked tending to her.

"What?" he asked, noticing her smiling.

"Nothing…I'm just…happy. At this moment, at least. I know that once I start thinking again and taking it all in, I'll be a mess for sure. But right now, being here with you makes me happy."

"I'm glad I can help," he smirked, placing the bowl and towel on her nightstand. "But you should probably get some rest. Your father should be back soon." When he started to stand up, she reached for his hand, holding him back.

"Please, don't go," she murmured, her eyes sad. She had no way of knowing the devastating effect that one look had over his willpower.

Resigned that he wouldn't be able to persuade her or himself otherwise, he sat back down, his hand still in hers. "Okay, I won't."

She smiled sleepily, the overwhelming exhaustion beginning to take its toll. She tried to force her eyes to stay open, and to stay focused on him.

"Talk to me, so I can stay awake until my food comes."

"What would you like to talk about?"

"I don't know, anything. Whatever comes to mind." She fought against a yawn, not wanting him to see just how tired she really was.

"Your father seems to…approve…of us." He looked strained as he remembered the older man's words and just how much they had startled him.

Capri smiled happily. "Yes, he does."

"I was prepared to prove myself to him if I had to," he added with a small grin. "Even if he told me I had to get up and sing karaoke in front of everyone, and I hate singing, I'd still do it."

"You'd do that for me?" Capri giggled, her eyes closing momentarily as she tried to picture him singing.

"I would do that, and a lot more," he murmured, watching her eyes flutter open and closed as she fought to stay awake.

"I should tell you…I wanted to say something to you yesterday…couldn't…" She sighed, her eyes closed, her words so quiet he had to lean in closer to hear her clearly.

"What was it?"

"I'm pretty sure…that I'm…in love…with you." She said the last words on an exhale, her lips curved into a gentle smile as her mind drifted into the darkness of sound sleep.

He was too speechless to bother keeping her awake any longer.

"This has been a very troubling time for all of us here on Euphora, but I'm afraid it's in danger of getting much worse."

Thea stood before everyone at the dining table, her voice stern and her presence ominous. "In light of yesterday's events, I have called you all before me to supply not only information, but explicit instruction."

Capri sat between her father and Rian at the table, nervousness clear in her eyes. She held Rian's hand underneath the table, as much for support as for comfort. She felt better knowing his hand was there for her to hold if she ever needed it. And with the seriousness of the situation, she knew she was definitely going to need it in the time ahead.

Around the table was everyone she knew since Euphora had become her home. The Muses, with the ability to inspire creativity, intelligence, and clarity of thought, were holding hands, looking nervous and afraid. Even their children looked uneasy, especially Tobias, who sat with his head lowered and his eyes glued to the table in what Capri assumed was shame. Thea had forgiven him, of course, because Capri had survived. But that didn't mean everyone else had. Capri decided when she had a chance, she would speak to him. She wanted him to know that she didn't blame him and that she would love to be friends. She had a feeling he could use a friend, and if he would allow her to help, then she most certainly would.

The Fates, masters of life and death, seemed edgy and distrustful, and were surrounding Nyxa protectively, who looked distraught and miserable. No one blamed her for her sudden emotional outburst which had resulted in the death of her husband, but Capri sympathized with her anyway. To know that the man she had loved, Brock, had been wrongfully accused and then banished, and that she had believed him guilty all this time, must be hard to swallow. Especially since the man who framed him was also the same man who slid cozily into her life afterwards to supposedly "pick up the pieces."

Beside Rian sat Brogan, who was staring resolutely at the table in front of him, his face stonily blank. Capri had no idea what was going through his mind. She wasn't sure if he needed someone to talk to, or if he wanted everyone to back off. She'd leave it up to Rian to take care of him, since he knew Brogan best. After all, they were the last two Furies, and they were going to need to rely on each other for everything.

Across the table from her sat Rohan, one hand clutching Serendipity's on the table. He looked particularly distressed and flustered, and Capri wondered what he would do once Brock returned home, which she assumed he would certainly do now that he was proven innocent.

Rhiannon, Liam, and Lucian were next to him. Lucian looked severely troubled, much like her own father, but Liam and Rhiannon both looked curious and eager for information.

And then there was Blythe. Capri had spoken with her briefly that morning when she had awoke, only to find her friend a bundle of emotions. Blythe wasn't really sure what to think about all of the startling revelations, and she kept switching between being violently angry, weeping hysterically, laughing uncontrollably, and getting lost in deep silences. Capri knew it would take time for her to adjust to the truth, but until then, she could at least be happy to know her father would be coming home to her, an innocent man after all.

"We have all been deceived and wronged, and we have all paid the price in some way." Thea glanced around the table, her eyes resting on everyone in turn. "Most of us, including myself, are shocked and appalled by the actions of one of our own. It is thanks to Capri that we have found out the truth of Balgaire's deceit. Therefore, I feel we should all toast in her honor, thanking her for being a crucial part in solving this investigation." Glasses suddenly appeared on the table, filled with rich red wine. Everyone reached for a glass and lifted it high, much as they had done when Capri had first arrived home months ago. She couldn't stop the blush that came over her face as everyone toasted her and tried to hide behind her glass as she sipped.

"Now, back to the matter at hand," Thea continued, setting her glass back down on the table. "It has come to light that Balgaire was working with a demon named Dante to execute all of his plans. Many of you recall who Dante is, but there are more of you here who do not know of him. I feel it is my responsibility to inform you, despite my prior resolve to never mention his name again in this castle."

There was hushed whispering around the table at her words, and she waited patiently. Capri shot a worried glance at Rian, who reassuringly squeezed her hand. When she looked back up at Thea, she saw Mother Earth watching her closely.

"Capri, Rian informed me that you were saying strange things while you were possessed, things that didn't make sense to either of you."

Capri nodded, her brows creasing with worry.

"Well," Thea continued, her eyes hardening, "what you said made sense to me, and that was perhaps the precise moment I came to the realization that we were dealing with more than just an average demon. Do you remember the exact words you said?"

Capri shook her head, and turned to Rian, who nodded as he spoke. "*You will suffer as I have suffered, an outcast, disposed of like trash, not worthy of being a Dryad because of dirty blood.*"

"Thank you, Rian." Thea bowed her head slightly before turning to the group at large. "To those of you who remember Dante, these words will make a lot of sense."

Around the table, the adults nodded solemnly, all looking uneasy.

"And for those of you who don't, let me explain." She took a deep breath before continuing, as though fighting against herself and her own principles to muster the courage to tell the story. "Brock's mother, Bristol, was the Fire Dryad before her son was born. Many of you remember her. She was feisty, devil-may-care, and foolish. But when she settled down with one of our Enforcers and gave birth to Brock, I thought all of my doubts about her were proven false. She was fiercely devoted to her son, and very proud of everything he did. But when he was ten years old, she started to lose interest in this life. I don't know what started it, but she began disappearing for weeks at a time, doing God knows what, and when I approached her about it, she threatened to leave and never come back." Thea chuckled darkly, shaking her head. "As you all know, threats do not work with me. I told her to leave and that I would raise her son Brock to replace her. I thought that by threatening her she would see reason and stay, but just the opposite happened. She left, leaving her son behind, and I didn't see or hear from her for nearly a year. Then one day, she came back, and she had a baby boy with her. She started begging me to forgive her, until I had to ask her why she needed my forgiveness. I, after all, had told her to go without fear of reprisal, and I was fully prepared to take her back. But then she held out the baby for me to see, and surprisingly, she told me the truth. And the truth was by far worse than anything I had ever expected of her. For all of her faults, I would have never dreamed her capable of committing this act. But she had. A child had been produced. A child that was half Fire Dryad and half demon."

Everyone sat in stunned silence as Thea let the weight of her words sink in. When she continued, it was clear just how painful the memory was to her.

"I think of you all as my children. I watch you grow up, start your own families and then eventually pass away. I have high hopes and expectations for all of you, and so it breaks my heart every time one of you falls. But even though it hurt, I had to do what was best for everyone. Bristol had broken one of my cardinal rules, and there was no possible way I could forgive her. And so I had to banish her and the boy, and raise her other son, Brock, myself."

"You have got to be kidding me!" Blythe said loudly, her face open with shock and disgust. "My grandmother slept with a demon?"

Thea nodded grimly. "Unfortunately, she did. And because of her bad decisions, you have never known her. I'm sorry to say you never will either, as she passed away about five years ago."

Capri's eyes shot to Blythe, gauging her friend's reaction to the news. But Blythe merely sat in silence, lost in her own thoughts.

"Most of you were young when all of this happened, but I'm sure you can remember my message to you. I do not tolerate any interaction with demons, unless you are trained to deal with them. And the reason is because things like this can happen. Bristol was not the first, but I hope she will be the last. Her son, the baby born of a demon father, was named Dante. He is, without a doubt, the most dangerous creature on this Earth, and he will attempt to destroy everything we are merely out of spite."

Thea's voice wavered a bit on the last word as she fought to maintain her resolve, but Capri could tell that fear for her home and her family was tearing her apart inside.

"Dante's powers are exceptional and unique. Not only is he able to produce and manipulate fire the way only a Fire Dryad can, but he can also change from human form into demon form, thus giving him the ability to possess. He is extraordinarily intelligent, but he is also extraordinarily evil, as all demons are. This makes for a lethal combination, and it will require all of our strengths to ensure he is brought to justice. Some of you may be wondering why I didn't destroy him the moment Bristol brought him to me as a baby. And the truth is that I couldn't, both morally and physically. I cannot kill any of you because you are a part of me, and doing so would be to destroy myself. Despite everything, he is still a Fire Dryad, and consequently it is not within my powers to kill him. Therefore it will be up to one of you to destroy him, once he is caught."

"I'll do it." Both Rian and Blythe said at once, each rising to their feet. They immediately turned and stared at each other, eyebrows raised.

Thea smiled, her eyes warming as she watched the two of them. Both so proud, so tough, so resilient. Both of them would be able to do it, no questions asked. Knowing that fact, and knowing she could count on them, comforted her more than she could say.

"Time will tell which of you will have the honor," Thea told them as they sat back down, eyeing each other cagily. "Until then, I have contacted a close personal friend of mine, Jackson Murphy, who is a demon bounty hunter. He has agreed to find Dante for us, capture him, and bring him here. At that point we will decide what to do with him."

"Wait, wait, wait…a demon bounty hunter?" Blythe snorted, her eyes flashing. "Who the hell does this guy think he is? Let me go, I'll find Dante and kill the bastard myself. Save your money, Thea."

"As much as I appreciate your…eagerness, Blythe, I cannot risk sending you by yourself. I need you here. Besides, don't you want to be here when Sebastian and I bring your father home?"

"Of course. But I can do both. I'll see my father when you guys bring him home, and then I'll leave to go hunt down my evil half demon uncle. Everyone wins."

"Unfortunately I cannot allow you to do that. This is something that requires a professional. Jackson Murphy is the best at what he does, and I have full faith in his ability to hunt down Dante." She eyed Blythe meaningfully, her lips curving as the younger woman nodded. "Now, since we are all up to speed on the situation, why don't we eat?"

That night after dinner, the mood in the parlor was lively, to say the least.

Capri found herself immersed in conversation, those around her both curious and sympathetic over what she went through with Balgaire. She was asked dozens of questions, to the point that she began to feel dizzy from spinning around from one person to the next. Her father, normally unswervingly protective of her, was busy being questioned and sympathized over himself in regards to his finding out the truth about his wife's death and his daughter's disappearance.

Capri managed to catch a quick glimpse of Rian in the corner speaking privately with Brogan. She saw the two of them grasp each other in a hug, just as Liam and Blythe grabbed her, pulling her away from Rohan and Serendipity.

"Gosh, you're sure the celebrity again." Blythe grinned, her eyes intensely golden. "Honey, you gotta stop getting into trouble."

"I don't try to, believe me." Capri laughed, hugging Blythe close. When they broke apart, her eyes were round with wonder. "Would you really have left to try and find Dante?"

"Damn right. I'm still gonna try and find a way to get Thea to let me go. I don't know about this Jackson Murphy guy…a demon bounty hunter, give me a break!"

Liam punched her playfully in the shoulder. "You really think that demon is going to be scared of a little pipsqueak like you?"

"Hey!" Encouraged, Blythe hooked her right arm over his neck and dragged him down to her level, her grin quick and mischievous. Liam tried to struggle, only to find her hold much stronger than he anticipated. "I can take on a man twice my size no problem. And as for a demon…" She let him go, and Liam winced as he rubbed the back of his neck. Blythe turned to Capri and winked before forming three fireballs in her hands and proceeding to juggle them. "We'll just have to fight fire with fire." With that, she pitched the fireballs one at a time into the fireplace, which erupted in a shower of sparks each time one of the fireballs disappeared into the flames and smoldering embers.

Capri clapped appreciatively, and Blythe bowed deeply.

"I have to say, if this uncle of yours ever does have the displeasure of meeting you, he's going to get more than he bargained for." Liam put his arm around Blythe and grinned down at her proudly. "You'll give him hell, darling."

"I know." Blythe kissed his cheek enthusiastically before turning back to Capri. "We all will."

"Capri?"

She turned around to see Rhiannon, looking pristine as always in a trim and tailored black skirt and jacket.

"Hi, Rhiannon." Capri smiled sweetly as the other girl approached her. Blythe immediately turned away, dragging Liam along with her, heading over to the windows where Lucian and Sebastian were deep in conversation.

Rhiannon watched the two of them leave, her eyes on Liam for a brief moment before she focused back on Capri.

"You must be relieved to finally know the truth about what happened with you and your mother."

"More than relieved, really."

Rhiannon smiled, but the emotion didn't quite reach her eyes. She looked for a moment like she wanted to say something, but she didn't know quite how to say it.

"When they told us you were missing, my first thought was that you had run away. I don't know why I thought that." She laughed halfheartedly as she shrugged. "I guess I just felt that if I were in your shoes, I wouldn't have been brave enough to come to this strange place at all, much less stay after everything that has happened to you."

"There is nothing in the entire world and beyond that could make me leave this place, Rhiannon." Capri reached for the other girl's hands, holding them tightly in her own. "You have my word on that."

"Good, because if you left again I don't know what we would all do." Her lips curved into a smile, her sage eyes lit in amusement. "There's something about you that brings out the best in all of us. I still can't believe you got Blythe and I to get along without either of us even realizing it. That was fun, while it lasted, anyway."

"What do you mean?"

"Well, after what happened at the party with my father and Blythe…she and I have once again burned that bridge. I don't blame her, but I have to stand behind my father, despite how poor his judgment can be sometimes. And with Brock coming home soon, I imagine that the tension will get worse before it gets better. My father and Brock get along worse than Blythe and I do, and that's saying something."

"I'm sure things won't be as bad as you think," Capri reassured her with a smile. "We have always been meant to be together, the four of us. You're my family, and if I have to be the glue that holds us all together, then so be it." She threw her arms around Rhiannon, who seemed momentarily caught off guard. However, after a second's hesitation, she hugged back, relishing this simple gesture of friendship.

"Capri?" Rhiannon chewed her bottom lip as she pulled away, her eyes focused on something over Capri's shoulder.

"What is it?" Capri asked, worried she had done something wrong. Rhiannon smiled as she sighed. Glancing back at Capri, she stepped back just slightly. "I think your knight in shining armor is waiting for you by the door."

Capri turned and saw Rian standing just inside the door, watching her intently. She felt the familiar jolt rush through her at the sight of him, and she couldn't help the bright smile that came over her face. Leaving Rhiannon, she maneuvered through the crowd, making her way over to the door.

When she reached him and took his outstretched hand, he pulled her into the darkened corridor, lit only by torches on the stone walls.

She started laughing as they stopped, only to have it cut off as he pulled her into his arms and kissed her fully. Her arms wound around his neck, her body pressing into his. It was almost desperate, a bit greedy, yet undeniably tender. When he pulled away, he rested his forehead against hers, his eyes closed. She took a deep, calming breath, hoping to settle her rapidly beating heart.

"Do you remember what you told me yesterday before you fell asleep?" he asked gently, his lips tracing over her eyelids, her forehead, her cheeks.

"Mmm...no, what did I say?" she murmured, her lips curving as he pulled away. When she opened her eyes, she noticed the amusement on his face.

"You must have the worst memory of anyone I've ever met." He chuckled, his hand reaching up to cup her cheek.

"My memory is just fine! I was just really exhausted yesterday." She pouted a bit, unsure why he was teasing her.

"You not remembering what you said makes me wonder if you even meant it." His eyebrows rose as he stared at her, a playful smile crossing his mouth.

Puzzled, Capri stepped back from him, crossing her arms defensively. "If you would just tell me what I said, then I'll let you know if I meant it or not."

"You said you were in love with me."

Her mouth fell open as she felt heat flood her cheeks. "Oh, well..."

Embarrassed, she averted her eyes and stared at the floor, silently wishing she had a hole to crawl into and escape.

When he stepped forward and tilted her head up with his fingertips, she cursed herself for being a fool. What had she been thinking? Of course he didn't love her, he couldn't...

She braced herself for his words, afraid it would break her heart. "I've never said those words to anyone in my entire life, Capri." He shook his head as his eyes searched hers. "And no one has ever said them to me. Until you."

"I–"

"Shush." He covered her mouth with his finger to quiet her. "Just listen. I wasn't sure what to think when you said it yesterday. I was scared, but not because I didn't like what I heard. I was scared because I understood at that moment that I loved you too."

"You do?" Her eyes widened in honest surprise.

"Yes, I do."

He laughed when she leapt into his arms, but he held her close all the same. She was, quite simply, his light. The one thing left shining in the darkness that had come to surround him. God, he had missed her.

"Come on, let's go for a walk before they come looking for us."

She pulled away, positively glowing. "Okay."

Taking her hand into his, he led the way out into the courtyard. Above them, the night sky exploded with stars and the moon shone brightly, illuminating everything with a soft, blue glow.

They walked along the cobblestone path, hand in hand, and Capri felt a happiness rise within her that she never knew was even possible. Her life, which had been virtually meaningless months ago, was now so perfect she wondered what she had ever done to deserve it. She had a true home, a father who cared for her, and now Rian, who against all odds loved her as well. It was almost more than she could handle, but she knew she would do everything in her power to keep her miracle now that she had it. Because that's what all of this was, essentially. It was her miracle.

They sat down on one of the many benches in the courtyard, this one open to the sky above so she could gaze at the stars. She tilted her head back and did just that, her eyes searching the heavens, her heart full.

After a moment, she turned to him, a sudden thought occurring to her. "Are you and Brogan going to look for Dante, too?"

"We will, but not in the way that Murphy will be looking for him. We have to notify our human contacts to keep an eye out for him, and we will try and track him using what resources we have here." He looked disappointed, but she felt extremely relieved.

"I'm glad you won't be leaving." She smiled tenderly as she watched him.

"Even if I did, it would be the wrong thing to do. Brogan and I have a duty to defend Euphora, and if one or both of us leave, you will be unprotected. I could never allow that."

Capri nodded, acknowledging that despite how perfect everything seemed at that moment, there was still more to overcome. Dante needed to be found and brought to justice, and even though she wouldn't have a direct hand in it, it still affected her and those she loved.

"So do you think this bounty hunter will find Dante?"

He smiled, his eyes sparking with that same excitement she had noticed before whenever he discussed demons. It was his life's work and his passion, after all, to keep any and all demons at bay.

"Jackson Murphy is the best there is. He used to be an Enforcer before he decided to go rogue and hunt demons on his own. Normally Thea wouldn't allow that, but Jax is too good at what he does. So don't worry, if anyone can find Dante, it's him."

"That's good." She sighed, feeling marginally better. "I hope I get to meet him someday. He sounds…interesting."

"You might not like him as much as you think, but I'll let you be the judge of his character when you meet him."

"Why wouldn't I like him?"

He couldn't help but be amused by the simple innocence in her expression.

"He's arrogant, unapologetic, and rough around the edges. But, he's also extremely intelligent and invaluable as a demon hunter."

"I see…well, I would still like to meet him, even if he is… rough. Too bad Blythe already doesn't like him." She looked troubled as she remembered how her friend had mocked the demon hunter without even knowing him. "I hope they get along okay."

"Even if they don't, he won't stay long after he's caught Dante," Rian said absently, distracted by a strand of her hair that had fallen loose beside her face. He tucked it behind her ear, noting how she still blushed when he touched her. He had no idea why he enjoyed it so much.

"You never asked me about it, but I feel I should tell you," he paused, his eyes meeting hers. "I was eight years old when you were taken. I remember you offering me a flower that night, just as I remember refusing to even look at you. I have always regretted it, but it was easier then to just ignore you. I wasn't allowed to make friends; that wasn't what my purpose was. I was born to be a warrior and a protector, cold and detached, and my father always made sure I knew that. And so I ignored you, and when I found out you were gone, presumably dead, I cried for you. The only other time in my life that I cried was when my mother died."

She felt her own eyes fill with tears as she silently watched him, her heart full of an emotion she couldn't quite describe. It was somewhere between sympathy and a deep, resounding regret for something she knew she had no power to change.

"You have no idea how relieved I was when I found out you were alive, and back home. And when I first saw you, it felt as though no time had passed. You were so much the same, yet I knew I should leave you alone. But once again, you were persistent." His lips twitched into a smirk as he reached up and brushed away a tear that had fallen down her cheek. "So thank you, for opening my eyes and giving me something I never thought I'd have. For once in my life, I am no longer cold."

Humbled beyond words, she threw her arms around him and held on tight. Feeling it wasn't enough, she slid into his lap and crushed her lips against his, pouring everything she had into the kiss.

He kissed her back, his hands fisting in her hair as she curved into him. Her hands wandered up his chest, grasping at his shirt as she felt herself letting go, losing herself completely to the moment. She needed him to know, without words, that she was his.

Maybe it was the effect a kiss under the moonlight had on her mood, or maybe it was the insurmountable emotion his words had evoked inside of her, but quite suddenly and unexpectedly, the wind began to blow.

And blow it did, quite fiercely in fact, howling around them with a stunning and unmatched power. It whipped through her hair and circled the bench, sending leaves soaring into the star studded sky.

She broke the kiss, startled by the interruption. But when she realized that she felt the rush of the wind not only on her skin, but in her heart, she knew it had been a reaction deep within her soul. Somewhere, beyond the gift of blood in her veins and the heart that beat full with life and power, was the Air Dryad, freeing itself from all boundaries.

An astonished laugh escaped her throat as she rose to her feet, pulling him with her. Sensing the panic and uncertainty in him, she cupped his face in her hands and merely smiled.

"Coming home gave me a purpose; it gave me a reason to find the strength within myself that I never thought was there. For once in my life, I am no longer weak." Her voice seemed to resound and echo within the roar of the wind as it swirled around them, a cyclone circling them like a protective cocoon. Her eyes darkened in the light of the moon from a light gray to deeper pewter, and he seemed momentarily mesmerized by the unbridled power she radiated.

Inhaling deeply, she closed her eyes and tilted her head back, her chest falling as she exhaled. Bit by bit, the howling of the wind disappeared, until it was as if it had never existed.

When she opened her eyes, all was calm and quiet, and she could hear the chirping of crickets and the song of frogs echoing once more through the courtyard.

"I think you have always been strong, you just didn't know it." His voice shook a bit as he spoke, a fact which amused her. Knowing she unsettled him was a special kind of feminine magic. "It took a lot of strength to stay calm when Balgaire tried to take you. And it took a lot of courage to attack him when he had a gun to your head. You could have died, but you fought back instead of giving in." His hand trailed down her neck gently, caressing her skin as his eyes held hers. "This time, it seems, you saved my life."

"I guess I owed you, didn't I?" She laughed, secretly amazed that her plan had worked at all. "The truth is, I thought about dying, and it scared me. But the thought of you dying scared me much more." She tilted her head into his hand, enjoying the feel of his warm skin against her cheek. "Almost my entire life I've lived without the fear of losing someone I loved, because there was no one I loved. As far as I knew I had no family, no one to care for me. I had no idea just how staggering it was to feel this love inside of me and to have it threatened. I suppose those feelings make people do things they otherwise wouldn't, and in my case, it made me do whatever I could to protect you from him. To protect all of you from him."

In the gentle light of the moon, she could tell he was measuring her, weighing her words. After a moment, his eyes softened, and when he spoke, she felt his words echo deep inside her very bones.

"You came to us a fragile, broken little thing," he murmured, leaning in to kiss her gently. "Who knew you would be the one to save us all?"

# THE DRYAD QUARTET CONTINUES

## ALSO LOOK FOR BOOKS THREE & FOUR

Nothing can compare to the exhilaration of discovering, at last, a mode of release for the imagination. Mine came, after years of struggling to visualize my creativity, in the form of the written word. I found myself with my nose constantly in a book, absorbing the life of the characters and the beauty of the setting. It was intoxicating, to say the least, and the only thing I knew was that I wanted to give writing a shot, and take the thousands of characters and storylines in my head and put them down on paper and form them into something real and compelling.

In truth, I'm just a girl from a small town north of Los Angeles with an imagination for days and thank goodness a keyboard at my fingertips. And even though my husband thinks I'm a nerd and my mom is undoubtedly my biggest fan, at the end of the day I'm loving life and enjoying giving breath to the characters living in my heart and sharing with others all of the creativity I can harness.

I believe in true love and I've always believed in happy endings. And that is just the beginning of the story.

*K*